D1046588

A SMILE ON THE FACE OF THE TIGER

BY LOREN D. ESTLEMAN

THE AMOS WALKER NOVELS
A Smile on the Face of the Tiger
The Hours of the Virgin
The Witchfinder
Never Street
Sweet Women Lie
Silent Thunder
Downriver
Lady Yesterday
Every Brilliant Eye
Sugartown
The Glass Highway
The Midnight Man
Angel Eyes
Motor City Blue

THE DETROIT NOVELS
Thunder City
Jitterbug
Stress
Edsel
King of the Corner
Motown
Whiskey River

THE PETER MACKLIN NOVELS
Any Man's Death
Roses Are Dead
Kill Zone

OTHER NOVELS
The Rocky Mountain Moving Picture Association
Peeper
Dr. Jekyll and Mr. Holmes
Sherlock Holmes vs. Dracula
The Oklahoma Punk

WESTERN NOVELS
White Desert
Journey of the Dead
City of Widows
Sudden Country
Bloody Season
Gun Man
The Stranglers
This Old Bill
Mister St. John
Murdock's Law
The Wolfer
Aces & Eights
Stamping Ground
The High Rocks
The Hider
Billy Gashade
Journey of the Dead

NONFICTION
The Wister Trace: Classic Novels of the American Frontier

SHORT STORY COLLECTIONS
General Murders
The Best Western Stories of Loren D. Estleman (edited by Bill Pronzini and Ed Gorman)
People Who Kill

LOREN D. ESTLEMAN

A SMILE ON THE FACE OF THE TIGER

OF THE

TIGER

THE MYSTERIOUS PRESS
Published by Warner Books

A Time Warner Company

Nobles County Library
407 12th Street
Worthington, MN 56187-2411

378575

This book is a work of fiction. Names, characters, places, and incidents are the product of the author's imagination or are used fictitiously. Any resemblance to actual events, locales, or persons, living or dead, is coincidental.

Copyright © 2000 by Loren D. Estleman
All rights reserved.

 Mysterious Press books are published by Warner Books, Inc., 1271 Avenue of the Americas, New York, NY 10020.

Visit our Web site at www.twbookmark.com

 A Time Warner Company

The Mysterious Press name and logo are registered trademarks of Warner Books, Inc.

Printed in the United States of America

First Printing: August 2000

10 9 8 7 6 5 4 3 2 1

Library of Congress Cataloging-in-Publication Data
Estleman, Loren D.
    A smile on the face of the tiger / Loren D. Estleman.
        p.   cm.
    ISBN 0-89296-706-4
    1. Walker, Amos (Fictitious character)—Fiction. 2. Private investigators—Michigan—Detroit—Fiction. 3. Detective and mystery stories—Authorship—Fiction. 4. Detroit (Mich.)—Fiction. I Title.

PS3555.S84 S57 2000
813'.54—dc21   00-022284

Nobles County Library
407 12th Street
Worthington, MN 56187-2617

For the Paper Tigers:

Goodis and Woolrich and Dewey and Kane,
Hamilton, Prather, McCoy, and Spillane;
Marlowe, McGivern, Miller, McBain,
and hundreds of others, too many to name.

The author wishes to thank the staff of John King Books for a cook's tour of one of Detroit's best institutions.

Although the personnel herein represented are fictional, this store is a most agreeable fact.

1

Bang! Bang! Bang! Bang!
Four shots ripped into my groin, and I was
off on the biggest adventure of my life . . .
But first let me tell you a little about myself.

—Max Shulman,
Sleep Till Noon (1950)

I thought I'd never see her again. But never is longer
than forever.

The beveled-glass door of the downtown Caucus
Club opened just before noon and drifted shut against the
pressure of the closer, the way things move in dreams
and deep water. While that was happening, Louise Starr
stood in the electroplated rectangle of light wearing a

white linen jumpsuit with matching unstructured jacket and a woven-leather bag on one shoulder. She had kept her pale-gold hair long, against the helmeted utilitarian fashion; in another six months most of the women who glanced up from their menus and kept on looking would be wearing theirs the same way.

She had lost weight. She hadn't needed to, but the loss hadn't done her any harm, just trimmed her down from a steeplechaser to a racer. I guessed tennis or badminton, although it might have been the white outfit that suggested it. I couldn't see her in leotards and a sweatband at Bally's with her hair in a ponytail. In any case the progressive-resistance machines would have surrendered without a struggle.

Inside the entrance, she paused to adjust her pupils to the muted light, then spoke to the man at the reservation stand, a plump sixty with a silver hairpiece and the knowing eyes of a vice cop. He nodded, body-checked the young waiter who stepped forward to offer assistance, and led the way to the corner table where I sat fighting a fern for my drink. In three-inch heels, she managed to stand a full head taller than her escort without towering. She was five-eight in her bare feet. I had seen her barefoot. I rose.

"I'm afraid our brunch has turned into plain old lunch." She leaned across the table and kissed my cheek. When she straightened she left behind a light trace of foxglove. "I had no idea the entire state of Michigan was under construction."

"Roadwork is our fifth season. How was your flight?"

"High. Which is what I intend to get as soon as possible. What are you drinking?" She got rid of her bag, slid out her chair, and sat down before the headwaiter could get his hands on it.

"Chivas." I sat.

She wrinkled her nose. She'd acquired little creases at the corners of her eyes since the last time we'd seen each other. They suited her, like everything else with which she came into contact. The eyes themselves were violet. "Bacardi, straight," she told the waiter. "We'll order food later. Unless you're famished." Her brows lifted.

"I had a big breakfast."

"When did this start?"

"Don't worry, I haven't reformed. I missed supper last night."

"A tail job?" The waiter had dematerialized, but she lowered her voice anyway.

"Novocaine. I broke a tooth on a fist."

"Business or personal?"

"It was an affair of honor. My family tree came up."

"You ought to consider another line of work."

"Do you think this one was my first choice?"

The waiter brought her Bacardi in a square glass with a thick bottom. "What should we drink to?"

"Telephones and airplanes."

We clinked glasses. She sipped, set hers down, and sat back. She wore a tiger-eye on a thin chain around her neck and earrings to match. No other jewelry. I remembered she was allergic to gold. "You look good, Amos. Gray is your color."

"I'm not wearing gray."

"I know."

I drank. "Are we going to be that kind of friend that exchanges over-the-hill gifts on birthdays?"

"No. I'm sorry. You really do look fabulous. Men still age beautifully while women just fall apart. You'd think after what's happened these past twenty years things would change."

"That won't float either. You know you're beautiful because every day strangers stop you on the street to tell you. You didn't need to come all the way out here to hear it. How are things in publishing?"

"Worse than ever. Three one-million-dollar advances went out last Christmas for books that didn't even make the list in the *Phoenix Sun*. Returns are running around eighty percent. All the big houses have pulled in their horns."

"Things can't be too bad if they flew you first class."

"How did you know I flew first class?" She smiled then. The sun came through the stained-glass partition behind her. It was probably coincidence. "Did you call the airport?"

"You were late. I can't afford the Caucus Club."

"Admit it, you were worried about me. I'm not with the firm anymore. I have my own company now. I thought you might have heard. *Publishers Weekly* gave me two pages last month."

"I dropped my subscription. *Soldier of Fortune* offered me a telephone shaped like a Claymore for signing up."

"What's a Claymore?"

"An explosive device. So is hanging out your own shingle in a bear market. What happened on the job?"

"You know Eddie Cypress?"

It wasn't a name I expected her to drop. It was like seeing Princess Di spit on a commoner. "Just what was on CNN. Glad Eddie never worked Detroit that I heard. He killed fifteen men on contract and the feds let him walk for turning state's evidence against Paul Lippo for ordering one hit."

"*Court TV* fell in love with Glad Eddie and so did the talk shows. He goes to a better barber than most hit men and doesn't have a cauliflower ear. The publisher told me to put in a bid for his memoirs. I told him I didn't offer money to terrorist organizations or cheap hoods. He fired me."

"That what it said on the pink slip?"

"The official reason was insubordination. I could have gone to NOW or Fair Employment Practices and sued to get my job back. I didn't. I was thinking of quitting long before Glad Eddie. Getting canned meant I could raid the inventory without guilt. I signed two *New York Times* bestsellers and a Pulitzer Prize winner right out from under them. They cried salty tears and threatened to sue me for industrial espionage."

"Congratulations. Want me to write *my* memoirs?"

"True crime's dead. Newspaper-clipping hacks and the Simpson case killed it. I wouldn't take a chance on it even if you weren't kidding. I need a detective."

"The last time you hired me it didn't turn out the way you wanted."

"If that's true I don't remember. What I remember is you delivered."

My glass was sweating on the polished tabletop. The ice cubes had melted. The restaurant was ducted for air conditioning, as was the rest of the Penobscot Build-

ing, but it wasn't scheduled to be turned on for another week; the summery weather in late May had taken
the whole southern part of the state by surprise. I signaled the waiter and asked Louise if she wanted a fresh
drink. She shook her head and the waiter went back
for another Scotch. I was getting the kind of service I
never got alone.

"I raised my rates," I said. "You might have to hike
up the cover price on your books."

She leaned forward and rested her chin on her hands.
"I'll let you in on a secret: Book prices rose ten years
ago when the cost of paper went up. Paper came down,
books didn't. I'll fold your fee into the profit."

My drink came. I raised it. "Here's to the lending library."

"Libraries? Love 'em. Guaranteed sale." She lifted hers.

When she set it down the playfulness was gone. "I'm
in a bind. I guess you could call it a book bind. One
of my bestsellers isn't selling as well as expected. The
other's blocked, he says, and the Pulitzer winner never
cracked the list on his best day; I only signed him for
the prestige, and as the man said, you can't eat that.
To hedge my bet, I put the rest of my money on an
old warhorse. The warhorse jumped the stall."

"I can't boost sales and I'm not a psychiatrist, so
breaking the block is out too. It has to be the warhorse."

"His name is Eugene Booth. He was big in the fifties.
PBO's."

"What's a PBO?"

"Paperback original. Two bits a pop, sleazy cover art,
cheap paper. Dames, gats, stiffs, striptease. He and his
colleagues corrupted a generation." The creases deep-

ened at the corners of her eyes. Aside from that her face was solemn.

"I read one or two when I was a kid. I thought he was dead."

"So did everyone else, until he sued a fly-by-night California publisher last year for bringing out a new edition of one of his early novels without permission or payment. The wires picked up the story, and suddenly he was hot again. An entire generation has grown up since he lost his last contract. He's part of that whole tailfins-Rat-Pack-lounge-lizard-swingers revival. Three of his titles are in development in Hollywood right now. I saw it coming the day the story broke. I tracked him down through a friend with the Associated Press and signed him over the telephone."

"He's still writing?"

She shook her head. "He's seventy and in poor health. He hasn't written a word in forty years. Even in his heyday he had a reputation as a drunk. He missed deadlines, reneged on contracts, submitted unpublishable copy and had to be browbeaten into rewriting it. In nineteen fifty-nine he assaulted an editor in a New York office. That was the last straw. When he sued the publisher in California he was living on Social Security and minimum wage, managing a trailer park in Belleville. That's near Detroit, isn't it?"

"Your plane almost landed on it. This Booth character sounds like the Babe Ruth of risks."

"It wasn't as if I was counting on him to deliver a new manuscript. The contract was to reprint *Paradise Valley*, his best-known novel, with an option on three others if he sold through. Here." She took her bag off the back of her chair, reached inside, and laid a squat glossy rectangle of cardboard and paper on my side of the table. It was almost square.

I picked it up. The aged paperback was dog-eared and the orange spine was cracked, but the cover still glistened beneath a coat of varnish. The scene painted on the front took place in a rumpled bedroom. A rough customer in a wrinkled trenchcoat and a fedora stood in the foreground in three-quarter profile with his broken nose showing. In the background, centered, a blonde crouched facing him in a scarlet slip with one strap dangling, threatening him with the jagged end of a shattered bottle. Behind her a window looked out on a street in flames and shadowy figures armed with rocks and clubs darting about in the flickering light. Fat yellow letters in upper- and lower-case spelled out *Paradise Valley* across the top. Eugene Booth's name, much smaller, clung to the lower right-hand corner.

The edges of the pages were dyed yellow. The pages themselves were brown and brittle and covered with fine print. A great deal more money had gone into the lurid package than into the book itself. The copyright date was 1952. "Bloody Melee on the Streets of the Motor City!" read a blurb on the back. I held it out.

"You can keep it," she said. "Collectors are paying as much as a hundred for it in good condition. Consider it a bonus if you take the job."

I laid it aside. There was a chance I'd be giving it back at the end of the meal: Work and old friends, coal oil and Kool-Aid. "I think it's one I read. Takes place during the race riot in forty-three."

"We were planning to issue it in hardcover, on acid-free paper, with a jacket painting by a major African-American artist. It's powerfully written, although salacious, and the macho posturing is unintentionally funny. Anyone bothering to reissue this kind of thing a couple of years ago would have been obliged to advertise it as a camp classic, and maybe sold five thousand copies, tops. Then the Library of America brought out a two-volume deluxe set of James M. Cain, Jim Thompson, Horace McCoy—Booth's peers—and pronounced it a national treasure. That was the beginning of the comeback."

"If Booth skipped out *after* you signed him, why don't you just go ahead and publish it?"

"That's just it. He canceled the contract. He returned the advance check uncashed, along with this note."

She handed me a trifold of cheap gray stock from her bag, creased and yellowed at the corners, with THE ALAMO MOTEL printed at the top. The brief paragraph had been typewritten in elite characters on an old machine whose keys needed realigning; the *a* and the *o* in particular had seceded nearly far enough to start their own typewriter.

Mrs. Starr:
Much as it sticks in an old hack's craw to refuse a buck, I hope you'll be kind enough to tear up our agreement. A gelding ought to know better than to try to breed.

Gene Booth

The signature was a thick scrawl in watery ink from a fountain pen.

I sniffed at the coarse paper. Bourbon. That was a nice touch. "Signature check out?"

"It matches the one on the contract, except for the nickname. He signed Eugene. Otherwise it wouldn't have been strictly legal. I called the trailer park, and got a stranger who said he was the temporary manager. He said Booth quit last week and moved out. I looked up the Alamo Motel—it's on Jefferson Avenue—but nobody I spoke to there had ever heard of him. They didn't have a registration card in that name."

"The Alamo's a rathole. I doubt it has its own stationery these days. This sheet is older than you are. What about the envelope?"

"Plain drugstore, no return address. Detroit postmark. Should I have brought it?"

"You just told me everything it would have." I read the note again. " 'A gelding ought to know better than to try to breed.' What do you think that means?"

"A number of things, none of them very cheerful. He must be a wretched man."

I folded the note along its creases and stuck it into the paperback like a bookmark. "Photo? Description?"

"We never met. We did everything by telephone and the mail. I had plans to set up a publicity shoot in a month or so. I couldn't even find an old picture on the Internet. He seems to have been allergic to cameras."

"He might have a record."

"He might. It wouldn't shock me. Many of those PBO writers were odd ducks, misanthropes and misfits. They rode the rails, picked lettuce, bellhopped, went to war and were changed by it; some of them served time on chain gangs. The stuff they wrote was too raw for the cloth trade. They got away with more in paper because that whole industry wasn't respectable to begin with. That's why they're so popular now. The rest of society has caught up with them."

I jingled the ice in my glass. "Even if I find him he won't want to come back."

"Finding him is only half the job. I want you to learn why he backed out. If I know what the problem is, maybe I can help fix it."

"You do want a psychiatrist."

She finished her Bacardi and touched her lower lip with a little finger. The lacquered nail was rounded to accommodate a computer keyboard. "I admit I thought of you because of the Detroit connection. But you're perfect for this job. You're the kind of detective Booth wrote about; the kind they say doesn't exist in real life. He's sure to see that. If you can get him to trust you, you can find out what's wrong. I'm sure of it."

"Two Model T's chasing each other on the Information Superhighway," I said. "Talk about your photo ops."

"It's not a publicity stunt, Amos. I need Booth." One hand gripped the other on the table, the knuckles pale against the tan. "My severance package and 401K went into the rent on the office suite. I floated a loan to cover the advances I paid out. I turn forty again this year. I'm too old to go back and start from the bottom."

"I heard your joints creaking all the way from the street."

She said nothing.

I picked up *Paradise Valley* and looked at it again,

front and back. It didn't mean anything to me beyond an interesting read. I slid it and Booth's note into my inside breast pocket. It had been a long time since a paperback had fit there. They were coming much thicker now, and cost twenty times more.

Louise knew what the gesture meant. She smiled, unfolded her hands, and got the waiter's attention. He brought menus bound in aubergine suede.

"We are offering a summer special on barbecued spareribs," he said.

I said, "It isn't summer."

"I'm aware of that, sir. Our chef is under the influence of the weather."

Louise handed back her menu. "I'll have the ribs."

I ordered the London Broil. When the ribs came, charred at the ends and drenched in rust-colored sauce, I said, "You shouldn't have worn white."

"That's what my ex-husband said." Her smile turned wicked. She shrugged out of the jacket, rolled up her sleeves, and tucked her linen napkin into her collar. She polished off half a rack with her fingers and never got a spot on her. Some people are like that. I can't walk past an Italian restaurant without ruining a good necktie.

2

When the waiter took her credit card, Louise asked him to call for a cab. I offered to drop her off at her hotel. She shook her head.

"I'd rather you got to work right away. Anyway, I'm staying with a friend in Hazel Park. I'll be there through the end of next week." She gave me the telephone number.

I wrote it down and got up to help her with her jacket. "Old friend?"

"Too young to be old. She's the local sales representative for my former place of employment. I mean

to steal her as soon as I can afford to hire sales reps."
She smiled. "Did you think it was a man?"

"Does it matter what I think?"

She studied me for a long moment. Then she shook
her head again and slung her bag over her shoulder.
"Oh, no. I've edited Washington politicians whose faces
I could read easier."

"I'm a riddle wrapped in a mystery with a crunchy
almond center." I went out with her to the canopy to
wait for the cab.

When a caved-in Black-and-White took her away,
leaking exhaust out of everything but its tailpipe, I went
for a stroll. I had some research to do, but it was too
nice a day to go straight back to the office. I headed
up Woodward with the sun on my back, smelling the
concrete heating up and feeling the Beastie Boys in my
feet from the monster speakers in the back of every
third car that passed me. The odd convertible top was
down, fluorescent-pale legs stuck out of short pants
that had lain in drawers since September, and everywhere I looked the city of Detroit was beginning to
creep out of its horned winter shell; but not so far that
it couldn't shrink back in at the first sign of a rogue
snowflake.

In Grand Circus Park I found a section of bench the
pigeons hadn't targeted, took off my coat, and sat down,
stretching out my legs and pressing my shoulders against
the dry weathered wood of the slats. I slipped the old
paperback out of the coat and opened it. Five or six
pages would give me the writing style, and through it
a glimpse of the writer.

I'd read ten chapters when a shelf of steely cloud

slid in front of the sun and touched my face with its
metallic shadow. It was the story of Roland Clifford, a
white Detroit beat cop badly injured while trying to
protect three Negro defense-plant workers from a racist
mob during the riot that swept the city in June 1943.
The blurb on the back cover announced that the narrative was based on fact, but no straight journalism I
had read about the incident approached the visceral
power of Eugene Booth's unadorned fiction. The sentences were lean and angular, as if they'd been scratched
onto the page with a needle, and the story moved
along as if it had been prodded by the sharp tip.

When I'd sat down, I had shared the park with a
woman and two children and a number of downtown
office workers in their shirtsleeves, eating sandwiches
from greasy paper sacks and reading on the grass. Now
I was alone. I marked my place with Booth's note and
walked back to the lot where I'd left my car. The wind
had shifted from Windsor, cold off the river. I didn't
pass a single pair of shorts on the way.

I'd had a green spring. A lawyer representing a local
trucking firm had retained me to collect affidavits from
witnesses to an accident involving one of its drivers in
Indiana, a college basketball coach whose wife had
walked out with their joint savings account hired me
to bring back the wife or the money, or just the money
if I couldn't do both, and a computer software store
where I'd worked undercover ten days on a case of
employee theft had decided to pay me for the month
they thought it would take me to stop the bleeding.
That and the lawyer's retainer and a few other jobs

made up for getting stiffed when I told the basketball coach his wife had earned every penny for sticking past the honeymoon. He clipped me in the mouth in lieu of paying, and got a receipt in the form of a dislocated jaw.

The money went into a crown, the retirement fund, a bottle of good Scotch, new magazines for the waiting room, and the Olds Cutlass, which now had a rebuilt carburetor and stainless steel pipes, handily disguised by dents and chalky paint. I use it to nudge supermarket carts out of parking spaces and blow off troopers on the interstate.

I didn't need Louise Starr's job. Only half of it was my specialty—the missing persons half—and anyway I'd been thinking of driving up to the Upper Peninsula for a couple of weeks to look up an old cop acquaintance who liked to fish, and let my beard grow. I could always start another retirement fund. She'd figured that might happen, and that was why she'd come in person. It's much easier to say no over the telephone, without the violet eyes and the foxglove.

I had a customer outside the office reading that month's *Forbes*, but it was a divorce case. I told him to try the marriage counselor on the fourth floor. It's a three-story building. When he left I unlocked the door to the inner chamber, pried up the window to let out the trapped heat, oiled the old nickel-and-iron fan for later, and sat down behind the desk to burn some offerings on the altar of the god of standard operating procedure.

Louise's information was a pale carbon of a rough sketch done from someone's faulty memory. Eugene Booth had married once, in 1954, and been widowed within two years, no children. He had been honorably discharged from the U.S. Army at the end of the Korean War and had outlived his parents and his only sibling, a brother named Duane. He had worked for a number of newspapers before his books sold and held down a slew of odd jobs, emphasis on *odd*: sparring partner, hardware clerk, chainsaw salesman, slaughterhouse worker, florist, mortuary attendant, volunteer fireman, grease monkey, floorwalker, apprentice exterminator. I could have gotten most of that off the back of one of his books. For an update I called my contact in the Michigan Secretary of State's office, who brought up a recent driver's license for Booth comma Eugene comma No Middle, in five minutes, complete with picture. He said he'd messenger it over. I said I'd money him later. Armed with an official description I called all the area hospitals, starting with the VA, and determined that no septuagenarian white male of Booth's height and weight and coloring had been admitted under that name or any other within the past week. The singsong Indian voice I got at the Wayne County Morgue looked under all the sheets and reported the same thing. All the John Does were either too young or too black.

Booth's Social Security and army pension checks went to a post office box in Belleville. The next ones weren't due until the first of June.

It was getting chilly in the office. The building superintendent had switched off the furnace on May 15 and wouldn't turn it on again before November. I leaned the window shut and sat back down and read three more chapters of Booth's book, but the bloody business in the

old black area of town known as Paradise Valley just
made me restless. I put it back in my pocket, got my
car out of the best space I'd had since someone bought
the abandoned service station across the street, and made
a research trip to John King Used & Rare Books.

The drab four-story building that sticks up like a blunt
thumb from West Lafayette near the John Lodge Expressway was moved there when the interstate came
through in 1947, God knows why. It's a hundred years
old, but there are holes all over the city skyline where
older and better-looking structures have been pulver-
ized by the wrecking ball. It had been a glove factory
in the thirties and forties, then an empty building after
gloves went the way of Jackie Kennedy's pillbox hat.
That was when John King bought it, tore out most of
the partitions, reinforced the interior walls, and filled it
top to bottom with books on every subject, from the
wit and wisdom of Yogi Berra to the post-metamorphal
changes in the vertebrae of the marbled salamander,
and by authors as varied as Sinclair Lewis and Louis
Farrakhan. You can smell the decayed paper and
moldering buckram from the far end of the parking lot.
It's a scent well known to bibliophiles, archaeologists,
and private detectives who spend much of their time
in records offices and basement file rooms.

In the dank interior I climbed a short flight of steps
to the sales counter, where a tall young woman with
the profile of an African princess directed me to the
second floor. This was a vast space divided by stacks
of books on wooden shelves with fluorescent troughs
suspended above the aisles. A youngish compact man
in glasses and a necktie on a denim work shirt led me

to a shallow room off the stairs. The door was secured by a piece of wood stuck through the handle with KEEP OUT PLEASE written on it in Magic Marker.

I thought for a moment I had penetrated to the center of the Denver Mint.

He drew out the piece of wood and let me inside. "The books are arranged by catalogue number. That's the bible there on the window ledge. I'll be out here if you need me, shelving books. I'm always shelving books. We process two thousand books per week."

"I brought this one with me." I showed him the battered copy of *Paradise Valley*.

A lip curled. "We'd charge about a buck for that downstairs."

"Someone told me it was worth a hundred."

"Not in that condition. What you see in here is as good as you'll ever find. The idea was to get literature into people's hands cheap. That didn't mean using vellum and good parchment. On a quiet night you can hear the paper crumble."

"So books aren't forever."

"Books are. The material they're printed on isn't. That's what makes the rare titles so rare."

He left me, although from time to time I saw him looking at me through the glass half-wall that separated the room from the rest of the floor. He must have thought I was a rival dealer.

The paperbacks lined the walls and free-standing cases in solid banks of silver and yellow and black, depending upon the signature color each publisher had chosen for its spines. Each was pocketed in its own glassine bag with a round price sticker pasted on the back. Opaque plastic shades dulled the sunlight coming through the tall outside windows as a further precaution against early demise.

I hefted a three-inch-thick volume off the ledge beneath the glass wall. Its warped cover read *U.S. Paperbacks 1939–1959*. The information inside was listed alphabetically and numerically under publisher headings, cross-indexed by author, title, and catalogue order number. I looked up Booth's name and found ten titles listed under Tiger Books. I scribbled the numbers into my notebook, returned the volume to the ledge, and turned to the stacks.

The system took getting used to. The books were numbered chronologically, and since few authors were prolific enough to offer a series of new titles in a row, tracking down the entire work of one writer involved skipping from shelf to shelf. After some confusion over why Gardner should occupy the spot next to Thompson, and what Woolrich was doing cozying up to Adams, I got the rhythm at last and wound up with three Booth books from those on the list: *Deadtime Story*, *Tough Town*, and *Bullets Are My Business*. All the covers appeared to have been painted by the same artist. He had a weakness for broken-nosed brutes and blondes in torn lingerie.

When I emerged from the room, relieved to be breathing a greater volume of oxygen among the odor of mummy wrappings in the larger space, my guide approached on the trot and punched home the piece of wood. Now the books were safe from everyone but John Dillinger.

"There are six more I'm looking for," I said.

"All we can do is promise to call you if any come in. You can make out a want list at the counter and leave your number."

"What are the chances I'll fill it?"

"Ten, fifteen years ago, not bad. These days it's John Grisham, Stephen King, Anne Rice. Bushels and bushels of romances. We have to turn them away. But you never know: Someone dies, his children clean out the old house, find a box in the attic, and bring it down to see what they can get. Sometimes we strike gold."

"When someone dies."

He adjusted his glasses. "There are more ghoulish ways to make a living. It isn't as if we perch on a dead branch."

"Who would shelve the books if you did?"

The three books came to fifteen dollars and change. There had been two copies in stock of both *Tough Town* and *Bullets Are My Business*, which apparently weren't as hard to find as *Paradise Valley*. The African princess arched her brows. They made perfect half-circles above her large clear eyes. "Are you a collector?"

"Yes." Bills and bruises. "The fellow upstairs wasn't impressed."

"He's a nice guy, but paperbacks aren't his thing. He prefers to spend his time in the rare book room in the other building, oiling the leather bindings. This is the man you want to compare notes with. He comes in once or twice a week to add to his want list." She found a business card under the counter and laid it in front of me. "You can keep it. Everyone here has memorized all his numbers by now."

The information was printed vertically, the way they were doing it now to include fax and cell phone and pager numbers and e-mail addresses and websites. One more communications breakthrough and they'll have to add a second page. Centered, at the top:

LOWELL BIRDSALL
Systems Analysis

I had a flash of a bald fatty in a *Star Trek* shirt, smelling of Ben-Gay. I thanked her and parked the card in the dead end of my wallet, next to the scratch-and-win tickets I got with ten bucks' worth of Unleaded.

3

I'd read enough for one day. I poked the slim paper
sack containing the three books into the glove compartment and tickled the big 455 engine into grumbling
life. The new carburetor fed it a good mix and the exhaust bubbled pleasantly in the shiny pipes. When I
let it out on the Lodge, the last thirty years beaded up
and rolled off the long hood and nubby vinyl top like
rain. I switched on the AM radio hoping for Jan and
Dean and got a gang of grumps complaining about
taxes and the Detroit Tigers. I turned it off and let the
wind whistle.

I slid past the orange barrels on the Edsel Ford just

ahead of rush hour and exited at Belleville, a low-slung community of strip malls, tract houses, and brick apartment complexes doing their best to look like English manor homes with only picture postcards and old C. Aubrey Smith movies to go by. The farther west you travel on the Ford, the less the place matters; but everyone has to have someone to look down on, and so the citizens of Belleville look down on Romulus, which lies to the east, directly in the flight path to Wayne County International Airport.

The White Pine Mobile Home Park was Eugene Booth's last known employer and place of residence. The directions I'd gotten had left out a stop sign. I turned too early and drove a couple of miles through flat farmland broken up by mounds of raw earth where subdivisions were going in before I came to a T and retraced my route. I finally found the park, across from a neighborhood of large older houses with tidy lawns and a glowering aspect, like you always see where developers have moved too fast for a community grievance committee to form. The only pines in view were the ones painted on the sign that identified the place. If any had ever stood there, they'd been cleared to make room for the trailers.

The sun was out again, its rays bending through the curvature of the windshield, yet my hands felt cold on the wheel. I'd driven that same car into one of those places once before and things had not turned out well. It had been a long time ago, but I had shot a woman, and I couldn't think about it without feeling a dull ache in the precise spot where the bullet had gone in.

An Airstream trailer parked just inside the entrance had an enameled OFFICE sign screwed to it. It was a fourteen-foot silver bullet with an outside staircase built incongruously of filigreed wrought-iron. The door made a sound like an empty beer can when I knocked on it. The same callow male voice I'd heard on the telephone earlier invited me to enter.

Everything inside was built to scale except the occupant. A midget chipboard desk stood in front of a louvered half-window with a miniature refrigerator placed within arm's reach. A chintz-covered loveseat pretended to be a sofa against a painted Sheetrock partition separating the office from what was probably a downsized living quarters at the opposite end of the trailer. There was a two-drawer file cabinet too small for the bloated file folders that had drifted on top, and a perky little buzzer of a battery-operated fan pushed air into the face of the young man seated behind the desk talking into the telephone.

"No, Mrs. Mishak, I didn't get a request to hold all package deliveries to your trailer. Mobile *home*, I'm sorry, Mrs. Mishak. Yes, Mrs. Mishak, I realize a pile of packages outside your trailer—your mobile *home*, excuse me—outside your mobile home while you're away is bound to get rained on and invite burglars besides. No, Mrs. Mishak, I'm not calling you a liar, I'm sure you made the request. Unfortunately, Mrs. Mishak, I *don't* know where it is, because I've only been on the job a week, the man who took the request is gone, and I'm up to my *ass* in paperwork I can't find." He stopped talking, blinked. "I understand,

Mrs. Mishak. I'm sure the owner will be happy to take your complaint. Have a nice day, Mrs. Mishak."

He hung up, bent over the telephone, and shouted: "It's a *trailer*, you fat old sow! You're fifty years old and you're living in a fucking box on wheels!"

He was too big for that office, but it wasn't the office's fault; he was too big for most rooms that didn't have frescoes painted on the ceiling. He ran about two-fifty in a plain cotton BVD undershirt with his dirty-blonde hair in a ponytail and blue barbed-wire tattoos encircling his biceps. The biceps were as big around as buckets. The artist would have had to go back for more ink. He had a small gold hoop in one ear and a little yellow stubble on his chin, but he smelled of clean sweat and unscented soap. He was in his early twenties.

"I'm betting she knows all that," I said. "She's just dumping the bag out on you."

"How the hell would you know?" A pair of blue eyes narrowed to paper cuts.

"Because I take that kind of call all the time. You don't have the corner. The only good thing about it is while I'm talking to people like that I'm not burning good gas driving clear out here from Detroit to talk to jackasses like you who don't know who their friends are."

He flexed both arms and I looked around for something to throw at him that wouldn't just bounce off. There was nothing big enough in the trailer. Then he blew out a lungful of air. The tension went out with it. He nodded. "You're the detective. Sorry about that. Here." He opened the little refrigerator, took out two

Stroh's, twisted the top off one, and thumped the other down on my side of the desk.

I twisted the top off mine and we clinked. The beer was ice cold. Moisture had beaded up on the glass. "You didn't get that tan behind a desk." His skin was burned as brown as the bottles.

"Up until last week I cut the hedges and mowed the paths between the trailers. That suited me just fine. All I had to deal with was thistles and poison ivy. I'm just filling in here as a favor to the owner. When this gig's finished he's going to take care of my dog while I'm at Disney World. If I can't find one that isn't housebroken I'll buy one and un-housebreak it. Even at that he'll have less shit to deal with than I do."

"Booth left in a hurry, did he?"

"I don't know about that. He just didn't give much notice. He had this big old bucket of a Plymouth and he just threw a suitcase and a portable typewriter into the back seat and drove away. He didn't peel rubber and he wasn't looking back over his shoulder. I couldn't see him doing that even if he was in a hurry. You could have cut off somebody's head and put it in the drawer where he kept his bottle and he would have just opened it and frowned because he'd have to move the head to get to the bottle. He wasn't the hysterical type."

"Sounds like you knew him pretty well."

"Just to talk to and drink a couple of beers with when it got too hot out to work, like we're doing. I'm closer friends with that bitch Mishak than I was with Booth."

"What did you talk about?"

"Sports and politics. He thought most politicians were full of shit and most professional athletes didn't take enough. He wanted to set up a transfusion." He had a high thin laugh. It irritated him more than it did me and he poured beer on top of it. In addition to the barbed wire he had a tattoo of a Kewpie doll that stuck out its belly when he bent his arm.

"He didn't say anything about himself? A couple of beers every now and then is usually good for a little autobiography. A bottle in the drawer is better."

"That was a gag, on account of he said he was a tough-guy writer. If that's autobiography, I guess you got me. All I ever saw him drink was beer, and no more than two of those at a stretch. I never saw him drunk. What'd he do, write himself a check and sign it Stephen King?"

"Nothing like that. Someone wants to give him money and I'm supposed to find out where to send it. There's a few bucks in it for you, too, if you can help."

"That's an old dodge. Just how few?"

I folded a twenty around one of my business cards and pushed them across the desk. He leaned back and poked them into the change pocket of his jeans without looking at either.

"I've already spent half as much time with you as I did with him all told," he said. "Those old guys don't talk about themselves much. I only found out he was a writer because I caught him pecking away once on that beat-up old typer and asked him if he was writing the Great American Novel. He slammed

down the lid and said half a dozen guys and one
woman already beat him to that. He said the people
he wrote about spent all their time bedding blondes
and kicking down doors. Then he started talking about
the shitty Pistons."

"He's writing again?"

"Hell, it could've been a letter to Ma Bell. He got
that lid down so fast I couldn't swear it wasn't a
sewing machine. I had one beer and got out. I felt
like I'd walked in on him jacking off."

I was sitting in an orange plastic scoop chair that
stuck to my back. The tin trailer was as hot as a kiln.
The little fan was blowing me a raspberry. I rolled
the cold bottle across my forehead. "So far all I'm
getting for my twenty is a bad case of B.O."

"He left some stuff behind. It's in a box in back.
I can get it."

He stayed put after saying it and I looked at him
until he put down his beer and got up and slid around
the partition. He had to stoop to keep from collid-
ing with the headliner and the trailer shifted on its
springs when he walked to the other end.

While he was gone I applied beer to my insides
and the container to my outside. All over the park
windows were open. Somebody was whistling, somebody else was hacking up last night's smoke, the Jef-
fersons were moving on up to the East Side, a kid
with a cardboard ear was blowing a trombone. What
sounded like a neighborhood soccer game was going
on someplace where trailers had not yet gone in,
complete with body blows and adolescent voices trying out their Martin Scorsese vocabulary. It was an-

other spring, and here I was pushing around Andrew
Jackson and waiting for him to push back, just as I
had been doing in January.

The big man came back carrying a fiberboard carton with the big Seagram's 7 stenciled on it in red.
When he plunked it down on the desk I lifted my
chin to see over the open top. It looked like the
usual junk people leave behind. If it were worth anything at all to anyone it would have gone with them.
That's the trouble with detective work. You have to
find out where they went to get a look at the things
that might tell you where they went.

"Just books and cassette tapes," he said. "The books
are falling apart and even the cassettes are held together with Scotch tape; he must have played the hell
out of them. His taste in music was all over the map."

He sat down to finish his beer while I reached inside without looking, grab-bag fashion, and brought
out a flat rectangle of stiff plastic. The cassette was
played three-quarters through. The label read LYNYRD
SKYNYRD. Yellowed strips of transparent tape were
folded over the corners.

I went back for more. Three cassettes this time:
Reba McEntire, Santana, an album of Christmas songs
played on bagpipe by the Scots Greys military band.
The top corners of each wore strips of tape. My host
must have been a CD man not to know what that
meant.

Not that it meant anything that would do me any
good. I dropped the tapes back into the box and sat
back. "Was he chummy with any of the residents?"

"Not if he was smart. A lot of them are retired.

Their kids don't come to see them and all they need is a friendly excuse to drop into the office and bend your ear for three hours. Then there's the scum that gives trailer parks a bad name. If you snuggle up to them you run the risk of getting nailed as an accomplice in a beef for receiving stolen goods, and if you get on their blind side you can wind up with a couple of slugs in you." He lifted his bottle to his lips, but he didn't swig from it. "Well, there was Fleta Skirrett."

"You made up that name." But I was reaching for my notebook and pen.

"I don't have that much imagination. She lived in thirty-six, over in the next row. Not bad to look at, if you like your meat fat. Booth went over there to make repairs two or three times a week. Nothing breaks down that often. None of the trailers here are more than ten years old."

"Romance?"

"All I know is he never put on a clean shirt to visit any of the others."

"Thirty-six, you said?"

"Until last month. She was starting to get a little screwy, cranking up the TV late at night and leaving her keys in the door. After the cops found her wandering down Merriman in pink mules and a flannel nightie her family came and got her. She's in a home somewhere now, I guess."

"No forwarding?"

He shook his head. "She picked up her Social Security checks from a box at the Belleville Post Office. You might try there."

I wrote *Fleta Skirrett* in the notebook and put a question mark next to it. While I was doing that the telephone rang. "What else have you got?" I asked.

He shook his head, said hello into the receiver, said "Shit" under his breath, then: "Yes, Mrs. Mishak. The furnace?" He leaned back and turned his head to read the thermometer mounted outside the window. "No, Mrs. Mishak, I don't guess it *would* be firing, seeing as how it's eighty-two degrees outside. Well, if you're cold, why don't you open a window in your trailer and let some of that heat in? Motor *home*, I'm sorry. . . ."

I left him holding the receiver in one hand and gripping the neck of his beer bottle with the other in a stranglehold.

4

R ush hour had the area by the throat when I got
away from there, and I smoked a third of a pack
of cigarettes while creeping along in the crush after the
driver of a 16,000-pound tractor-trailer rig fell asleep,
jumped the median, and plowed into the outbound traffic heading west. A medevac helicopter from the University of Michigan Hospital drifted down near the scene
as passing drivers slowed to a crawl to get a glimpse
of tangled steel and spilled brains. It would do as an
outlet until bear baiting came back into fashion.

A tired female clerk at the Belleville Post Office had
told me Fleta Skirrett had filed a change-of-address

from a P.O. box to the Edencrest Retirement Home in
Marshall, eighty miles west of Detroit, but that Eugene
Booth still maintained his box in Belleville. That was
a break I hoped I wouldn't need; staking out the lobby
the third of the month in case Booth came in for his
government checks was right up there with having my
prostate examined.

After the traffic jam broke up I bailed out at a suburban mall with a Best Buy and bought a cheap tape
player from a hyper young salesman in a Tasmanian
Devil necktie. Back home I shooed a salesman out of
the office who wanted to set me up with a DNA test-
ing kit, drew a leaf out of the desk to put my feet up
on, and finished reading *Paradise Valley* in one sitting.
Officer Roland Clifford, the hero of the story, was
beaten half to death by the lynch mob, who had then
taken the three innocent black defense workers from
his custody and torn them apart. The final trial scene,
during which a pale and angry Clifford, his head shaved
and bandaged, gave testimony against the defendants,
was even more tense than the violence. The story came
to an end with the conviction of the three ringleaders
and Clifford's promotion to detective sergeant. From
there he had gone on to lieutenant, then inspector,
and finally precinct commander, and following his retirement had appeared often at ceremonies with various black community leaders as a symbol of racial
harmony. He had been dead ten years and the NAACP
and the Detroit Chamber of Commerce were discussing
changing the name of a section of Outer Drive to
Roland Clifford Street in his honor.

That last part was straight history, and postdated

Booth's book. The narrative ended in a seedy resort motor hotel on Black Lake near the tip of Michigan's middle finger, with Clifford reading about the verdict in the newspapers while recovering from his injuries. It wasn't really a happy ending; the blameless dead were still dead, and the rage and intolerance that had led to the tragedy continued to bubble beneath the surface of the World War Two homefront. Whatever rays of hope found their way into Booth's world did so through a dirty window.

Dusk was drifting in. An old building is the most efficient telegraph system in the world: On all three floors empty swivel chairs rolled to a rest, file drawers boomed shut, light switches snapped off, stairs creaked under feet heading heavily home. In a little while the cleaning service would arrive, and then would begin the jet-engine whine of vacuum cleaners and whoosh-whoosh of the superintendent's broom on the foyer floor as he cycled the dirt and twigs and dead butts back to the street. There was nothing keeping me there except the thought of an empty house and two pounds of hamburger thawing in the sink. I switched on the gooseneck lamp, reached into the John King bag, came out with *Deadtime Story*, and read six chapters. This one was about an accountant on the run from the Mafia, or the Syndicate, as Booth called it. The accountant was a decent guy who happened to be good with numbers, and whose love for recording long columns of figures and magically transforming them into sums at the bottoms had obscured the realization that he was working for a mob boss who contracted murder as casually as a cab driver ordered a hot dog in a diner. When an attempt was made on the accountant's life to shut him up, he woke up and took off with the books.

I stopped reading just as he and the ledgers were fleeing north of the city in search of a place to hide. My eyes were scratching in their sockets, but that wasn't why I stopped reading. Something had begun to grow, and I thought that if I kept reading it would shrivel. I tried to look at the thing, but it stopped growing when it was being watched. I needed to quit thinking about it. Whatever it was, it would have to finish fleshing itself out in the dark, like a potato.

I'd brought in a fistful of cassette tapes from the box the trailer park manager had given me. I put batteries in the tape player, selected one of the cassettes at random—*George Takei Sings the Best of the Beatles*, or some such thing—poked it into the slot, and hit the play button.

Buying blank cassettes can be expensive if you're in the habit of doing a lot of recording. Audiophiles who are always taping music off the radio or transcribing it from compact discs and long-playing albums often stretch a dollar by buying pre-recorded cassettes at yard and garage sales, snapping Scotch tape over the holes on the top corners where the tabs have been removed to avoid accidentally recording over the title tracks, and using them in place of blanks. I'd done it myself and had a number of cassettes in my collection that looked just like the ones that had belonged to Eugene Booth. If what I had in the player sounded anything like Mr. Sulu's rendition of "Yellow Submarine," or Patsy Cline if she was more to the preference of a seventy-year-old tough-guy writer, I'd wasted Louise Starr's money at Best Buy.

What I had was silence, a lot of it, then the whir of air stirring around a microphone, followed by what might have been the legs of a chair scraping a floor and then a groaning sigh like a soul crying in hell or an old man sitting down. A throat got cleared, a long gargling acceleration broken in the middle by a cough, sharp as a pistol report. Some fumbling with the mike, then a low fuzzy bass that might once have been rich and pleasant, the voice of a fair roadhouse singer-pianist before too much whiskey, too many cigarettes, and three or more trips too many around a rundown block had hammered it into that dull monotone you hear at last call and over the loudspeaker in the eleventh inning of a pitchers' duel:

"Midnight, now, past curfew. Even the sirens are tired and sound as if they want to go home. They're saying . . . What the hell are they saying? What do they ever say besides 'eeyow'? Jesus, Booth. And why's it have to be midnight? Nothing ever happens at midnight except lousy poetry and a trip to the can. If that's the best you can do you might as well write a crappy horror novel and let 'em stick a skull on the cover. All the really horrifying things happen in broad daylight. Well, hell, there's my opener: 'All the really horrifying things happen'—no, *truly*—'All the truly horrifying things'—no, no, fuck that, that's a goddamn romance word. 'All the really horrifying things happen in broad daylight.' Drink to that." Rattle of an old-fashioned church key against a metal bottle cap, sharp gasp of carbonation released into the air, then the gurgle and the little sucking sound of lips pulling away from the neck of a bottle. I could almost smell the beer. " '. . . happen in broad daylight.' Paragraph. 'Hollywood doesn't think so. Movies with murder in them have to start at night or they waste too much footage getting to the melodrama. That's unless they can get Gable or Cooper; then the sky's the budget. But this isn't a story for Cooper or Gable.'

"Note: Substitute someone contemporary for Cooper and Gable; Cruise and some other twerp. Mustn't limit the readership to old farts and blue-haired ladies who don't mind if a little acting gets in the way of the special effects. How to do that without taking people out of the story? Put Cruise in their heads and they'll shit the first time someone climbs aboard a streetcar. This is harder than I remember." Something creaked; a man's weight shifting in his seat. "Three minutes gone. At this rate I'll finish behind Margaret Mitchell and that old bat who wrote about the ladies' club. . . ."

He picked up his rhythm a little later, dictating whole paragraphs with only a few pauses to substitute a word or rearrange a phrase. Some of it had a familiar ring and I realized I'd read some of the same material in *Paradise Valley*. I'd heard somewhere that when a writer begins to plagiarize himself he's on his way out. I couldn't credit it. There always seemed to be three or four people on the bestseller list who had been writing the same book since the beginning of their careers. He opened and emptied two more bottles of beer while I was listening, but the alcohol didn't appear to affect his speech or his thinking. A system accustomed to hard liquor absorbs plain hops like a bar rag. Anyway, apart from an interesting glimpse into the interior machinery of the creative mind, I didn't get much out of that tape or the one I substituted for it a little later, aside from the conviction that the thing that was growing like a potato in the moist dark corner of my subconscious was still putting out sprouts. I decided to go home and not think about it a little longer. I deliberately left behind Booth's books and the cassettes and the player so I wouldn't be tempted.

I forgot about the dusty old books in the fiberboard carton on the back seat, though. It caught my eye when I got out in my garage, but I have an iron will. I left it there all the time I was preparing meatloaf from my grandmother's Gypsy recipe and all through dinner. It was no help. The point was not to think about Eugene Booth at all and I couldn't not do it with the paraphernalia sitting ten feet away on the other side of the firewall. I washed down dinner with a second bottle of beer and went out and lugged in the carton.

Sitting in my one good armchair in the living room drinking my post-prandial Scotch, I hoisted one of the cloth-bound books out of the carton beside the chair and opened it in my lap. The spine was split and the paper gave off a smell of dry must that reminded me of the air in John King's bookshop. The title, *Causes and Repercussions of the Detroit Riot, June 20–21, 1943*, was as catchy as a yarn worm on a paper hook. It was a privately published report addressed to Frank Murphy, former Detroit political strongman and then justice of the United States Supreme Court, prepared by an associate professor of Social Studies employed at Wayne University, since renamed Wayne State. Following the title page was a 133-page chronological history and statistical breakdown of the situation and events that had culminated in the day-and-a-half racial brawl that swept the city while the Second World War was in full cry. The upshot, once the population figures were weeded out and the demographic vocabulary was rendered down into plain English, was that the close proximity of Negro and white defense workers in the converted automobile plants had created friction that burst into flames following an altercation between a white and a black motorist on the Belle Isle bridge. In flat pedantic language, the educator managed to make the deaths of thirty-five people—twenty-nine of them Negroes—over a thirty-six-hour period sound as dull as the annual mean rainfall in British Honduras. Without footnotes or statistics, Booth had managed to do far more with just one image: a scene of a carload of transplanted white Kentuckians quartering the neighborhoods for black prey with shotguns across their laps. The picture was seared into my memory as if the ghost of Francisco Goya had been summoned forth to paint it in scarlet and indigo; as if I had witnessed the act that had inspired it.

Booth, or someone who had owned the book before him, had been impressed enough with the report to highlight whole sections in yellow. Some whole pages were set off in this way, so that it seemed it would have been much easier to strike out the passages that held no interest and save the rest.

The next book I looked at covered the same subject, but more sensationally. It was shabbily bound in dirty green cloth with the cardboard corners poking through, with a tattered paper dust jacket painted in orange and black, showing comic caricature black faces with banjo eyes being pursued by a single redheaded Neanderthal in a torn BVD undershirt carrying a black-jack. Gore dripped from the letters of the title: *Hell in Detroit.* The copyright was August 1943, but I didn't need it to recognize a slap-up job intended to capi-talize on a hot story before news from the foreign front dumped water on it. The prose did that. The author's name, Jack McCord, had pseudonym all over it. Who-ever he was, whatever name he'd signed on his checks, he was in love with exclamation points and italics. Booth or his predecessor hadn't bothered to highlight a single one.

There were four more books in the box, three of them trade paperbacks with creased and thumb-smeared covers. One was a mainstream novel about the riot, written by an author whose name I recog-nized, in a style that was both literary and restrained. The others were standard histories of Detroit. A high-lighter had been used on chapters dealing with the riot. The novel wasn't highlighted. Booth—and I was sure it was him now, unless he'd acquired all the books from one man with one pen—only plagiarized himself.

The first day of any missing persons investigation is mostly catch-up. You have to find out who a man is and where he's been and what he's been up to be-fore you can find out where he's gone. I only had a little of the first three, but then I'd only been work-ing since lunchtime. The books might have been left over from his original research for *Paradise Valley*, except the three trade paperbacks and the hardcover literary novel had all been copyrighted years after Eugene Booth had stopped writing professionally, and the yellow highlighter pen hadn't yet been invented when he was laying the groundwork for his paperback thriller. Nor had cassette recording tapes, but he had been dictating something onto them that sounded a lot like *Paradise Valley*, albeit with a twist that was new and if anything more sinister.

Sinister. A Eugene Booth word if ever there was one. I was tired from all the driving and talking and reading, but if I went to bed in the frame of mind I was in I'd be lucky not to have that rough droning voice playing through my head all night. I heard plenty enough voices as it was.

I dumped everything back into the carton, swept the dust off my lap, and turned on the TV. The sitcoms were too shrill and I didn't understand the teenage soap opera, so I watched the second half of a theatrical movie that had been carved open to insert commercials and then the eleven o'clock news as far as the weather. The forecast for tomorrow was more of the same, good weather for driving. That made up my mind for me and I turned in knowing what I was going to be doing the next day.

Lying between the cool sheets I thought I knew too much about where Eugene Booth had been just before he sent back Louise Starr's check and lit out with his portable typewriter and too little about where he'd been and what he'd done between finishing his last novel and coming to work at the White Pine Mobile Home Park. That meant at least another day of catching up, and moving in the wrong direction to boot. Whatever good it did me or didn't, it would have something to do with an old woman in Marshall who was losing her mind.

5

Eugene Booth was waiting for me on the floor of my office when I got in at eight. Standing in the doorway I tore open the manila envelope from the Michigan Secretary of State's office and looked at his face on the duplicate of his driver's license, broad and flushed under a good head of iron-gray hair, brushed straight back and receding at the temples. He wore square glasses with heavy black rims and the scowl people used to assume for official photographs before the people who took them loosened up enough to tell them to smile. He had a strong thick nose that looked as if it might have been broken once, although I'd have to

see it in profile to be sure. He reminded me of someone. I couldn't think who. I had the odd sensation that
whoever it was I didn't know his name.

Included was a Xerox copy of Booth's motor vehi-
cle registration. He was driving a 1979 Plymouth, mint
green, with a white vinyl top. I figured I'd know it
when I saw it.

I went to the desk and stood there long enough to
call Louise at the number she'd given me and file my
report. A fresh chirpy voice answered and put her on
right away. It was all business. She thanked me and
said I didn't have to call again unless I had something
important. I was in a hurry to get on the road to Marshall. When I cradled the receiver three minutes after
I'd dialed I should have felt relief.

An excavation crew had erected a twelve-foot pile
of red earth on the asphalt of the deserted service station across the street where I usually parked my car.
They were going to scrap the subterranean gasoline
tanks so they wouldn't collapse under someone with a
good lawyer, fill in the hole, knock down the glazed
brick building that had been boarded up for years, and
put up a KFC or something similar in its place. With
the casinos and the new baseball park coming in downtown, the center of the city had begun to pry open its
gummy eyes and gape its toothless mouth in a yawn
and stretch its wasted limbs toward the sun. I didn't
know how long my little building would be able to
hold out, with its gargoyles on the roof and its fossil
on the third floor. For the time being I was using whatever meter I could find and feeding it quarters every

two hours or so, just in case the doctor's caduceus I had clipped to the visor didn't work.

Somewhere past Belleville and the site of my interview with the groundskeeper-turned-park-manager, the Edsel Ford stopped being the Edsel Ford and became plain old I-94. It hadn't been resurfaced since it was built to ferry defense workers to the Ford B-17 plant at Willow Run, and now M-DOT crews were sweating day and night to peel it down to its original concrete and build it back up from bedrock. At that hour the traffic was light coming from Detroit and I didn't lose much more than ten miles an hour waiting my turn to thread through the lane closures and temporary shunts to the inbound. Rollovers and running gun battles were confined to peak traffic times.

It was two and a half hours to Marshall and I made it with the help of a local jazz program on NPR and then a Ted Hawkins tape in the deck to avoid the news from the current hotspot in the eastern hemisphere. There were long stretches of flat green farmland dotted with stately old barns in various tragic stages of disintegration, with here and there a sprawling multiplex theater sprung up from what used to be a drive-in, bravely trying to fill all its parking spaces; they'd have had to program a new *Batman* and three or four *Titanic*s, and even then they'd have room left over for Woodstock. What we do best in America is waste space.

Marshall was founded by German farmers, and the city fathers work very hard to remind people of the fact. A long winding route leads off the expressway and through the business section, dominated by an enormous restaurant built along Bavarian lines, with ex-

posed timbers and *Wienerschnitzel* on the menu. With
it behind me I consulted my scribbled directions briefly
and turned down a tree-shaded cul-de-sac lined with
modest brick houses and ending before a long low
L-shaped building of golden brick with ornamental shut-
ters on the windows and EDENCREST RETIREMENT HOME
painted in elegant script on a sign pegged to the front
lawn. There was paved parking for twenty cars, half of
which was taken up by what were probably employee
vehicles; the visitors' slots stood as good a chance of
filling up as any of the multiplex lots.

I parked next to an EMS unit that was doing its best
to look like an ordinary van, with its Christmas-tree
lights placed discreetly between the head- and taillamps,
got out, peeled my shirt away from my back and shook
it, and put on my sportcoat. I used my reflection in
the glass door in front of the building to adjust the
knot of my tie. Older people in general interpret a little formality as a sign of respect.

The place was air-conditioned, but the temperature
wasn't more than three or four degrees lower than outside; the elderly chilled easily. A light fresh potpourri
had been laid in over the Lysol. A door marked OFFICE
stood open to the right and I entered a small room
with two visitors' chairs on steel frames and a painted
steel desk. Tacked to the wall a bright-colored poster
with a photo of a killer whale flashing its baleens in-
formed me that I was dressed for any occasion as long
as I was wearing a smile. A leathery-faced young woman
with tightly coiled red hair smiled up at me from behind the desk, setting the example. She wore a yellow
T-shirt with a smiling sun printed on it and had been

writing on a sheet attached to a clipboard braced against the desk when I came in. White plastic letters snapped to a nameplate on my side of the desk read MRS. MILBOCKER. She transferred the smile to the card I gave her, then returned the smile to me.

"The detective," she said. "Did you have any trouble finding the place?"

"No, your directions were fine."

"I'm glad to hear that. So many of our guests' families seem to get lost and don't show up."

"That's the policy, is it?"

"It has to be. Once you start to chew over human nature it's difficult to be cheerful for the sake of the guests. I don't imagine your work is all that different."

"I only have to be cheerful for my own sake. It's easier on the smile muscles."

"They say it takes fewer to smile than it does to frown. The people who say that never worked in a retirement home." She glanced down at the clipboard. "It's Miss Skirrett you wanted to see?"

"It is. I still do. Is she up to receiving visitors?"

"She's holding court in the TV room. I'll take you."

Mrs. Milbocker had large hips in tight faded jeans with a daisy stitched on one hip pocket. I figured her for a flower child during the Age of Aquarius. We walked briskly down a wide hallway with stainless steel rails on both sides. The door to each numbered room was painted a different color, probably to assist confused residents in finding their way back to their rooms. She stopped to touch the wrist of a bony old man in a heavy sweater who was dozing in a wheelchair and yell a glad word into his hearing aid. I was pretty sure

she'd been looking for a pulse. He came awake, lifted
his trifocals to see her at a better angle, and asked
when they were serving supper.

"It's morning, Mr. Goldstein. Lunch in two hours."

"Shit, I'll be dead by then." He went back into his
fetal curl.

"Mr. Goldstein was the first American on Corregidor,"
Mrs. Milbocker said as we resumed our journey. "He
can still smell it, he says. He says that's the part the
movies can't get, the stink of blasted-open bodies."

I said, "I imagine you learn a lot in this job."

"If we could harness the life experience in this one
building, we'd be on Mars by now."

We made a wide circle around a knot of residents
gathered in front of a pair of double doors secured
with a cable lock. Most of them were in wheelchairs.
Two or three stood grasping the steel wall rail as if
letting go would pitch them down a steep cliff. The
women's hair was coiffed in a variety of exotic styles;
practice for local beauty-school students. Most of the
men wore bright golfing caps with fuzzy balls on top.

Mrs. Milbocker said, "I gave up trying to shoo them
away from the lunch room my second week here. They
start drifting toward it exactly two hours before each
meal. Most of them don't have watches, and the ones
who do never look at them. They just know. Poor
dears, we try to keep them occupied and entertained,
but eating's the only thing that holds their interest; eating and looking forward to eating. When it doesn't interest them anymore we know they're getting ready to
leave us."

"It must be tough to watch."

"It is if you think about it. I stopped doing that my *third* week. These days I think of it as working in a hotel: They check in, they check out."

"I notice you don't call them by their first names."

"I didn't learn that here. My parents taught me. It's called respect. Here we are."

We'd stopped before a doorway without a door. The room inside was a little larger than the average living room, with armchairs and sofas upholstered in green and yellow and orange Naugahyde arranged in front of a cabinet TV set with a twenty-three-inch screen. A morning show was playing, with a fat comic in a chef's hat showing the perky blonde hostess how to boil eggs, but the sound was off. A couple of the residents in the seats were watching the screen, but three or four others were looking at a woman who was even fatter than the comic, sitting on the end of the orange couch jingling the ice cubes in a tall glass of what looked like iced tea and talking with both hands. Her hair, teased, sprayed, and dyed cotton-candy pink, brought back memories of Carroll Baker, but her fat face and the massive arms jiggling out of the holes in her sleeveless yellow dress belonged more to Gertrude Stein. A pair of silver-framed glasses on a chain around her neck lay horizontal on her bosom. The long story she was telling about the time her girlfriend locked the keys in the car when they were crossing the Straits of Mackinac on the ferry amused her more than it did her listeners, but what should have been a foghorn bray of a laugh issuing from that flesh mountain was a tinkly little-girl giggle, hardly a bubble in the stream of her

high breathy Marilyn Monroe speech. Coming down the
hall overhearing her I'd thought a cartoon was playing.

I'd come into it in the middle, but it didn't seem to
be much of a story, and I wasn't the only one who
thought so. Those who joined in when she laughed
missed a beat, reacting more to her glee than to the
detail that had prompted it. The entertainment lay in
watching her entertain herself.

I took advantage of a brief pause while Fleta Skirrett sipped iced tea to murmur in Mrs. Milbocker's ear.
"I was told she was beginning to lose it."

"This is one of her good days. Last Monday she
walked all the way from her room at the end of the
building to the front door stark naked. She'd have kept
right on walking if I hadn't happened to glance up as
she passed the office."

The fat woman finished her story on a high squeal-
ing note. While she was taking a breath and before
she could start telling another, Mrs. Milbocker approached and put her hand on her shoulder. "Miss Skirrett, this is Mr. Walker. I told you he was coming to
see you today?" There was hope in her tone.

"I remember." It came out testy; evidence that the
stories were true. She looked up at me with unfocused
eyes, but would not put on her glasses in that company to see what I looked like. She smiled with well-
fitting teeth. "Would you give an old fat woman a hand?"
She offered one loaded with junk jewelry, with bright
pink polish on the nails.

I took it and braced myself, but she rose with the
kind of easy grace you only see in people who have
been accustomed to moving around extra tonnage for

a long time. She had on a perfume that put me in mind of a gift shop loaded with porcelain gnomes and pillows embroidered with hearts. She gave my hand a squeeze before letting go. Her palm was as moist and squishy as a shower cap.

I thanked Mrs. Milbocker. She smiled in response, cast a last considering glance at Miss Skirrett, and left us, checking vital signs on the way.

"My room's just down the hall. Now, don't you go getting any ideas about closing the door with just us two in there." Fleta Skirrett's voice twirled up into a hysterical titter. The other residents laughed at her laugh and redirected their attention to the cooking lesson on TV. No one bothered to turn up the sound.

I accompanied the woman in the yellow dress down the hallway to a purple door near the end. She wore her stockings rolled to mid-calf with flesh spilling over the tops like dough. On the way she waved at a woman shuffling along the rail with a hump and a frizzy permanent, and a man in a white belt and shoes and two kinds of plaid looking out a window at a humming-bird buzzing around a feeder on a squirrel-proof stand. Neither of them paid any attention to her.

The purple door led into a small bedroom. A pink-and-white crocheted coverlet dressed up a bed with plain head- and footboards and a tropical fish with red stripes and a big tail shaped like a scimitar circled the inside of an old-fashioned round bowl on the bureau. Color Polaroid shots of what might have been nieces and nephews in drugstore frames covered one wall along with older black-and-white snapshots of people in hats and overcoats standing next to automobiles with bulging fenders and bug-eye headlamps. A painting, done boldly in oils, occupied a gilded plaster frame on the wall opposite. The frame had been expensive when it was new, but now there were white chips on the corners and old dirt and grime caked black in the ridges and between the petals of the florets.

I wasn't interested in the frame. An original painting is rare in such surroundings and I stepped up for a better look. The scene struck a bass chord I felt in my testicles. I saw again the broken-nosed profile of the rough customer in the trenchcoat in the foreground, the overdeveloped blonde in the red slip waving a broken bottle in the background center—the sweet spot— the bedroom strewn with books and clothing, and dark elongated figures running hunched over amid the flames burning outside the window; only this time everything was eight times larger and I could see the heavy combed brushstrokes in the thick paint. It was the original illustration from which the cover of *Paradise Valley* had been reproduced.

Like many seriously overweight people, Fleta Skirrett was light on her feet, tiny ones with painted nails in woven-leather sandals; I didn't know she was standing right behind me until I smelled her gift-shop perfume. I felt her breathy whisper on the back of my neck.

"That's me, all right," she said. "I was a blonde then. We all were; Monroe was just getting big and we thought a bottle of peroxide was all that stood between us and Hollywood. God, I'd kill for a butt about now. Got any?"

6

You were a model?"

In the time it took me to reshape what she'd told me into a question, she'd flounced over to a platform rocker upholstered in flowered chintz and lowered herself into it with the same grace she had used getting up. She put on her glasses, smiled at what she saw, and said, "You might try not to look so surprised. Just because a girl turns sixty and puts on a few pounds doesn't mean her feelings can't be hurt. How about that cigarette?"

She was banging hard on seventy, but her fat filled in the wrinkles. I shook a Winston out of the pack and went over and held it out. "I'm out the window at the first siren."

"I'm not a charity case. I'm paying rent on this dump and if I feel like smoking it up I'll build a campfire on the rug." She leaned forward to let me light it, then sat back and tilted her head to one side to blow smoke out the corner of her mouth. "You might close the door and open the window, though, just to avoid upsetting a nurse. They're delicate creatures, poor dears."

I saw it then, when she mentioned the nurses: the feral look of the woman wielding the broken bottle. You never outgrow enemies in this life. Near the end they all wear white and drape stethoscopes around their necks.

The window was one of those horizontal jobs that tilt out on pivots. I tilted it and walked over and shut the door and leaned back against the bureau and lit a cigarette for myself. I didn't want one especially, but the generation she belonged to never let a lady smoke alone. We took turns tipping our ashes into a squat turquoise-painted Mexican pot that was supposed to contain a plant on a round some-assembly-required pedestal table beside the rocker. That made me an ash brother and someone to confide in. A fine gray powder coated the top of the black potting soil inside. No plant had grown there in a while, only butts.

"Edencrest seems like a nice place," I said. "Modeling must have paid well even back then."

She spat smoke. "It's a rathole with a fresh coat of paint. My Social Security just covers the rent. I made more in tips waiting tables. But waiting tables won't get you into the movies."

"Did you get into the movies?"

"Plenty of times. All it cost me was the price of a ticket."

"How'd you wind up posing for paperback covers?"

" 'Wind up' is right. I came to the agency hoping to do magazine covers. That's how Lauren Bacall and Audrey Hepburn started. I shot lingerie spreads for catalogues for almost a year. Eleven months into my career I was still parading around in my undies with my head cut off in every shot. When they told me the art director at Tiger Books had requested me for a cover I thought I was on my way. The address they gave me belonged to the Alamo Motel. You know the Alamo?"

"I know the Alamo." I saw Eugene Booth's typewritten note to Louise Starr on Alamo stationery. I took in a lungful of smoke to keep my body from vibrating.

"It ought to go on the National Register of historical fleatraps. The architect, if it ever had one, designed bus stations and none of the owners ever changed anything but the lightbulbs. 'Fleta,' I said, 'you're in the arts. Van Gogh worked out of an attic.' So I go in and meet the artist and he hands me a slip two sizes too small to squeeze myself into. I'm coming up on my second year in the business and I'm still modeling underwear. I think that's when I realized Lana Turner had nothing to fear from me."

"That was the *Paradise Valley* cover?"

"Mm-mm." She shook her head, sucking on the filter tip. "*Truck Stop*. You never heard of it. It was the first Tiger title not to go into a second printing. The guy that wrote it made a bigger noise when he threw himself out of a window at the Book-Cadillac. It didn't help sales, though. I didn't work for six months after that. The goddamn editor that bought the book blamed it on me. He said I scared away customers. I looked too intimidating. I wasn't ladylike enough holding a forty-five automatic as big as a Frigidaire."

"How'd you get back in?"

"Gene requested me. He liked the *Truck Stop* cover and he wanted one just like it for *Paradise Valley.*"

"That's Eugene Booth?" We were coming to it now.

The feral look returned. She took the cigarette out of her mouth, picked a shred of tobacco off her lower lip, and flicked it into the clay pot. "What's your interest in Gene? Is he in trouble?"

"Just the opposite. I'm working for someone who wants to give him money."

She managed to make a giggle sound like an arid chuckle. "Just because the catalogue hacks cut my head off doesn't mean I never use it. I read some of the books I posed for; I still had hopes and I didn't want to get myself tied up with pornography or commie propaganda. It was the fifties, remember. Decency still had a good reputation. Anyway, I read some of the books and in every one of them the detective claimed he wanted to give the guy he was looking for money. That was the magic word. It was a lie every time."

"It usually is when I tell it. Not this time. A New York publisher wants to reprint *Paradise Valley.* The money's good, but Booth gave it back without explaining why and pulled out of the trailer park. I'm supposed to find out where he went. If he still doesn't want the money, that's okay, but this is New York we're talking about. They can't understand why anyone would turn down hard cold cash. I'm supposed to ask."

"Good luck, brother. Gene wouldn't tell you his blood type if he was bleeding all over his shoes."

"You must have done all the talking all those times he came over to visit you in your trailer."

"Mobile home. Nobody wants to spend their golden years in a trailer." She took one last drag that ate the cigarette up to its filter tip. "Got any more of those? One just wakes up my lungs. The second's for nourishment and I need a third to put them back to sleep."

"Enough of them could put them to sleep for good." I gave her the pack. There were only a couple left.

"I heard that." She lit one off the butt of the first and poked the butt out of sight in the potting soil like a plant stick. "That's our government for you: Subsidize tobacco for two hundred years, then tell us it's bad for us and we have to quit, but they don't say how. I gave up coffee when they said it raised my blood pressure and drinking when they said it hurt my liver. Now they say coffee cures migraines and liquor unclogs the blood. If I smoke long enough they'll tell me Camels cure rheumatism. Any chance you could steer some of that New York money my way? I'm thinking of writing my memoirs. You know I slept with Dali."

"Really?"

"Well, he said he was Dali. I couldn't figure out what he was doing painting Bulldog Drummond. Seriously, I could use some extra for smokes. My Social Security checks go direct to the cashier."

"I got you from the new manager at the park for twenty. What will a carton get me?"

"Twenty's as much as I got for a week of holding still in my unmentionables. Five of that went to the chiropractor. Bone-crackers aren't so cheap anymore."

I started to put a new fifty on the bureau. She told me to put it in the top drawer, what was she, a prostitute? I parked it on top of a stack of neatly folded blouses. She sure liked yellow.

"Gene got me into White Pine," Fleta Skirrett said. "I had a real nice room at my niece's, my own bath, but I couldn't stand her husband. He was a TV pitchman, little bald twerp who kept waiting for L.A. to call. Never did anything around the house, Nancy even had to cut the grass when she came home from work. I stuck it out; no place else to go. Then I read in the paper where Gene was suing somebody and I remembered we used to get along okay when I was posing. The paper said he was managing at White Pine. I called him there. He was glad to hear from me, thought I might be able to help him out with his suit. I don't know how. All I had to do with the book was what's on that wall. I didn't even finish reading it; too depressing. I was nine when the riot broke out and I remember my mother being too scared to let my brother and me outside to play. We lived clear up in St. Clair Shores, miles from the trouble."

"My folks were the same way during the riot in sixty-seven, and I was older than you."

"We're past due for a third. Anyway we met for lunch, and I guess it was pretty clear an old fat woman wasn't going to be much use, but I couldn't help telling him my setup. He said there was a vacancy at the park and he could get me a deal if I didn't mind living in a mobile home. I said I wouldn't squawk about a cardboard box if it didn't come with my niece's husband."

"Was he propositioning you?"

"It wouldn't have bothered me if he was. I'd have put out, too. It's been a mighty long time, and Gene is a good-looking man. The itch doesn't go away when you pass fifty. It just gets harder to scratch."

She was growing younger; and I thought of the broad battered face in the photo on Eugene Booth's driver's license. But someone had to fall for the pugs or there wouldn't be so many of them. "I take it from the use of the subjunctive case you and he weren't an item."

She showed off her well-fitting teeth. They might have been all hers at that. "Subjunctive. I know what that is. You've hung around a few writers yourself. No, he wasn't trying to get into my pants, and he didn't. It was just a friendly deal. All the people his age who lived at White Pine were miserable or dull or both. Usually both. A tin box in a row of them is okay for starting out but rotten for ending up. All he ever heard around there was complaints. That's part of the job, but you sure don't want to have to listen when you're with the people you call your friends. If he'd tried to strike up anything social with any of them, he'd have gone as dotty as me."

"I haven't heard anything dotty so far." I got rid of my Winston. It had taken me twice as long as she, and her second had burned down almost as far as the logo. That breathy voice was pure vaporized nicotine.

"What a sweet thing to say. My family says I'm nuts.

I wouldn't care about that, but Gene thought so too. He was the one who told me to come here. It seems I took a little walk one night and he was afraid I'd finish up under a bus. He said, '*You* might not mind, Flea, but a cliché like that would be an insult to me.' He calls me Flea. Guess 'cause I'm bugs."

I smiled. My teeth weren't fitting as well as hers and I'd grown them myself. "What did you talk about when he came to visit? Was he writing?"

"I never heard him talk about writing even when we were young. I didn't know many writers, but all the painters I knew either talked about their work all the time or anything else but. Gene belonged to the second group. At White Pine, he talked about his dead wife, the army, his brother, some of the jobs he'd had; I guess what most men his age talk about. He loved his wife, hated the army, got along okay with his brother. Oh, and he liked to fish, but he said he hadn't been fishing in years. The rest of the time he sat and listened to me chatter on. Pretty dull, huh? I guess we weren't so much different from the others after all."

"His brother's name was Duane, wasn't it? I heard he'd died."

"Gene never said and I didn't ask. You don't, you know, at our time of life. It's tactless. He always spoke about Duane in the past tense, so I guess he did."

It was all wearing thin. Either her personality or the surroundings were leeching all the freshness out of the morning. I thought about showing her Booth's note on the Alamo letterhead, about a gelding knowing better than to try to breed. It stayed in my pocket. I had the thought it was something he wouldn't want her to see.

What that had to do with anything, I didn't know to the tenth power.

"How is it you were friends when you modeled? You said you didn't know many writers."

"I didn't. I met him through Lowell. Gene used to drop in to watch him paint. They admired each other's work. When Gene's books started selling and his publisher wanted to commission a better-known artist in New York, Gene said no. He refused to sign a contract until they agreed to have Lowell do all his covers."

"Lowell?"

"Lowell Birdsall." She waved twelve ounces of zirconia in the direction of the painting on the wall. "They didn't sign them in those days. Potboilers, Lowell said. Something to pay the bills while he was waiting for the Louvre to call."

I couldn't figure out why the name was familiar until I remembered the business card in my wallet. I peeled it out. "Lowell Birdsall," it read. "Systems Analysis." It listed five numbers and none of them was an address. I showed it to her. "I got this from a clerk in a bookstore. She said he's a collector."

She slid down her glasses to read over the tops, then shook her head and pushed them back up. "That's his son. Lowell died years ago. Junior used to sneak in after school, hoping to catch me undressing for work. I still get Christmas cards from him. He's living in his father's old studio in the Alamo."

7

On the way out I leaned into Mrs. Milbocker's office to thank her again. She smiled up from her clipboard. Her leathery face broke up into deep lines.

"Character, isn't she?" she said. "Sometimes I think if some of our livelier guests channeled the energy they spend being charmingly eccentric into just plain living, they wouldn't need Edencrest. But it could be I'm being eccentric myself. It rubs off."

"What did you do before this, traffic cop?"

"Just the opposite. I stole cars and stripped them and sold the parts for drug money. This started out as five hundred hours of community service and ran into six years and counting."

"The system works."

"The system works for those who would've found their way out without it. But if it weren't for this job I'd probably be wearing a gold blazer and selling real estate. Gold doesn't suit my complexion."

"Are you hungry? How's the food at the German place?"

"Yes, and not bad. Unfortunately I have to eat here. The guests become paranoid when they don't see me sharing their creamed corn. I'd invite you, but they'd think you were sent here by the state to shut us down. They've been uneasy ever since we prosecuted an orderly last year for attempted molestation."

"Just as well. I'm addicted to chewing."

"Try the wurst platter."

I left her to her clipboard and went out past a middle-aged couple heading inside with a picnic basket. The woman was reminding the man that this could be Dad's last birthday.

"Bullshit. He's had more last birthdays than the Kennedys."

At the restaurant I got a table under the Hohenzollern coat-of-arms. I was going to order the wurst platter right up until the waitress asked me what I wanted. I lost courage and had pork chops instead, but I washed them down with beer from a bottle with a Valkyrie on the label.

All the way back to Detroit I was aware of the thing growing like a potato in the unlighted bin behind my brain stem. Something Fleta Skirrett had said had fed

it, but I didn't know what. That kind of thing was happening more and more lately. I'd considered taking a
mail-order course in self-hypnosis, but I was afraid I'd
forget how to snap myself out of it.

I did some business back at the office. The answering service said a lawyer had called to ask me to check
out a client's story. I called him for the particulars,
wrapped the thing up in two conversations lasting three
and five minutes respectively, typed up my report along
with a bill, pounded a stamp on the envelope, and slid
it into the OUT basket. There were no messages from
Louise Starr, so Eugene Booth hadn't resurfaced while
I was in Marshall. By then the pork chops were making me sleepy, so I switched on the electric fan and
stuck my face into it and when I was alert enough to
ask questions and listen to the answers I dialed one
of the numbers on Lowell Birdsall's business card. I got
a dreamy kind of a male voice that I had to separate
from the Sinatra ballad playing in the background. He
awoke from his dream when I mentioned Eugene Booth
and told me he'd be out between four and five but
expected to be home the rest of the evening—Room
610 at the Alamo Motel—and looked forward to showing me his collection. He sounded like an only child
with his own room.

I had a couple of hours to kill, so I settled a heel
into the hollow I'd worn in the drawleaf of the desk,
crossed my ankles, and opened *Deadtime Story* to the
spot I'd marked with a spent match.

Following a number of adventures on the road, some
of them in the company of a beautiful female hitchhiker who happened to put her thumb out at just the

right time, the accountant on the run from the mob stopped at a rustic motel in the northwoods. There by the pulsing light of a cheap lamp running off a sputtering generator he wrote a note of explanation to the special prosecutor and wrapped it and the incriminating ledgers in butcher paper. The beautiful hitchhiker, who was staying in the next cabin, had to be persuaded to agree to deliver the package, knowing that they might never see each other again. She didn't get ten miles before she fell into the hands of the Mafia boss's henchmen, from whom the accountant was forced to rescue her. At the end, torn and bloodied, he and the woman marched into the special prosecutor's office, placed the package in his hands, and went out without waiting to be thanked, eager to get to a justice of the peace who would marry them.

It was a tight, suspenseful story, and if the love angle was predictable there was something about the villains, their flat vernacular and working habits, that suggested the author had borrowed them from life rather than the movies or the pages of his competitors' books. I wondered where in his herky-jerk resumé Booth had come into close enough contact with the breed to collect their idiosyncrasies like blood samples. It left me thirsting for more Booth. I saved *Tough Town* and *Bullets Are My Business* for later and poked another tape into the cassette player.

" 'He was too tired to think,' " he dictated in his scratchy monotone, " 'or maybe he just didn't want to. He drank from the flat pint and sat outside the wobbly circle of gasoline-generated light and watched the moths hurl themselves against the glass as mindlessly as waves smacking the shore. And he didn't think, didn't think.' " A bottle gurgled, lips pulled away from it with a kissing sound. "Okay, Tolstoy, you've got your beginning and your end. Now all you have to do is write twenty chapters to stick in between."

I'd been half-dozing, the raspy sentences grinding the edges of my subconscious with no meaning. The drinking noises and the slight lift in his tone when he'd stopped dictating snatched me awake. One phrase had come through, but I'd needed the hand up to realize its importance. I rewound the tape and played back the passage. At "gasoline-generated light" I hit the stop button. I picked up *Deadtime Story* and paged backward from the end, past the touching scene in the adjoining cabin when the woman clutched the bundle of evidence to her breasts in lieu of the man she loved, to the one in the accountant's cabin. Once again he grimly wrapped the ledgers and scribbled the prosecutor's name on the slick white paper in the throbbing light of a lamp hooked up to a generator. There were moths there as well.

The ending he'd dictated wasn't that much different from the end of the original version of *Paradise Valley*; the last scene in that one took place in a motel on a lake. He liked to write about anonymous lodgings in remote locations. Someone else knew about some other things he liked. The potato was ripe.

I called the Edencrest Retirement Home and got a nurse who said Mrs. Milbocker was busy at the opposite end of the building. I said I'd hold. I listened to Burt Bacharach for twelve minutes.

"This is Mrs. Milbocker."

"Amos Walker again. Can you put Fleta Skirrett on the telephone?"

"I can't, Mr. Walker. She had an episode."

The receiver creaked in my grip. "What kind of episode?" She couldn't have died on me. Booth would have scorned to write a scene like that.

"Nothing serious. She forgot she ate lunch and accused a nurse of plotting to starve her to death. She became so agitated we had to sedate her. You won't be able to talk to her before tomorrow morning."

"How late is your shift?"

"We're shorthanded. I'm on until midnight."

I gave her my home number. She already had the one at the office. "If she wakes up tonight, ask her where Gene Booth likes to fish."

8

The Alamo Motel clung to its spot on West Jefferson Avenue like a half-dead bush to the side of a cliff. It offered four tiers of rooms exactly the same size, entered from outside by way of elevated boardwalks with open staircases zigzagging between. The nearest thing to a renovation it had undergone in recent years was a brief period during which the *M* in *Motel* had been replaced with an *H* on the sign in front; an attempt to lure conventioneers from the Westin and Pontchartrain hotels downtown. It hadn't worked, and after a while the *M* had gone back up to reassure transients they'd have a place to park. Jungle growth sprouted through cracks in the asphalt lot, green grunge and hornets' nests occupied the brass-plated carriage lamps mounted on the outside walls above the doors to the rooms. That was as much life as the place showed most days.

I parked next to a handicapped slot where a Dodge truck stood on blocks with a young elm grown up through its front bumper and mounted the stairs to the top floor. The original owner's aspirations showed in the numbering of the rooms: They started on the ground floor at 300, jumped from 310 to 400 on the next, and ended on the fourth floor at 610, where Lowell Birdsall lived. The idea was to make forty rooms seem like more than six hundred. It didn't stop the owner from going broke when the Edsel bottomed out. The Fraternal Order of No-Necked Sicilians had owned it for a couple of years, intending to run it into the ground and burn it for the insurance, but it was a stubborn organism that refused to lose money beneath a certain level, and they sold it for what they had put into it. Now it survived as a combination welfare hotel for permanent residents and a stopping-place for visitors who wanted something a little more private than the Y but didn't mind sharing their quarters with a few silverfish. Both the fire marshal and the building inspector overlooked the code violations at the request of the police, who enjoyed the convenience of knowing where to look when the mayor needed a drug bust.

In front of 610 I leaned on the leprous iron railing to finish my cigarette and watch the shadows cross the Detroit River on the other side of Jefferson. At that hour the Windsor skyline looked like a row of books of uneven heights and thicknesses. It was the only spot on the North American continent where you could look across at a foreign country without seeing either wilderness or tattoo parlors. I snapped the filter end at the homebound traffic and turned around and knocked on the door.

The man who opened it didn't look like the son of an artist or a systems analyst or a man named Lowell Birdsall. He was built like a retired professional wrestler going to fat, with rolls of slackening muscle straining the neck of his clean white T-shirt and a dusting of stubble on his shaven head. His ears lay flush to his skull and he had no eyebrows, so that the top half of his face was frozen in an expression of perpetual surprise. A black smudge of moustache and goatee beard covered the lower half. He looked as if he could take me, but he'd have had to climb a stepladder to do it. His broad chest, thick arms, and great muscular thighs belonged to a six-footer who'd been put through a trash compactor.

"The P.I.?" he greeted. "May I see your license?"

I showed him the photo ID. His goatee drooped.

"That's all there is to it? I thought there'd be a seal or something."

"That's Eagle Scout." But I took pity on him and let him see the half of the wallet with the sheriff's star attached. He gathered up his chin then and nodded. I stepped around him into the nearest thing to a combination museum and indoor amusement park I'd ever seen in a tiny apartment.

One wall was painted white to set off the art that decorated it. Original canvases and movie posters in metal frames plastered it from ceiling to floor and from side to side, waging a war of primary colors toward a single objective: enumerating the variety of ways in which a man and a woman can put each other in mortal jeopardy. I saw guns and broken bottles, saps and baseball bats, Tommy guns and in one instance a machete, all raised and ready to spill the maximum amount of blood onto the Deco carpet at the base of the display. Red lips snarled on the women, Cro-Magnon brows beetled on the men in a blown-up comic-book parody of animal emotion stood up on its hind legs and wrapped in a trenchcoat or lacy lingerie. A connoisseur now, I recognized Lowell Birdsall Senior's brushstroke on a couple of the canvases, but the others, cruder and more angular, must have set his son back several months' pay at collectors' shows and specialty shops.

It was a hell of a thing to fall asleep looking at, but the pull-down ring belonging to a Murphy bed socketed into the wall opposite said that was how Birdsall found unconsciousness every night. He probably dreamed in cadmium red, phthalo blue, and titanium white.

Someone had taken down the plaster from the other walls, ripped out the laths, and installed shelves between the studs. I looked without wonder at the unbroken rows of Pocket Books silver, Penguin green, Fawcett yellow, and all the other trademark spine colors, arranged not alphabetically by author or title, but by catalogue order number. An additional forty or fifty occupied an original drugstore revolving rack with a Dell Books decal on each of the crossbars. There was a bondage theme on the cover of *The Hound of the*

Baskervilles. I couldn't remember such a scene anywhere in Sherlock Holmes. The room smelled musty
despite the efforts of a small dehumidifier to slow the
decay.

Birdsall crossed the room silently on white-stockinged
feet—his loose-fitting jeans, like his tight T-shirt, were
white too, like the uniform of an orderly in a burn
unit—and lifted the needle from a long-playing record
on the turntable of a cabinet phonograph. It was a vintage machine with two built-in speakers and shiny panels of amber-colored Bakelite streaked with black. June
Christy stopped singing with a squawk and we were
left alone with the hum of the dehumidifier.

There wasn't room for much more furniture, but it
was all period. A laminated table held up a Domino's
box and a glass that looked as if it had contained but-
termilk, with three tubular chairs upholstered in shiny
red vinyl drawn up to it. There was a loveseat covered in nubby green fabric with gold threads glittering
in it standing on skinny black-enameled steel legs and
a yellow wing chair with a tri-colored hassock that re-
sembled a beach ball. If a beatnik didn't come bop-
ping through the door in the next five minutes I was
going to be sore.

A laptop computer lay open on the loveseat, looking as if it had dropped from outer space into Ozzie
and Harriet's living room. That would be what paid the
rent.

"It's the most complete collection in private hands in
the Midwest," Birdsall was saying in his dreamy voice.
He was looking at the books, not the furniture. "I turned

down twenty thousand just last year from a collector in California."

"Twenty thousand." There were cracks in the ceiling and I could hear the toilet running in the bathroom.

"What would I do with money? Just spend it, probably on books, and start all over again. You don't get to own the largest collection in the world by going back to the gate at my age. Do you collect?"

"I'm reading Eugene Booth now."

"I might have guessed. Read him a lot, I bet. You look like you stepped right out of *Bullets Are My Business*. Tiger Books, number nine-fourteen. It's at seven o'clock."

I glanced at the spine. "I've got it. I'm mostly interested in *Paradise Valley*. Fleta Skirrett told me your father painted the cover."

When he smiled, wrinkles stacked his face clear to the top of his head. He wasn't that old; his skin was just dry from rooming with a dehumidifier. I wondered if he ever went out, except to buy more books and launder his whites. "How *is* Fleta? I had the biggest crush on her when I was thirteen."

"Most complete in the Midwest. She told me."

"I saw her at Dad's funeral. She got fat. Living's hell. But on the cover of *Paradise Valley* she'll always be as beautiful as nineteen fifty-one."

It was an opening, but I didn't jump through it. Once a man starts talking about what he likes, you're in the box with a fastball heading straight for the sweet spot. "Is that why you collect?"

"Partly. Life goes fast. Faster now, thanks to that." He gestured at the laptop. "You want to hold on to something, and you think if you don't do it, no one else will. Then it's lost for good. Did you know that more than seventy percent of the books published originally in paperback between nineteen thirty-nine and nineteen sixty are moldering away, with no publisher offering to step forward to reprint them? I'm more in the way of a curator."

"That puts you in the arts. Just like your father."

"My father was a son of a bitch."

I looked at him. His face and scalp were as smooth as a ball bearing. The smile-wrinkles had left no trace. I asked him if I could sit down. He indicated the yellow wing chair and moved the computer to make room for himself on the loveseat. He sat with his knees together and his hands on them. Big hands, they were; wrestler's mitts. He must have had trouble negotiating a keyboard with those banana-size fingers.

"He cheated on my mother with all his models. I never blamed the models—brainless creatures, mostly, sleeping with all the wrong people to get ahead. I mean, *artists*, come on! Nobody with genuine talent has ever been in a position to give anybody else a leg up. They're too busy looking for their next meal. No, the blame begins and ends with my father. He got so he wouldn't even bother to change shirts before he went home. Most people remember the smell of their mother's perfume. I can't separate it from all the others. She killed herself when I was in college. The state police said it was an accident. She ran her car into a bridge abutment on I-75. There were no skid marks."

"I'm sorry."

He shook his head. "That's his line, and he never

said it. He wore a black armband for a fucking year. It got him laid even more. And the older he got, the younger they got. He blew out his heart at seventy-eight plowing a sixteen-year-old redhead. I didn't go to see him buried."

"But you live in his old studio, and you collect books whose covers he painted."

"I'm Lowell Birdsall's son." The smile he made didn't stir so much as a wrinkle. "I collect the same models he did, and for the same reasons. The rent's cheap enough to allow me to do that. The only difference is I just look at them. I'm a virgin, the oldest in Detroit."

The dehumidifier lapped up moisture through the silence. I showed him my pack. He shook his head again.

"Please don't. It's very dry in here."

I put it away. "I'm looking for Eugene Booth on behalf of his publisher. Fleta Skirrett said he and your father were friends. Have you stayed in contact?"

"Not since my mother's death, when I stopped going home to visit. Actually, before that. After Booth's wife died, he started double-dating with my father and his models. He used to drop by the house to visit, but he stopped coming eventually. I think he was ashamed to look my mother in the eye. My theory is he knew my father didn't care, so he decided to feel bad enough for both of them. That's why I read his books. He had a decency I didn't get to see very often. It runs through even his most hardboiled stories."

"Miss Skirrett used the word *decency* too. It seems to have been important to both of them."

"As much as money to a poor man. Writers and artists and actors and models have been looking for respectability since Shakespeare. But Fleta can tell you more about Booth than I can. They live in the same trailer park."

"Not anymore." I told him Booth had left and Fleta was living at Edencrest.

"The waiting room," he said.

"It seems nice."

"They all seem nice. Some of them are. It doesn't change the fact that nobody leaves under their own power. She's a courageous woman. It's Booth who ran away."

"I think I know which way he ran."

"So do I."

We shared that through a little humming pause. I ended it. "You go first."

He spread his big hands on his knees. "When I was a boy I was too busy hating my father and ogling the women he painted and went to bed with and hating myself for ogling them to pay much attention to the books he wrapped them around. It's ironic that I spend most of my income filling these shelves. The original typescripts were always coming through here, with the scenes the publishers wanted illustrated marked off for him to read. Booth used Alamo stationery he stole to save on paper. I don't think Dad ever read any of them all the way through, and he probably threw them out after he got what he needed. The typesetters had copies and no one thought they'd ever be worth anything. If I'd pulled just five or six of them out of the trash, I could sell them now and finance my whole collection. Anyway, I've read them all since in the form most people saw them. You can learn a lot about a writer by reading all his books one after the other. Patterns establish themselves. I knew Jim Thompson had an anal fixation before I found out he suffered from severe hemorrhoids, and I figured out Cornell Woolrich was homosexual before the literary revisionists started in on him. Sooner or later, every one of Eugene Booth's heroes drift up to northern Michigan to think things out in some cheap rented bungalow in the woods. There was usually a lake nearby. He was a Thoreau wannabe. You'll find him in some Walden up north."

"The question is which one. Fleta Skirrett said he liked to fish. Did you ever hear him say where he liked to do it?"

"Black Lake. It's up by Hammond Bay. He used to go there to write. I heard him tell my father once he couldn't write about a city while he was living in it. He had to go where there weren't any car horns to hear them clearly enough to describe the sound. Of course, that's when he was writing. He hasn't produced a thing since fifty-nine."

"He's writing again. His replacement at the trailer park gave me some tapes with his dictation on them."

He got excited. His smile went clear over the top of his head and down into his shirt. "That's the best news I've heard since they found an unpublished novel by W. R. Burnett. I'm surprised you're not halfway up I-75 by now."

"He mentioned Black Lake specifically in *Paradise Valley*, but it didn't register until I read another book and heard the tapes. He didn't say which motel. There were probably several of them even then. By now there are dozens."

His brow went slick in thought. Then he got up and went to a shelf packed with orange Tiger Books spines, pulled out a book, and removed something in a glassine envelope from inside the front cover. He returned the book to the shelf and faced me, holding the object flat to his solar plexus with both hands. They completely covered it.

"He sent my father a postcard when he was writing *Some of My Best Friends Are Killers.* That was in fifty-six, a few months after he lost his wife. I found it in Dad's papers when I was getting ready to sell the house. It's the nearest thing to a letter he had from Booth."

I waited, but he didn't bring it over. I sat back and got very tired. "How much?"

"I want an advance reading copy of the new book when it's ready. And I want the tapes with his dictation."

"I can probably arrange the reading copy. I can't give you the tapes without Booth's permission."

The muscles worked in his forearms. I couldn't figure out where he got his exercise unless it was from climbing stepladders in bookshops. "Well, will you ask him when you talk to him? I'll give him a good price and promise not to go public with the contents. I'll sign a paper to that effect."

"I'll ask."

He came over and held out the item. I took it and looked at it without sliding it out of its transparent envelope. It was a postcard with a canceled three-cent stamp in the corner, postmarked *Black Lake, Sept. 12, 1956.* The handwriting, in faded brown ink, was Booth's:

Lowell,

Fishing's good, writing stinks. Thinking of turning my Smith-Corona into a boat anchor.

Gene

The other side was a hand-tinted photograph of four rectangular one-story log cabins strung out to the right of a fifth with a red neon VACANCY sign in the front window. A sign shaped like an Indian arrow hung by a pair of chains from a horizontal post above the door: WIGWAM MOTOR LODGE.

"Is it still there?"

"The local chamber of commerce will know if it is."

I fanned myself slowly with the card. I wasn't hot. My hand needed a cigarette. "Lonely place to go when your wife just died."

"I doubt he got any fishing in at all, despite what he said on the card. He probably worked the whole time. The rage would have eaten him up otherwise. It got bad enough later to destroy his career."

"Why rage?"

"Well, from the way she died." He stared at me browlessly, reading the same empty expression on my face. His goatee dropped. He gathered it in too far and had to work his lips loose to speak. "I thought a detective would know. Allison Booth was murdered. The police never found her killer."

9

Remind me to unload all my stock. When *you* start looking prosperous, the economy's getting set to slide the other way."

I said, "Now, is that nice? I put on the new suit just for you."

Lieutenant Mary Ann Thaler conned me through the slight correction of her oversize glasses. She barely needed them and probably only wore them to blunt her cheerleader good looks. This season she was wearing her light brown hair short, with springy bangs arcing out over her forehead. She wore no makeup apart from a little pink lipstick and had on a fitted taupe linen shirt and pleated khaki slacks, huaraches on her bare feet with clear polish on the nails. The unlined charcoal blazer she would wear to cover the holster behind her right hip hung on the back of her desk chair. She was stretched out on the fabric-covered sofa she had finally earned for her office at Detroit Police Headquarters, with her ankles crossed and the *Michigan Penal Code* bound in red braced on her lap.

"It's a good suit, too, for off-the-peg," she said. "You need a woman to pick out your ties. Red on white with navy is too J. Edgar Hoover."

"Is that a proposal?"

"Only in the ashes of your dreams. The man I marry won't know a nine-millimeter Glock from a German musical instrument. He'll buck the eight A.M. traffic on the Ford and come home every weekday at six with a healthy fluorescent tan. Saturdays he'll burn brats on the gas grill out back and take me to see Julia Roberts."

"Sunday you'll blow out his brains and then yours." I pointed at the book. "Someone else check out the new John Grisham?"

"I'm studying for the bar, thank you very much."

"You a lawyer? I can sooner see you hooked up with the Poindexter in the chef's apron."

"Me too. I just want to look good on the stand."

"You couldn't help but." I looked out the window. Another stinking beautiful day was sliding in from Windsor. I had no excuse not to make the four-hour drive up to Black Lake. "I need a favor."

"Frank Lloyd Wright tie, navy and gray, with maybe a little white to pick up the shirt. You can get it at Hudson's."

"Not the favor. I need a rundown on an old murder case."

"Give me a date."

"June something, nineteen fifty-six."

She turned a page.

"Too far back?"

"Investigating cases that took place before I was born isn't police work. It's studying history. That far back we don't even bother to put it on computer. I'm not going to spend all my lunch hours this week fighting the crickets for the old files in the basement. I've got allergies."

"I'd do it myself if I could get clearance."

"Go to the newspaper section in the library. All the murders got press then. They were still a novelty."

"That's on the agenda, but I need the real details too. Reporters get everything right except the story."

"Well, I'm not going to the basement." Another page got turned.

"John around?"

"Inspector Alderdyce is on vacation. You can get a good deal on Florida in May. Next Christmas he's going to Iceland for the blubber festival."

"You're in a good mood. Shoot anyone today?"

"It's still early."

I headed for the door. "I'll be at the library. Call me there if you need a detective."

"Let me know if you crack it. It'll look good on the stats when we ask the council for more money."

I took my time turning the knob and opening the door. All I got was the slithering sound of another page turning. I almost had the door closed when she spoke again.

"Who got murdered?"

"A woman named Allison Booth."

"Tomorrow soon enough? It's Casual Friday. I can wear jeans and a sweatshirt. It's dusty down there."

"Tomorrow's fine. Thanks, Lieutenant. Sorry about that detective crack."

"Like hell you are."

I dropped by the library anyway. Scrolling through June 1956 I got so bogged down by the clothing advertisements and what was playing at the Roxy I almost missed the story when it surfaced on the 14th. Mary Ann Thaler had a Felony Homicide cop's low opinion of the state of current affairs; one run-of-the-mill murder didn't command much more space under Eisenhower than it did last week. A woman's unidentified body had been found slumped in the basement window well of a restaurant on Coolidge early that morning with fifteen stab wounds in the chest and abdomen. She was fully clothed, so rape was not suspected, but there was no purse nearby and her pierced ears wore no rings nor her wedding finger a band despite evidence that one had existed, so the police were treating it as a mugging. She was a tall brunette who appeared to be in her late twenties.

That was what the *News* said. The *Free Press* played it down even more, slugging it in the police column along with a service station stickup, a pinch for aggravated assault, and a flashing in Grand Circus Park. There she was about thirty with auburn hair. Hearst's

Times blew it up to a column in the same section with a strip-joint bust in rural Oakland County and a nasty editorial cartoon featuring Adlai Stevenson, but apart from referring to the victim as "a raven-haired beauty of perhaps 22," and doubling the number of stab wounds, it didn't leave me any more enlightened.

Two days later, when the woman was positively identified, the story jumped to all three front pages, along with a photograph that some enterprising newshawk had probably swiped off a mantel and put on the wire. Allison Booth was attractive, in a well-bred way that would never have done for the women who posed for Eugene Booth's covers, dark hair piled atop her head bouffant style, high cheekbones, and strong unplucked brows. Her marriage to a popular local author got her a good spot just below the fold, but when no leads developed within a week the item fell back inside, then away. A dismemberment by the river and a scheduled visit by Clare Boothe Luce—no relation—to address the women's auxiliary of the Detroit Rotary Club took its place. I learned that Allison Booth had last been seen buying a cocktail dress and some cosmetic items at the downtown J.L. Hudson's the evening before her body turned up. The purchases were left for delivery. She didn't drive, no one remembered seeing her on a bus or a streetcar, and no taxi drivers came forward to claim her as a fare. The medical examiner reported that she had been dead since around sundown, and that she had not died where she was found, but had been transported there from somewhere else and deposited in the window well. That made it different from the standard robbery-murder, but not enough to give it legs or to

prompt the press to demand action when the case dead-
ended. Her husband was questioned, but he had been
in New York City for two days meeting with his publisher and didn't return to Detroit until the police called
him at his hotel.

I had gotten most of it from Lowell Birdsall Jr., but
seeing it in print made it real, like one's first glimpse
of a painted corpse in a casket. I wound the crank of
the microfilm reader through to the end of the spool,
but there was nothing more. My watch read 9:40, too
late to thread on another that morning. I had just enough
time to report to my client in person before heading
north. It looked as if I was going to get in that fishing trip after all.

Hazel Park is best known for its raceway, an oval track
where frozen-faced jockeys the size of children bounce
on sulkies behind trotters in what is arguably the most
corrupt sport after football and the Korean Olympics.
At one time it was owned by Joe Zerilli, a recognized
member of the national board of directors of the Cosa
Nostra. Now it's split up more democratically among
the remnants of the late Detroit mayor's political machine and the local casino interests. Laying a wager before the comfortable-looking middle-aged women at its
windows is not quite as pointless as betting on professional wrestling, but if you Know a Guy who Knows
a Guy you can plot out the whole day in the comfort
of your home as easily as predicting a Movie of the
Week.

To the residents, the raceway is just a square notch
cut out of the city's northeast corner, to be avoided

during peak traffic hours on race days but otherwise ignored. About fifty percent of them have never seen the track. They work in Detroit and fight the other cars and the orange barrels for the shortest route back home and couldn't care less if they were living next door to a bookie or an archbishop.

The address I got from Louise Starr when I called was written in fancy script on a simulated board of an aluminum-cased ranch-style house in a neighborhood filled with them off Nine Mile Road. The person who paid the taxes on the place hadn't gotten the word on how to regard the raceway: A silhouette in black-painted plywood of a horsedrawn carriage decorated the pull-up door of the attached garage and an iron jockey with its face and hands carefully re-enameled pink stood with its fist stuck out at the end of the composition driveway. The bing-bong of the doorbell disappointed me. I'd expected the trumpet fanfare from Belmont.

Louise opened the door barefoot, in black Capri pants and a matching sleeveless top that showed off the definition in her upper arms. She wore blush and eyeliner, but it took a trained detective to see it. Her eyes were a paler shade of violet in the morning light and her hair spilled like golden silk to her shoulders. Her feet were slender, with well-shaped toes; a rarer thing altogether than a beautiful face. There was no trace of foxglove. She would not apply it at home before noon.

I said, "Going Bohemian?"

"Why not? This is flyover country. The yokels never get to see a real live citizen of the Village outside *Breakfast at Tiffany's*." She smiled. "The publisher I used to work for really thought that. To him it's all crank telephones and Red Man signs west of the Hudson. Actually this is my work uniform. I'm editing scripts. Come in. I warn you, it's not for the squeamish."

The living room was done in shades of white and country blue, with baby's-breath slipcovers on the sofa and armchairs and magazines in baskets. A braided rug lay on the broad planks of the floor and ducks were taking off in pictures all around the walls.

"Isn't it hideous?" Louise asked. "Debra—my friend, the sales rep—rented the place over the telephone from New York, thought 'Park' meant she was moving out to the country, and hired a local decorator to do the house accordingly. She says she literally screamed when she saw it, but she can't afford to do it over again this year. I told her I'll redo it myself when I can afford to hire her. Fortunately her territory is larger than some European nations, so she doesn't have to spend much time here. Today she's in Milwaukee. I think I can find a glass without a pheasant on it in the cupboard if you're thirsty."

"Just water. I'm making a long drive later."

She went through a swinging door and I followed her into the kitchen. More blue and white, lacquered pine chairs with hearts cut through the backs and a table draped in chambray with lace trim. A wall clock shaped like a woodpecker twitched its tail to left and right for a pendulum. Louise took down a pair of diamond-patterned tumblers from a shelf over the sink, broke ice out of a tray in the refrigerator, and poured water into them from the tap. The cubes cracked when it made contact.

"I've always liked that noise," I said. "They really snap when it's booze."

She handed me a glass and raised hers to her left cheek. "They say a person who thinks and talks about drinking when he isn't actually doing it is an alcoholic."

"By that logic I'm also a sex maniac."

"I've never heard you talk about sex."

"Later. I'm working."

We went back into the living room, where she sat on the sofa and tucked her feet under her. A stack of loose pages, some rubber bands, and a thick pencil lay on the next cushion. I thought of Lowell Birdsall's laptop computer. She offered me the cushion, and that's the last time I thought about Lowell Birdsall for a while. I set down my glass, transferred the stuff to an end table, sat down next to her, and propped my elbow on the back of the sofa. I smelled soap on her skin, a light scent I couldn't identify. She sipped her water and smiled at me over the glass.

"You didn't tell me Eugene Booth's wife was murdered," I said.

She leaned forward to put the glass on a coffee table made from a wooden footlocker. When she sat back she wasn't smiling. "I didn't know. It wasn't in any of his publicity biographies."

"It wouldn't be."

"You'd be surprised. I once edited a crime writer whose mother was murdered while working the streets. He had it put on the dust jacket. The book became a bestseller."

"People gab about worse on talk shows for a lot less.

They didn't in Booth's day. It might have something to do with why he sent back the check and left."

"I don't know why. He married his wife in nineteen fifty-four. The things he wrote about in *Paradise Valley* took place eleven years earlier. He wrote the book in fifty-one. Anyway, all I want to do is reprint it. He doesn't even have to read the galleys if he doesn't want to."

"He's rewriting it. Or another book just like it. I told you about the dictation tapes yesterday."

"That has nothing to do with me. Although I'd be happy to talk to him if he wants to write an original."

"Stop being a publisher and listen. He never got over his wife's murder—he might have done it himself, despite the alibi he gave the cops, but if he did he didn't get over that either—and that's why he became impossible to work with and stopped publishing. I don't know what he did between then and when he went to work for the trailer park, but I'm betting it didn't have anything to do with writing; that part of his life carried memories too painful for him to live with. Then, wham, he's a hot property again, being courted by New York and signing contracts with publishers. It all comes roaring back like indigestion and he does the same thing he did forty years ago, only more politely: He severs all his contacts and disappears. Maybe it's coincidence, but if you start believing in that you're through in my work."

"But if your theory is right, why is he writing again now?"

"I don't know. Maybe he never stopped. Maybe it's the New York connection he couldn't take. If he didn't kill her, he might feel as guilty as if he had, because he was there when he should have been here protecting her. I'll ask him when I see him." I told her about the Wigwam Motor Lodge.

"His habits might have changed in forty years," she said. "Maybe he doesn't like fishing anymore."

"Maybe not. But it's a direction to go. I'm fresh out of others." I leaned across her for my glass of water and sat back quickly when I had it. I'd identified the scent of the soap she was using. It was the jasmine she'd worn when we first met. "I need a copy of *Some of My Best Friends Are Killers*. It's the book he wrote up north after his wife's death. It might tell me something. Have you got it?"

"I have all his books. I left it in New York with the others. *Paradise Valley* was all I thought I'd need. I'll have my assistant send it."

"Have her send it—"

"My assistant's a he."

"God bless Betty Friedan. Have him send it to me by overnight express in care of the Angler's Inn in Black Lake. I've reserved a cabin."

"Why there?"

"I got the name from the old wheeze who answered at the chamber of commerce. The current owners changed it when they bought the place twenty-five years ago. Before that it was the Wigwam Motor Lodge."

10

Setting aside mile after crawling mile of feverish construction and the odd idiot who thinks free use of the accelerator saves wear and tear on his turn indicators, a straight shot up Interstate 75 to the tip of the lower peninsula in good weather is one of the more pleasant things you can do in this life. I got away from the Detroit crush before noon, stopped for lunch an hour and a half later at one of a proliferating chain of restaurants that offer "homestyle cooking" in the dining room and stuffed animals in the giftshop, and took note of the scabbed-over remnants of a culture that has all but vanished from roadside America: a homemade sign advertising a drive-in zoo whose animals had died of old age, Indian artifacts touted on the side of a semi trailer parked thirty yards off the gravel apron to serve as a billboard, great painted Amish faces weathering off the ends of painted barns in the receding farm country. I counted down to the Mystery Spot from forty miles to two hundred yards, watched a line of heavy trucks waiting their turn on the scales, drifted wide around a man squatting to change a tire on his travel trailer, his shirttail standing straight out from his body in the slipstream. Roadkill and recaps littered the apron and a gaunt backpacker stood next to a mile marker holding a sign reading ST. PAUL, no hope on his stubbled face. A rock museum leaned at a crazy angle with its windows out and half its roof fallen in, leaving a dozen orphaned advertising placards strung out for sixty miles. It was all going to golden arches, convenience chains, factory outlet malls, and multiplex theaters selling the same bill from San Francisco Bay to the Gulf of St. Lawrence.

All except the hitchhikers. They had only turned in their bindlestiffs for duffels and abandoned the switchyards for freeway entrance ramps.

A hundred miles north of Detroit, the farms and subdivisions faded and stands of pine began to flank the highway. Up there most of the land was owned by the state and the National Forest system, with here and there a chunk carved out for a private log home that could have sheltered Davy Crockett, Daniel Boone, the Green Mountain Boys, and their families. Not that the lower classes weren't represented; there were whole stretches of tarpaper shacks with painted iron oil pigs attached to testify to the basic human need to import slums to God's country.

The aging female twitter I'd spoken to over the telephone had apologized and explained it was the policy of the Angler's Inn not to provide any information on its guests. She had admitted that two cabins were occupied at present. The fishing season was just getting under way and she expected to take more reservations for that weekend and to fill the place up by the end of the month. I'd given in to this hard sell and asked for a cabin.

"I can offer you one of the new ones. Most of our guests prefer the modern conveniences."

"How new is new?"

"We added two in nineteen seventy-four."

"So one of your current guests is occupying one of the original cabins."

"I'm sorry, sir. It's the policy of the Angler's Inn—"

"I'll take one of the older cabins. Does it have a bath?"

"A shower. The new ones have Jacuzzis."

I said I'd rough it.

From the exit, a broad two-lane blacktop led between more pines, past sprawls of Kmarts, Ben Franklins, and service stations whose gasoline prices dropped twenty cents in two blocks, then through an older business section with a couple of dusty giftshops, a movie theater that had been converted into an H & R Block, and a boarded-up furniture store. On the other side of town I caught glimpses of water shining like bright metal through more pines and passed a string of motels ranging from a Frank Lloyd Wright knockoff with a pool to a concrete bunker set back from an office in a Quonset hut. A quarter-mile of wilderness with signs offering lake lots for sale followed, then I was there.

The Angler's Inn was still recognizable as the Wigwam Motor Lodge in the old postcard. One of the four original cabins was missing, probably due to a fire, but the others hadn't changed and appeared well-maintained, with good roofs and a new golden finish on the logs. Two new units with picture windows stood to the left on a spot once occupied by pines, and some enterprising downstater had managed to convince the new owners that white vinyl siding would dress up the office and create parity with the Holiday Inn. The arrow-shaped sign above the door had been replaced by one close to the road spelling out the new name in pink neon with a trout leaping repeatedly over the top.

I looked for Eugene Booth's old Plymouth in the strip lot out front, but there was only a new GMC pickup with camper parked by one of the new cabins and a muddy green van trying not to take up too much customer space on the far edge. I pulled up in front of the office and got out. The air was ten degrees cooler here than in Detroit—cool enough for a jacket in the evenings—and there was a clean sharp smell of fresh water from the lake. The mere act of inhaling sliced the soft spot out of my brain caused by four hours of driving.

I stepped through an airlock into a shallow lobby with a rubber runner ending at the reservation desk. A six-foot-square tapestry covered the wall to the right, showing a wading fisherman in rubber pants fighting a piscatorial Moby Dick breaching at the end of his line. Opposite it was a display of mounted fish with lacquered scales and brass plates identifying their vanquishers. Tourist brochures shingled a rack to one side of the desk and there was an array of lures, flies, spools, and multiple-bladed knives for sale on the wall behind it.

There was no one behind the desk. An afternoon soap confrontation was taking place on a TV set beyond an open door to the left. I leaned over the desk, found a small tin file box on a shelf underneath the top, and was reaching for it when the TV suddenly went silent. Springs sighed and I straightened up just as a thickset old woman about five feet high came waddling out in a white canvas vest over plaid flannels and a bucket hat with hooks stuck in it. Orange curls boiled out from under the brim all around like Harpo Marx's. She had small sharp birdlike eyes without apparent need of correction, red lipstick, and round patches of scarlet painted high on her cheeks.

"Reservation for Amos Walker," I said when the sharp little eyes met mine. She lifted the tin box to the desk, found my card, and slapped it down on the desk with a plastic pen.

She watched me fill in the blanks. I was wearing jeans, sneakers, and a polo shirt; nothing so suspicious as a coat and tie or riot gear. "Fishing? I can sell you a license." It was the twitter from the telephone.

"Not yet. I'm planning on coming up later in the season. Thought I'd take a look around, pick my spot."

"You don't pick your spot. It picks you. That will be thirty-five dollars for the night."

I gave it to her. She put the cash in a drawer, took back the card, read what I'd written, and returned it to the box. I hoped she'd leave it there while she went to get the key, but she put it back down on the shelf, scooped a square brass key attached to a wooden tag out of the drawer, and tossed it on the desk. It skidded off the edge but I caught it.

"You're in Two. Actually it's One, but the old One burned down and we didn't change the numbers on the others. It's on the end. Sure you don't want a new cabin? It's got cable."

"I'm nostalgic. Guess I'm not the only one." I smiled. She stared. She was in no hurry to get back to her soap. I went out. A zinc bin with ICE painted on the hinged latch in big white letters stood outside the air-lock on the side nearest the two new cabins. That was handy.

The windows of Cabins Three and Four were shaded when I drove past to park in front of Two. If the man I was looking for was in one of them he'd walked there, as no more cars had turned in while I was in the office. I took my overnight bag from the back seat and let myself into a clean, cedar-smelling space with a buffalo-plaid comforter on an iron bed, a cheap yellow dresser with a plate-glass top, and a club chair of a vintage to match the cabin. Whoever had re-covered the chair last had selected a tough fabric with embroidered fishes on it. Fish hooks were printed on the curtains and a muddy lithograph of William Sidney Mount's *Eel Spearing at Setauket* hung on the wall above the bed in a glass frame that had cost more than the print. More fish swam about on the shower curtains in

the little bathroom. For a brief moment I was sorry I
hadn't brought tackle.

I had a view through the window of a piece of the
lake framed between towering pines and a public landing ending in a redwood dock. The reeds were bright
green and just above ankle height. By late summer they
would be the color of wheat and as tall as a man. An
experienced caster would wade far out from the shore
to avoid snagging his line among them on the back-
swing. I wondered if that was possible, or if the bottom dropped out too steeply for anything but a boat.
I tried to remember if I'd passed a marina; and then I
remembered I hadn't come up there to wet a line.

I blew some air, set down my bag on an Indian rug,
grabbed the plastic ice bucket from the bathroom, and
went back out. The same three vehicles were sharing
the lot. I wondered if the new units had managed to
pay for themselves in twenty-five years.

A scoop was attached to the zinc bin by a bicycle
chain. I filled the bucket, turned left instead of right,
and stuck my key into the lock of the new cabin in
front of which the pickup was parked. The New York
plate wasn't promising. The key went only partway in.
I rattled it for effect, then tried the knob.

The knob pulled out of my hand and I looked at a
man my height, but built more slightly in a denim shirt
and tan Dockers, cordovan loafers on his feet. He had
a New York Yankees cap pulled down to his eyes and
green sunglasses. The lower half of his face was slim,
tanned, shaved, fortyish, forgettable. He had a red cotton Windbreaker draped over his left forearm. That wasn't
worth noting, except it was covering his hand too, in

the way you carry a jacket when you don't want any-one to see what you have in your hand. From the length of the overhang it was one of the larger mag-nums, if not a .22 target pistol with a silencer.

The face below the glasses formed a friendly smile. He had nice teeth, capped and bonded. "Wrong cabin, sport?"

"Long drive," I said. "I'm punchy. I thought a little ice water would help. Sorry to disturb." I started to turn.

He put a loafer on the threshold and brought the jacket forward a couple of inches. "No hurry, sport. Here for the bass?" He spoke huskily, from the back of his throat.

I stopped. "No bass around here. Trout's my fish. They put up a better fight."

"Trouble is you got to have a frying pan all heated up on shore and clean and cook it right there. Every minute it's out of the water you lose some flavor. That's what my old man told me, anyway. I'm not a fisher-man myself. I'm just here for the quiet."

"Well, you found plenty."

"Not so's you'd notice. The frogs are driving me nuts. Whoever said it's peaceful out in the country must've been deaf."

"City boy." I grinned.

His smile flickered, then stayed. "Sin to waste good ice on just water. I got a bottle of bourbon that's too big for me. I was expecting friends but I guess they aren't showing up." He hesitated half a beat before the *aren't*. Somewhere under that tanned plastic finish was an *ain't* screaming to get out.

"Thanks. I'm cutting back. A friend told me today she thinks I'm an alcoholic."

"Your friend cares about you. You're a rich man, sport. Good luck on the water." He moved his foot out of the way and pushed the door shut in my face. The deadbolt snapped.

I went back to my cabin. I'd intended to pull the same gag on cabins Three and Four, just to get a look at my other neighbor in case he was in after all, but I wasn't sure how much the Yankees fan could see from his window. I decided to be true to my word. I left the bottle I'd brought in my bag, unwrapped a plastic glass from the bathroom, threw a handful of ice into it, and filled it from the tap. Sitting in the armchair sipping water I thought about the man in Cabin Five. I was pretty sure his voice wasn't that husky in real life, that he was disguising it in the same way he was covering his face with the cap and dark glasses and his gun with his jacket. I was even more sure we'd never met. That made no sense, because his smile was as familiar as my own.

11

With the sun dyeing the lake pink my skin started to jump. I'd been in the cabin almost two hours, pacing the floor and sitting in the chair and lying on my back on the bed with my hands behind my head, smoking and not drinking anything but water. I had the little thirteen-inch TV set turned on for company but with the sound off so I wouldn't miss hearing a car pull up to one of the other cabins, and if I didn't go out and skip stones I was going to turn fishy like the natives. I got as far as the door, then went back and took the Smith & Wesson Chief's Special out of my bag and snapped the holster onto my belt behind my right hip.

I almost hadn't packed it; I'd thought if a man couldn't catch his limit without artillery support he might as well stay home and eat Mrs. Paul's. That was before I knew about the guest in Cabin Five. I untucked my polo shirt and let the tail fall over the rubber grip.

The air was chilly coming off the lake. In a half hour or so I'd be able to see my breath. I pulled a zipfront jacket out of the car and put it on. The pickup was still there and so was the old van. Vehicles tend to resemble their owners. I could imagine the old woman in fisherman's gear driving the van, but the Yankees rooter didn't match up with the truck and camper any way I tried to do it. He was strictly high performance and low clearance, bucket seats and twelve cylinders or better to open. I'd taken note of the number on the license plate, but if it didn't belong to a rental or a borrow job I was a sleuth without instincts. Maybe he didn't have a gun. Maybe his left arm was in a cast and it embarrassed him. Except he wasn't the getting-embarrassed type, any more than he was the type to throw a sleeping bag into the back of a camper and take off north of 110th Street. And I still knew him from somewhere.

A hollow footpath worn down through the grass led to the redwood dock a hundred feet behind the motel. I walked out to the end and leaned on a painted piling and watched some gulls swooping at water-striders on the lake's surface, wrinkling it like a silk flag in a light wind. When they missed they cried, the sound like the creak of an old hasp. A lone fisherman in a mackinaw and an old slouch hat stood on the opposite shore, waggling a fly rod in the approved four-count rhythm between ten and two o'clock, or so I supposed; I'm a worm-drowner myself and never found the knack. I watched him for a couple of minutes before I realized it might be Eugene Booth I was looking at. My binoculars were in the car and from that distance I couldn't tell if it was a man in his seventies or a boy fourteen years old. Whoever he was, he was good. The red sun caught his wet line in a beautiful glittering spiral curve twelve feet above his head as he swung it like a lariat, feeding it by hand, and I could have watched until sundown without caring who he was if I hadn't heard a car door slam a hundred feet behind me.

I trotted back just in time to see a man fumble a big square box into Cabin Four, two doors down from mine, and kick the door shut. I had an impression of gray hair and glasses and a thick build in work twills, high-top shoes with metal hooks. Parked in front of the cabin was a twenty-year-old Plymouth, mint green with a white vinyl top. The plate matched with the registration I'd gotten from Lansing. The fisherman was home from the sea.

I glanced toward Five, just to see if the pickup was still there. It was, and as I looked, a movement in the window of the cabin attracted my attention. It was the shade sliding back into place.

12

I went back into Two. I wanted to wait for dark before I made my move. I wasn't sure why, unless it
was habit. If it weren't for Cabin Five I'd have been
knocking on Four as soon as the door closed.

The television was still playing without sound. A
teenage local anchorman mouthed words off a
TelePrompTer, a graphic showing behind him of a gun
clamped in a Popeye fist. I switched off the set. There
were more than enough guns at the Angler's Inn that
day. The air was damp cold and I cranked up the ther-
mostat attached to the radiator under the window and
put my hand on the rough metal until it began to get

warm. I hadn't eaten in six hours. I'd brought a Thermos and sandwiches wrapped in wax paper, but I left them in the sack. I wanted my blood going to my head where I needed it.

I stood at the window and watched the light recede from the surface of the lake. From that angle I couldn't see my fisherman, but he'd be reeling in his line for the last time and recovering his creel from the water if he'd caught anything. The water turned an eggplant shade of purple, then slowly went to black as if the shadows of the pines had spread to cover the lake, like a grounds crew unrolling a tarpaulin across the infield. I looked at my watch for no particular reason and had to snap on a lamp to read it. That was my signal to go visiting.

A twenty-five-watt bulb burned in a wrought-iron carriage lamp above the door to Cabin Four, illuminating little but itself and the brass numeral nailed to the door. The shade was still drawn in the window, but there was light behind it. Five was dark. I couldn't see what was going on in the window there, but the chances were better than fifty percent I was being observed.

I cocked my head, listening to the out-of-rhythm clacking on the other side of the door. It sounded like a machine-gunner getting bored. It was an oddly soothing noise, like the crack of an old-fashioned wooden baseball bat or the clip-clop of hooves hauling a hay-wagon. You hardly ever hear a manual typewriter anymore.

I hesitated before knocking. I'd forgotten which old poet had failed to finish his most famous verse because someone had knocked at his door.

The hell with it. He probably wouldn't have finished the damn thing anyway. I knocked, three sharp raps; a confident combination, but not threatening. When I write my memoirs I'm going to include an entire chapter on knocks, from the shave-and-a-haircut of the cocky, gum-chewing best friend to the heavy hammering of the cop in a flak jacket. I'd used them all.

"Yes."

No footsteps accompanied the response.

I had one of my business cards ready. I stooped and poked it under the door.

A long silence followed and I wondered if he'd seen the card. Then floorboards shifted inside, a leather sole scraped wood, and a shadow broke the light coming out above the threshold. There was a little grunt, as might be made by a man who didn't bend over without thinking about it first, then another silence that was longer than required to read the three words and two numbers printed on the card.

The deadbolt slid back with an oily snick and the door came open the width of a broad face with a hypertensive flush and glasses with heavy black rims. He had the same scowl he'd worn for his driver's license picture. A puff of whiskey came out with the cedar smell from inside.

"Your name is Walker?" It was the flat roughened baritone of the cassette tapes.

I showed him the state ID and my county buzzer. He tilted his head back slightly to use the lower half of his bifocals. He made the same grunt he'd made when he picked up the card. "Fancier than it used to be," he said. "You could still have fixed it up at Kinko's.

Where'd you get the star? That's illegal for a private investigator in this state."

"It wasn't when I got it. They forgot to ask for it back when the law changed. I'm working for Louise Starr." I put away the folder and showed him his note to her.

He grunted again. "I've still got a ream of that cheapjack stationery I stole from the Alamo. Don't know why I didn't toss it when I quit writing. Maybe I knew even then I'd wind up quitting quitting. What's the matter, couldn't she read? I sent back the check."

"She wants to know why."

"I couldn't make it any clearer."

" 'A gelding ought to know better than to try to breed.' If that's as clear as you're writing these days, it's no wonder you quit."

"That's the idea, Sherlock. I'm dried up. Spent. No more lead in my pencil. How clear do you want it? I can't write anymore."

"There isn't anything in the contract about writing. She was buying an old book."

"That's how it starts. They manage somehow not to lose money on it and the next thing you know they're beating down your door asking you to write something fresh. I made my peace with all that years before you climbed on an egg crate to peek through your first keyhole. I've got blocked arteries to my heart. I don't care to blow them fighting the same old battle."

"What were you typing just now, your grocery list? Can't read your own handwriting?"

"I'm just doodling. Just because a leg's been amputated doesn't mean you don't want to scratch when it itches."

"It must itch bad. You filled up half a dozen tapes dictating and wore out a highlighter researching the same history you already used to write *Paradise Valley.*"

His face flushed alarmingly deeper. "That weed-whacking son of a bitch. You've been to White Pine."

"It says on the card I'm a detective."

"Well, you did your job. You found me. Go tell Mrs. Starr no one's holding a gun to my head and I didn't join a cult. That way you get paid and I'm let the hell alone."

He started to push the door shut. I leaned against it, but he was ready for that and he was leaning from the other side. He was built closer to the ground and as strong as an ornery bull. I spoke into the narrowing gap.

"You're not either alone. You're being watched. And not just by me."

The door sprang back open. "Cabin Five?"

"That's the one."

He stood aside to let me in, then closed the door behind me and twisted the deadbolt home. He surprised me by not poking his head out to look at the cabin on the other side of the office. It made him seem a little less like a civilian.

Booth's cabin looked like mine. His bed was built on a maple frame, not iron, with fish inexpertly painted on the headboard, and a gateleg table with a straight-back chair drawn up to it stood in the spot that the armchair occupied in Two, with a fat lamp on it, good for tying flies or writing postcards. A Winslow Homer seascape hung above the bed. Aside from that there was the same machine-made Indian rug, the bathroom in the same place, the same curtains framing a slightly different view of the lake.

He wasn't tying flies or writing postcards. A battered old black portable typewriter minus its case squatted on the gateleg table with a tall stack of paper on one side and a shorter one on the other. I recognized the coarse yellowing Alamo stock and Booth's thick scribble on the wide margin at the bottom of a typed page. I also recognized the big red Seagram's numeral 7 on the label of the open bottle standing out of range of the typewriter's carriage. It belonged to the box I'd seen him carrying in earlier; the unopened bottles still inside were helping hold down one corner of the rug.

I smelled evergreen and whiskey and cigarettes. A pile of butts formed a dome in a copper ashtray on the table next to an open pack of Pall Malls. His suitcase, a scuffed old blue model with discolored white piping, was parked in the bottom of the narrow open closet with his twill jacket and a rumpled old raincoat suspended above it on wire hangers. The raincoat made me think of something, but I didn't know what. The radiator was starting to make headway against the evening chill. He'd have turned it up the same time I had mine.

Booth saw me taking stock. "Place hasn't gotten any prettier since Kennedy. It used to be done in early Geronimo. There was a peace pipe on the wall and a wooden spear and a squat butt-ugly cedar redskin with a hollow in his head for an ashtray. I loved it. I like this okay. You don't want anything beautiful or even tasteful to distract you. Almost anything's easier to look at than a blank sheet of paper."

"This the same cabin where you wrote *Some of My Best Friends Are Killers?*"

If I expected him to rise to that one he disappointed me. "At one time or another I wrote in all of them, including dear old departed Number One. Don't expect me to tell you what I wrote in which. Any old whore in a storm." He went into the bathroom and left the door open while he used the toilet. His prostate sounded healthy. "You one of these new non-drinking detectives?" he called out above the trickling stream.

"I'm not a new anything. I've got ice in my cabin."

"Well, it's not doing either of us any good over there."

I went out while he was washing his hands. The GMC truck was still in front of Five but there was no light coming from the cabin. Either he retired early for a city boy or he'd turned it off to improve his view through the window. I couldn't tell if the shade was still drawn.

When I came back with the ice, Booth had unwrapped a second glass from the bathroom and placed it next to his, which had some amber residue in the bottom. The fermented-grain smell was sharper than it had been. He'd made a fresh deposit while I was gone.

As he poured, his broken-nosed profile told me what I'd been thinking of earlier. It belonged to the tough in the trenchcoat on the covers of all his books. Lowell Birdsall had gone no farther than the author for his inspiration.

"I love that crack when the whiskey first hits the

ice," he said. "It's like the spring break-up in the mountains."

"I said something just like that this morning. The person I said it to said I talk too much about drinking."

"Woman, right? They're the ones that give a shit. I bet she had you all wrapped up in a rubber sheet taking the cure. Everything's a disease now. Me, I'm just a drunk. I tried writing this book on beer, but I couldn't fool it. You need at least eighty proof to break things loose." He pulled the chair out from under the table, turned it around, handed me my drink, and sat down.

I sat on the edge of the bed and lifted my glass. "What to?"

"Bullshit." He drank down a third of his glass. The ice prevented him from emptying it in one draft.

I sipped. The orange glow filled my head like a balloon. I should've eaten the sandwiches. I decided to take it slow. "So you are writing a book."

"I'm spoiling perfectly good paper. When I've spoiled enough of it I'll have something that may someday be a book. God knows we need another one of those. You know, Robert Benchley couldn't bear to spend more than a minute in a bookstore. He said someone wrote each book expecting it to be *the* book that would make all the others irrelevant. Then it went up on a shelf with the rest and he could hear them all calling to him. In the end he couldn't bring himself even to enter a store. Ordered all his books by mail."

"He drank himself to death, I heard."

"Drinking never killed anybody. There has to be a finger on the trigger." He took down another third.

That made me think of the man in the Yankees cap. "You knew about Cabin Five?"

"I had FBI agents following me everywhere I went for two years after *Bullets Are My Business* came out. My detective went to bed with a sexy communist and I didn't kill either of them. You get so you know when you're under a glass."

"I had a two-minute conversation with this guy by accident. If he's a fed he took a course on how to talk like a regular American."

"Never happen. They don't pick 'em for their imagination." He took a thoughtful sip, leaving some whiskey in the bottom of the glass. "You don't suppose your client is doubling up on you?"

I drank a little to look as if I were keeping up. "She's got faith in me. Besides, she can't afford it. She could barely afford to pay you the advance you threw back in her face."

"I didn't. You've got the note. Well, I'm buffaloed. I haven't been with a woman in ten years, so it isn't a jealous husband. Even if there were jealous husbands anymore. Country's gone so far toward hell if I wrote the way I wrote back when I could write, no self-respecting horny kid would bother to hide one of my books under his mattress."

"Maybe he's a fan."

"Maybe I'm Leo fucking Tolstoy." He drank up, then frowned at my glass. "There's dust on top of your booze, son. Don't tell me you're one of these punks drinks Jack and Coke." He twisted in his seat, scooped up the bottle, and refilled us both. His hand was steady enough to pour nitroglycerine.

"One of us ought to go easy. I'm pretty sure this guy is heeled."

" 'Heeled.' " He blew through his nose. "You've been reading too much Booth. You say he's got a gat, a heater, a rod, a roscoe, a piece? I never knew a cop or a crook to call it anything but a gun."

"That was before you guys changed the language."

"The language changes itself. You can't tip a can up over it and keep it in, that's the trouble. I've got a hundred brand-new pages that read like Middle English: Coffin nails instead of cigarettes, streetsweepers instead of shotguns. A car's a crate, a bodyguard's a goon, a corpse is meat. You should've seen what I went through when I had to write about a real heater or a crate or a hunk of meat in a skillet. Dames instead of girls. Well, women. If I ever called Allison a dame, she'd've brained me with Webster's Second."

He went silent then and drank. He wasn't as sober as he looked. Bringing up his wife had kicked the braces out from behind the canvas front. He let his chin fall to his chest. He might have been faking it to discourage questions. That made it time to ask one that counted.

"Did you ever find out who killed her?"

His head came up in millimeters, as if he were raising it with a winch. The shelf of crisp gray hair had fallen onto his forehead and his eyes glared out from under it through the thick lenses of his glasses with a sudden naked lucidity.

"She was just a stamp to them. A lousy one-center on a postcard. The bastards didn't even care who else read it as long as I got the message."

"What message?"

The winch let go then and his chin drifted back down. He made purring noises with his lips and the glass in his hand tilted, slopping some of its contents onto the Indian rug. I got up and took it from him and carried it and mine into the bathroom and emptied them into the sink. He was snoring loudly and with enthusiasm when I came back out; his head was all the way back now and I saw his molars. I screwed the cap back on the bottle. That would slow him down half a second.

I left the cabin and pulled the door shut until it locked. I couldn't turn the bolt. I hoped he'd wake up enough to do that later. I glanced toward Cabin Five. I made it a long look. The cabin was still dark and the pickup camper was gone. He had a quiet motor. I hadn't even heard him pull out.

13

The few hits of Seagram's I'd taken were still ringing in my skull. I wasn't hungry by then, but to absorb the alcohol I ate the sandwiches I'd brought and drank all the coffee in the Thermos before going to bed. The mattress was too soft and the springy metal slats creaked like ship's rigging whenever I turned over. It was going to be a long night.

Wrong again.

Something was knocking against the hull of my fishing boat. I lay on the deck staring up at the bright sky and tried to ignore it, but after a little silence the knocking came again: five rapid raps, confidence mixed with

impatience. It wasn't just a piece of driftwood clunk-
ing against the waterline.

I opened my eyes to the dazzle of the sun bound-
ing off the lake. I hadn't closed the curtains over the
window. Dust-motes swarmed like tiny bright golden
bees as far up as the exposed rafters. Out across the
water someone was trying to pull-start an outboard
motor and not having much luck; there would be a series of half-hearted pops followed by a clank-clank and
an emphysemic wheeze and then a pause before he
tried again. For a second I thought that was the noise
that awoke me. Then again the five knocks, blows now
with the side of the fist, hard enough to bounce the
panels.

"Eight o'clock, Petunia! Breakfast call! Rise and shine
and grab your pants."

I'd gone first for the Smith & Wesson on the belt of
my jeans crumpled on the floor beside the bed. Then
I recognized Booth's voice and swung my legs over
and pulled them on. I got to the door just as he started
knocking again. He stood there with his fist raised,
combed and scrubbed and bright-eyed with a clean
work shirt tucked into the same trousers he'd had on
the night before. His eyes were clear behind his glasses
and his face shone from the razor.

"You look like you just washed up on the beach,"
he said. "You need to cut down on your drinking."

I caught a whiff of eye-opener on his breath.

"You're not going to turn out to be one of those
pain-in-the-ass morning people, are you?"

"Only on vacation, son. I'm not a breakfast person
either, but there's a place in town that serves steak-

and-eggs cooked in lard like it's nineteen fifty-eight. How long will it take you to scrape off the top layer?"

"Give me fifteen minutes."

"I'll give you ten. It's a celebration. We outlasted Cabin Five. He was gone when I got up."

"He was gone when we went to bed. Maybe we were wrong. Maybe he was expecting somebody's wife and she never came and he went home. Maybe what I thought was a gun was a box of chocolates."

"You know what they say. You never know what you're going to get."

"The hell you don't. They put a chart right in the box."

"Don't trust it. I never worked from an outline even in the old days. Three minutes gone, friend. Try not to cut your nose off." He strode back toward Four, whistling. It's hard to whistle that consistently off-key. It is its own kind of perfect pitch.

Seven minutes later, doused with cold spray and shaved and tucking in a fresh sport shirt, I climbed into the passenger's side of his car, which he already had running. I'd decided at the last minute to leave the .38 in the cabin, hidden on the floor behind the radiator. If the Yankee was still around and his jacket had been hiding a gun, a shoot-out in broad daylight didn't seem his style.

Inside, the Plymouth smelled of stale tobacco and dust. A fine skin of Michigan road dust coated the dash and there was a cigarette burn in the vinyl above the ashtray, but apart from that the car was tidy and when he backed around and pulled into the road the engine ran smoothly and the gears meshed without hesitation.

He drove with one hand on the crossbar and a Pall Mall burning between the fingers of his other hand resting on the window ledge. The odometer read too low for a car that old; it had rolled over a couple of hundred miles back. Either the car had a new motor and transmission or he took better care of it than he did of himself. He drove two to three miles over the limit and switched off the turn indicator after it had served its purpose.

I said, "If you keep on like this you're liable to give senior drivers a good name."

He blew through his nose. "If the world made sense, everyone would add ten miles an hour to his speed for every year past sixty."

"I figured you'd be sleeping in after last night."

"I don't need near as much as I used to. That's the part that makes sense." He stuck the cigarette between his teeth and used both hands to wheel around a minivan waddling along at twenty. "Did I sing any of the old songs?"

He asked the question in a casual tone without taking his eyes off the road. I answered just as casually.

"Not a note. The years on beer don't seem to have softened you up any."

The little silence that followed said he wasn't satisfied. But he dropped the subject. "You wouldn't know it now, but this place used to be the fishing capital of the Midwest. I saw Cesar Romero drinking with his buddies in a bar once. He had on a week's beard and a dirty cap."

We were driving through the boarded-up downtown. A middle-ager in Spandex and a racing helmet was unlocking his bicycle from the lamppost in front of the local branch of a national bank chain and a woman carrying a plastic tub full of folded laundry stood on a corner waiting for the light to change. A pair of gulls skipped and flapped at each other over a wad of gum stuck on the sidewalk. I said, "I wouldn't hold out for Cesar, but it's still early in the season."

"Even then they'll be out at the malls. But what the hell. In ten years everyone'll be doing his shopping on the 'net and today's kids will mope around pining for the days when they used to hang out in front of the Gap. Meanwhile there's plenty of places to park downtown." He turned the corner and glided into the curb two doors down from a yellow brickfront with CAPTAIN KIDD'S painted on the front window in skirling letters.

The dim cool interior was done in a nautical motif, teakwood paneling and booths with spoked helms cut out of the partitions. Piped-in music tinkled out of a soporific piano. At Booth's request, a teenage hostess in puffy sleeves and a tricorne hat led us between tables to a deck out back beneath a canvas awning. On the way we passed scattered couples, one or two lone diners, and a tableful of white-haired men in baseball caps and cocoa straw hats, the last group haw-hawing over platters of bacon and mounds of fluffy scrambled eggs.

"Locals," said Booth. "I swear it's the same bunch that occupied the same spot twenty years ago, when this was Gus's Tavern and there was a moosehead hanging over where the salad bar is now. You wonder what they still have to talk about. *I* wonder what happened to that moosehead."

"Maybe that's what they talk about."

The land fell off sharply from the deck, giving us a view of the greater portion of the lake. It was Friday and several more fishermen were out, casting from the docks and wading offshore and rowing boats. An eight-footer with an outboard spluttered across, cutting a *V* in the silken surface. I hoped the ride was worth all the trouble the boater had gone through to get it started.

I decided it was. It was good there with the sun on the water and the green smell of the needles and something rustling down among the reeds, a muskrat building its den or a hungry fox looking for the first catch of the morning. It was a connection, and it was strong enough to pull a lot of people, men mostly, out of their offices and tractor-trailer rigs and the back seats of limousines and all the way up here in pursuit of a thing they could get cheaper and better prepared in a good restaurant close to home. Either that, or they couldn't stand the women they lived with.

A different girl in the same outfit took our orders for steak-and-eggs and black coffee and went away. Booth offered me his pack and we both took one and I lit us up. The first drag made me cough. I hadn't smoked unfiltered in years.

He noticed. "CBS bought the detective I used in *Bullets* in fifty-nine. The series tanked after thirteen weeks, mostly because Winston was the sponsor and all the good guys had to smoke filters. You knew who the murderer was the minute he lit up a Camel."

I grinned. "That was just about the time you got out of publishing, wasn't it?"

"I got out of publishing the way Trotsky got out of

Russia. I submitted a three-page outline for my next book to an editor I'd been working with for six years and he bounced it back without an explanation. I flew to New York to discuss it. He said *Some of My Best Friends Are Killers* hadn't performed as well as expected—that's how he put it, 'didn't perform as well as expected,' like it was a juggler or a dancing chihuahua—and he thought I should take a year or so off and find my inspiration. I said if I took a year off all I'd find would be my own death from starvation. That's when he said it."

Breakfast came. We sorted out blood-rare from medium-well and scrambled from over-easy—he liked his eggs to run from a harsh word—got our cups filled, and the waitress went off to see to the big group.

Booth covered his eggs with pepper. "Where was I?"

" 'That's when he said it.' "

"Yeah. He said all the great writers had to starve before they produced their best work. I hit him."

"With what?"

"His desk, I wish. I laid him out with a straight right, the same one that got me fired as a sparring partner. Gashed two knuckles on his teeth and had to get a tetanus shot. It was beautiful. Cops arrested me at my hotel, I did a weekend in the Tombs. Publisher dropped the charges, which was the dirtiest thing anybody ever did to me in that town. I'd have held out for a jury of writers and told them on the stand what that son of a bitch said to me in his office. After that the verdict wouldn't matter. That would have been the note to end a career on."

"I heard you missed deadlines and reneged on contracts."

"Everyone misses deadlines. I never backed out of a deal in my life. Who told you that—Mrs. Starr?" He didn't wait for the answer. "That's New York. It's the only civilized society in history that bought into the mythology it made up for itself. Well, there's Hollywood, but I said *civilized*. No, they didn't boot me for being unreliable. My books stopped making money. That's the only unredeemable sin."

My steak was as thin as a placemat and nearly as tough. I sawed at it until my wrists got tired and then I ate my eggs. They'd been cooked in lard, just as he said. I'd forgotten what a lethal dose of cholesterol can do for flavor. "Why did your books stop selling?"

"Why does anything? I started telling the truth. Did you read *Some of My Best Friends Are Killers*?"

"Not yet."

"Don't. Nobody wants fiction to be real. The people who buy books and go to the movies want the hero to snatch the heroine off the conveyor belt just before the buzzsaw gets her. My editor made me rewrite it. He was right. For what I wanted to say I should've written straight journalism, but I'd had my fill of that when I did it to eat while I wrote my books at night. Even after the rewrite there was just enough truth in it to turn away readers in herds."

"What did you want to say? Sometimes the hero doesn't get there before the buzzsaw?"

He nodded, chewing. "And when he does, sometimes he just turns up the speed."

*   *   *

Just then the sun wrapped itself in a sheet of cloud and it was no longer good on the lake. The surface looked tarnished. There wasn't a boat or a fisherman in sight. Thunder chuckled to the west, where the sky still looked clear. A sudden damp gust shook the awning. The waitstaff bustled out to strip the settings off the outside tables.

"These spring bumpers come in quick, but they blow through just as fast." Booth sipped from his cup and resumed sawing at his steak. "Huron swallows them before they turn into anything. Otherwise they'd plane everything flat clear to the Atlantic."

"Should we go in?"

"What for? Got something against getting wet? We're born wet." He grinned around a mouthful of eggs.

So it was going to be a contest. I sat back with my hair lifting in the stiffening wind. "People these days like more grits with their sugar. The kind of fiction you want to write might go over now."

"I thought about that."

"Is that why you're rewriting *Paradise Valley*?"

He picked up a slice of toast and buttered it. It had been about to blow off his plate. "Don't put too much store in what's on those tapes. I've got arthritis in my fingers and I thought I'd get more done if I tried dictating. I filled six hours and stopped."

"Didn't work?"

"It was too easy. They ought to outlaw anything that makes the creative process convenient. That's why so much shit gets written on computers."

"You didn't answer the question."

"I don't have to answer the question. I don't have

to sit here with you except I didn't feel like eating alone this morning. Just why escapes me now."

We ate for a while without speaking. A flat wave slid across the surface of the lake like a crumb-scraper.

"You were a cop?" He used the toast to mop the egg yolk off his plate.

"I took the oath. I never wore the uniform."

"Detroit?" I nodded. He swallowed. "My brother was a Detroit cop. Left to join the marines in forty-three. Jap sub torpedoed his troop ship one day out of Pearl. He never made it to the fighting."

"I'm sorry."

"It wasn't you sent that fish."

I finished my coffee. "How late in forty-three?"

"September."

"Was he in Detroit in June?"

He watched me over his cup. "He was on duty during the riot. That's what you wanted to know, isn't it?"

"He tell you anything?"

"I was his little brother. He told me everything. Including the stuff his watch commander told him not to tell. That's why he quit. It wasn't what he saw, exactly. It was what he saw and couldn't talk about. Except to me."

"What did he see?"

"Did you read *Paradise Valley*?"

"I read the one you published. I heard enough of your dictation to want to know more about the one you didn't."

The rain came then. It started as a swishing in the pines to the west and swept our way in a straight line as if it were slung from a bucket. It smacked the awning and ran down it and over the edge, splattering the deck and completely blocking our view of the lake. We went inside just as lightning flared and a long cackle of thunder let go overhead. The old men at the big table were still drinking coffee and laughing at the same stories. A number of the other diners who had finished stood inside the entrance looking out at the hard rain and waiting for it to let up. The lights went down twice but stayed on.

"We're in for some dark," Booth said. "Last time I was here we were out for three days. No, I invited you." Standing in front of the cash register he waved away my wallet and paid the bill. The hostess rang it up, hunching her shoulders at each snap of thunder.

I thought we were going to wait along with the others, but once he'd gotten his change and left a tip he turned up his collar, clutched it at his throat, put a hand on the doorknob, and leered at me. "Ready?"

I grabbed my collar and jerked my chin down in a John Wayne nod. We dashed out into the cold wash. It smelled of brimstone from the warm concrete.

We sprinted hard, but by the time we threw ourselves into the Plymouth's deep front seat, hooting like drunken kids, we were soaked to the bone. The wipers couldn't keep up with the downpour; they just smeared it over the windshield like glue. Waiting for it to slow down, Booth turned on the heater and let it warm up and then hit the blower to give us the illusion we were drying out. He was shivering, but when he caught me watching him he showed his teeth at me and winked. His was the generation that met everything, from a death in the family to a mortar blast at close range, with one eye closed.

When the curtain finally opened he tugged on the lights and swept the car into a tight U-turn in the middle of Main Street, heading back to the motel. He pressed down the accelerator as we straightened out and the car fishtailed. He let the wheel twirl through his fingers right, then left, then right again as he corrected. I couldn't tell if he was a good driver because he was good or because he thought he was. It's the kind of thing that can only be proven when you crash.

"Same drill," he said as the neon fish leapt into view up ahead. "You fetch the ice, I'll uncork the booze. Did you remember to turn off your radiator this morning?"

"I think I forgot."

"I didn't. First time I wished I had Alzheimer's. We'll meet in your cabin. I'm an old man. I talk better when I thaw out."

14

"For a long time I tried to be like my brother," Booth said. "He was ten years older, a champion sprinter at Central High. He had two letters of commendation in his police jacket and was up for a medal of valor after the riot. He turned it down. That's when I knew I had no hope."

It was dark in my cabin. The power was out and although it was just past 9:00 A.M. the window was black. When lightning streaked, the sky went platinum and I saw him sitting in the armchair with the hand holding his glass resting on the right arm. We had on dry clothes and the room was warm, but there was a damp smell that made me think of the tropics, where Duane Booth's ship had gone down in September 1943.

I was sitting up in bed with pillows bunched in the small of my back. My glass was on the nightstand and we each had a bottle so neither of us would have to get up to refill. I was closer to keeping up with him now that there was something in my stomach and Cabin Five was empty. Booth had brought the entire case; I'd asked if he was moving in and he'd said he wasn't sure about the roof in Four and wanted to keep his valuables handy throughout the crisis. I'd almost asked about the manuscript, but he was talking now at last and I didn't want to take a chance and grind down the starter.

"The riot was the war's worst blunder, and we had enough of those to lose the whole show if the enemy hadn't had even more," he said. "Ford and GM and Chrysler did what the government told them, put blacks next to whites from Kentucky and Tennessee and Mississippi and Georgia on the line for the first time and beefed up the security so there'd be no trouble in the defense plants; then when the whistle blew they threw open the doors and told them to go out and have fun. Half the police force was overseas, and what was left was too busy looking for Fifth-Column saboteurs to see how everyone else was getting along.

"It all busted loose on June twentieth, a Sunday. A gang of rednecks threw a Negro woman off the Belle Isle bridge, or maybe it was a gang of Negroes and a white woman; I don't think they ever did sort that one out. Anyway, rumors spread fast in the heat. Streetcars got dumped over, black dives in Paradise Valley were set on fire, people on the street, black and white, were beaten and gang-raped and shot. By Monday night there were more than thirty dead, most of them Negroes. Took five thousand federal troops to put it down. About six weeks later a governor's committee reported it was the blacks that started it. I think that's when the term *whitewash* was coined." He took a long draught. "Shit. Tastes like water. Let's see. Duane was on duty the whole time, partnering Officer Roland Clifford. You've heard of him."

"He's the one hero both the white and black communities agree on. There's talk of naming a street after him."

"Hitler had a street too. I saved the clipping from the *News*, because Duane was mentioned. I threw it out finally, but I still know parts of it by heart: 'Officer Roland R. Clifford of the Fifth Precinct was commended by the department for his heroic attempt to save three Negro defense workers from an agitated mob. With the aid of Officer Duane A. Booth, his partner, he stopped the Woodward Avenue streetcar at eight P.M. and removed the men, who were the only Negroes aboard, to give them safe conduct to their homes. On their way to the squad car, the two officers and their charges were intercepted by a mob of between twenty and thirty white males, who claimed that the three Negroes were responsible for an earlier atrocity and demanded that the accused parties be turned over to them for justice.'

"To hell with the journalese," Booth said. "I said before I had my fill of it. Clifford drew his gun and held back the mob while Duane hustled the three men into the car. Before he could get the door shut, a rock flew out of the crowd and hit Clifford in the head. He went down and the mob poured in and beat the shit out of Duane. When he and Clifford came to they were alone. They found the three poor bastards they'd been trying to protect hanging from three lampposts in the next block."

I drank whiskey and watched lightning bleach the inside of the cabin briefly. It made him look like a carved hunk of white marble.

"That's how you wrote it in the book," I said when he didn't continue. "You described it just as if you'd seen it yourself."

"No one saw it. That's why it's called fiction. I'm a better writer than anyone knows, me included. The way I wrote it, no one could believe it happened any other way. A year or so before Clifford died, the president came to Detroit and gave him a medal. He should've given me one, too. They won't admit it now, and they sure wouldn't have back when I wrote it, but that two-bit paperback made Roland Clifford. He'd have been forgotten along with all the other heroes who had the bad taste not to die when their names were in the headlines if *Paradise Valley* hadn't sold six hundred thousand copies, mostly to horny little boys who got themselves off on the rape scenes. Is it my fault one of them grew up to be president?"

"You're saying what you wrote wasn't what happened."

"You're a detective. That you are." He swallowed.

Rain clobbered the windowpane, the only sound. He'd either changed his mind about talking or had lost his train. I was about to introduce a new subject and work our way back when he went on. He'd fallen into the grating drone of the tapes.

"When I close my eyes I can still hear Duane telling it, just the way he told it to our mother and me in the dining room of the old place on Kercheval late that Monday night and never told it to anyone afterwards. Guess that's why I don't like closing my eyes for too long at a stretch. Everything happened just the way the papers said and the way I put it in the book, except for one detail. It wasn't Clifford who got knocked cold. It was Duane Adam Booth, his partner. And it wasn't a rock. It was the butt of Clifford's service revolver. He used it when Duane went for his own to push back the crowd. The three poor bastards were dead when my brother woke up."

"Clifford turned them over?"

"I doubt he wanted to. He was probably a bigot— everyone was, then—but he was no killer. He was just yellow, and a better mathematician than my brother. It was two against a couple of dozen and he turned coat to save his own skin; try translating *that* for the foreign market. Fortunately I didn't have to worry about it. I wrote it straight from the official police report. The one Clifford filed and Duane signed."

"Why? Start with Duane."

"Why did he sign it? It wasn't his first choice. He wrote a different report separately, then tore it up. His partner made it clear that if he went down, he wouldn't go down alone. None of the members of the mob that lynched those men was going to come forward and back Duane up."

"Still, it was just Clifford's word against his."

"Clifford had friends. He retired a full commander after twenty-five years with the department. Even a coward who gets to pose as a hero doesn't rise that far on reputation alone. The reputation was useful, maybe crucial, but it would've blown over in a year without someone in a position to nail it down every time the promotions list went up."

"City hall?"

"Don't be naive. What's city hall got to gain from a cop with gratitude? Who's left? Think."

"Oh, them." I emptied my glass. "It always seems to come down to them no matter what."

"The price of liberty is eternal corruption. Ask Russia." Liquid splashed in the dark. "Duane wasn't around to do it—he enlisted rather than spend the rest of his career telling the same old lie, then got killed—so I made Roland Clifford my hobby. For years I kept a scrapbook, starting with the riot piece.

"I don't know even now if the boys in the tight jackets had their teeth into him from the start or if they smelled money and swam in later. Whatever else you say about them, you can't say they don't learn from their mistakes. They got rich from Prohibition, then blew most of their profits lobbying against Repeal. It took ten years to regain their momentum. Then came the wartime black market. They turned meat and eggs and cigarettes and tires into cash, tons of it, but they knew the war couldn't last forever. When Roosevelt and Churchill met Stalin at Yalta, the Detroit boys held their own summit."

He stopped to light a cigarette. Twin match-flares

crawled on the lenses of his glasses. I almost jumped. In the dark I'd half convinced myself I was listening to his canned dictation.

"They drew up a plan to divert their gains into post-war rackets." He shook out the flame. "Gambling, unions, prostitution, entertainment. They needed protection from the law, so they bought it. Clifford was a sergeant when the war ended. A week after V-J Day he was promoted to the plainclothes division. The city averaged a dozen raids per election year, complete with front-page pictures of cops loading whores into paddy wagons and smashing one-arm bandits and posing behind tables covered with betting slips and cash. Sergeant Clifford managed to appear in all of them. The amount of money confiscated barely covered the cost of the raids. The people who went to jail were strictly blue collar: pavement princesses and pugs, door openers. Nobody important. The cash registers were chiming again next weekend."

"That doesn't prove Clifford tipped them," I said.

"I don't have proof for any of this. We're just two guys talking in the dark."

"I'll drink to the dark." I poured. "You've already told me more than you told Fleta Skirrett."

"You talked to Flea?" He chuckled, coughed. Sparks sprayed. He cursed and brushed them off. "I bet she told you she slept with Pollock."

"She said Dali. But she wasn't sure it was him."

"She doesn't know who she slept with last week, or if she slept with anyone ever. She's as nutty as a pup chasing its tail. Always was. The Alzheimer's is just an excuse. Good old Flea. She's the only one from back then I'd care to spend time with. Pink birthday candle in a cave, that's her. Doesn't light anything but itself, but looking at it takes your mind off the cave."

"What kept you from writing *Paradise Valley* the way Duane told it?"

"Life. It's overrated, let me tell you. Oh, I was hot to write the truth at first, but truth won't carry a book if you don't know how to tell it. I was a kid, and I had my mother to support after Duane died. Well, if you read my books, you saw the resumé. I hacked for newspapers, sold chainsaws and flowers, stood in for a punching bag down at the gym until the real sparring partners came back from the war, fifty cents a day and they threw in the iodine free. I changed oil, killed cockroaches, stunned cattle, and found out some things you don't want to know about what goes on in the back rooms of mortuaries. Just about the time I'd lived enough to write, Harry Truman tagged me for Korea.

"Korea," he repeated quietly; the storm was out over Lake Huron now and the wind had died to a whimper. "I found out something my brother never knew, about combat, and how you never kill a man without something in you curling right up with him. That was like losing Duane all over again. It was the same when I celebrated my forty-first birthday and realized my father never made it that far. Anyway the truth didn't seem so important after Korea. It wouldn't bring Duane back and, worse, it wouldn't sell. People wanted heroes. I gave them one in *Paradise Valley* and they lapped it up. *Deadtime Story, Tough Town, Bullets Are My Business*—three more books, three more heroes. They sold like candy. I bought Mom a new house in

Royal Oak. I met Allison and got married and moved out of the Alamo. Mom died after two years in the new place. I found out she'd put some things in storage that had belonged to my brother and I went over and claimed them."

The red eye of his cigarette brightened as he drew on it, then made an arc down to the ashtray. He thumped it out.

"How about you, Walker?" he said then. "Any brothers or sisters? Kids?"

"None of each."

"It's a bitch being the last of your line. I'd found out by then Allison couldn't have children. I didn't much care for them—little larval human beings, raise them as right as you know and then they turn on you and blame you for what rotten adults they turned out to be. Not the point. I looked at that pathetic pile of stuff that was all that was left of Duane: track trophies, term papers, junk from his police locker, the usual mess of compost; and I wondered if a stack of cheap books was all my life was worth and if it was worth even as much as that crap of Duane's.

"We didn't have the phrase 'midlife crisis' then," he said. "I might've laughed it off if we had. Nothing burns my butt worse than a cliché. What I did was get drunk. I stayed that way for fifteen years."

The overcast was wearing thin. Watery gray light gleamed on the lake and picked up the broken boughs and other trash that had collected outside. A soaked green-and-white patio umbrella stuck upside-down in the grass like a broken harpoon.

"So you went off on a bat," I said. "I'd say you were entitled. I don't know about the fifteen years."

"It's not them I'm curious about. I've got a clearer picture of them than I care to have. It's the first few weeks I can't call up. God knows who I talked to in that time and what I said. Whatever it was it got my wife killed."

15

The sun was back in place now. A pine bough, heavy with water and brushing the window, glittered with droplets like bits of broken glass left behind at the scene of a traffic accident. The lake was still choppy, with white foam frosting the waves, but as I watched, its color went from tarnished silver to bright sapphire. It was light in the room too. Eugene Booth sat with his hand wrapped around his glass, his feet in their heavy lace-up shoes flat on the rug, and the back of his head resting in a hollow in the upholstery that had been worn by a hundred other heads. His eyes were open.

"The police said your wife was killed during a mugging," I said.

"I've spent most of the last forty years telling myself they were right. It would've been easier if I didn't know what I know about the police." He turned the glass around in his hand, working it with his thumb. "Don't get me wrong. Most of the time they do a good job. When they don't, it's usually because someone won't let them or they're too busy with other things. Her purse and jewelry being missing gave them an easy out. You can't blame them for taking it. I wouldn't blame them if I didn't think it was in someone's best interest not to blame them for taking it."

"Someone being Sergeant Roland Clifford."

"He was a lieutenant then at headquarters. But I don't think it was him. The only thing he ever did on his own initiative was brain my brother with his revolver. From that point on he never had to make a decision for himself."

"What made your wife worth killing? If you were drunk and shooting your mouth off about what happened in forty-three, you were the obvious candidate."

"That's the point. If there's anything the fuckers learned from Prohibition, it's to avoid being obvious. I was a famous character by fifty-six. If it was my corpse stuck in that window well there would've had to be an investigation. They'd have had to throw someone to the wolves. Why risk it, if by taking out Allison they could put a cork in me just as tight as if they'd killed me? The joke was on them, though. I was more determined than ever to write the truth. That's when New York stepped in on their side.

"*Some of My Best Friends Are Killers* is about a police cover-up," he said. "I wrote most of it right here at the Wigwam. It might have been this cabin, although I think it was Number One, the one that burned down later. Did you say you read it?" He'd forgotten our earlier conversation.

"Not yet. I asked Louise Starr to send me a copy."

"Read Steinbeck instead. By the time it came out it was about one crooked cop and an honest police department that united against him when the hero presented it with the evidence. The cop didn't bear even a passing resemblance to Clifford. That editor I knocked out later talked me into watering it down; Legal was afraid of a lawsuit and Marketing said the book would just upset readers. Legally and commercially they were right. By then I was tired of grieving, tired of being angry. I'd discovered a sure-fire cure for hangover, which is to stay drunk. I caved. I rewrote it. I can't blame anyone for that but me. I never thought I could hate anybody more than I hated Roland Clifford. As usual I was wrong. He was a yellow son of a bitch but he was never as yellow as Duane Booth's little brother Eugene. I didn't even have an angry mob as an excuse. I was afraid of not being a success."

He tilted his head forward. His voice deepened:

> " 'There once was a lady from Niger
> who went for a ride on a tiger.
> They returned from the ride
> with the lady inside
> and a smile on the face of the tiger.' "

He laughed, coughed, drained his glass, and filled it again. The ice cubes had melted and he was drinking eighty proof.

"Freud was right," he said. "The more you fear something the more likely you are to bring it about. *Killers* tanked. Not because it was watered down, but because there was still too much whiskey in it. It was the first book I ever wrote drunk. It sure as hell wasn't the last. The last was *Concerto for Cutthroats.* I never even read it myself. Tiger Books wouldn't have brought it out at all except it was the last one I owed them on my contract and it gave them an excuse to get rid of me. It sold like anvils. Nobody else would sign me after that. The rest you know." He grinned baggily. "You like that? That's the first time anyone ever delivered that line outside of a book or a movie. Consider it your going-away present." He put down his drink in two draughts and got up. He stumbled and caught himself on the iron railing at the foot of the bed. The empty glass thudded to the plank floor and rolled around in a half circle. I got up to give him a hand, but he waved it off. He straightened himself with a hissing intake of breath, found the door, and went that way.

"So now you're writing *Paradise Valley* the way you wanted to before you went to Korea," I said. "That's why you sent back Louise's check."

"Yeah. Big-ass deal. Everybody's dead. Call it the last irrelevant act of a useless fucking life. Put that on my tombstone and piss on it." He groped for the knob, got it on the second pass, and went out, lifting his feet over the threshold as if it were two feet high. I stepped out after him and leaned on the doorframe until I saw he'd made it into his cabin.

Just then the lights came on in mine. I went back in and switched them off. He'd left his case of whiskey. I picked up my glass, which was still half full, but I didn't drink it. I went into the bathroom, wobbling on round heels, and dumped it out in the sink. I splashed my face with cold water—it was rusty and stank of sulphur, the electric pump having just kicked back on—then wobbled back out and threw myself on the bed. I had to put one foot on the floor to avoid riding the mattress. I hadn't been that drunk at that hour of the morning since college. I decided I hadn't the liver to be a writer.

I woke at noon, checkout time. My head was banging like a sheet of tin in a high wind. I killed the little travel bottle of aspirins, chased them with rusty water, and packed. That took two minutes since I hadn't taken anything out except my toilet kit and the clothes I'd worn. Oh, and the Chief's Special; I remembered it behind the radiator and put it in the bag. The shirt and jeans I'd had on that morning were still wet, so I rolled them into a bundle and stuck it in the plastic sack that had lined the wastebasket. When I had everything loaded in the car I went back in and looked at the case of Seagram's.

I doubted he was in shape to answer his door. My job was finished, I'd found Booth and learned why he'd sent back the check. He was good for three or four more hours of oblivion and I needed the drive time more than I needed to say good-bye. But he'd be sore as hell if I left the whiskey as a tip for the maid.

Three knocks, five knocks, shave-and-a-haircut; none of the codes worked. Pounding just confirmed how really cheesy the door panels were. I gave up and walked down to the office.

Someone was watching the news in the little room off the desk. The announcer was warning people not to touch power lines they found lying on the ground. A bony male party of about the same vintage as the woman who had checked me in was reading a water-damaged copy of *Sports Illustrated* in the captain's chair on the customer side of the desk when I came in. He glanced up over his half-glasses, put down the magazine, and heaved himself to his feet with enough force to lift a man twice his size; the heavy soles of his Red Wing shoes seemed to be the only thing that kept him from going through the ceiling. He went around a plastic bucket catching the water from a leak in the roof, got himself behind the desk, caught the key to Cabin Two on the first bounce, and looked me up in the tin box. He had on a white shirt and shapeless green slacks, no fishing gear, and combed his thin white hair sideways across his dry pink scalp. The nosepiece of his glasses cut into the skin of his great pink beak like baling wire.

"Oh, Walker," he said. "Package came for you this morning. Special delivery."

I looked at the padded six-by-eight envelope he placed on the desk. It had a New York City return address. It would be the copy Louise had promised me of *Some of My Best Friends Are Killers.*

It reminded me of the New York plates on the GMC pickup. I signed the receipt he handed me for the room and gave him back his copy. "What time did Cabin Five check out last night?"

I expected the lecture on the sanctity of the guests. Instead he said, "Cabin Five," licked a thumb, and went through the plastic dividers in the box until he came to it. "Receipt's still here. Guess he just left."

"That happen often?"

"Often enough to make us ask for cash in advance. Some folks are in a hurry, just leave the key in the cabin and take off."

"Ferris, you gossiping about the guests?" The old woman's voice rose above the TV announcer's.

"I'm telling him all about the orgy in Five." He pronounced it with a hard *g*. "Wimmen and likker and Mary Jew Wanna all night long. I think it was a rock group we had in there."

"No one's laughing, Ferris. Don't you go gossiping about the guests."

Ferris lowered his voice. "No one's laughed in thirty-six years. I was better off married to my dead first wife."

I grinned. "There's a box in Two belongs to the man in Four. You'd better give it to him when he wakes up." I put a five-dollar bill on the desk.

He glanced toward the open door, then folded the bill one-handed and stuck it in his shirt pocket. "Four? He's checking out today, I think." he pulled Booth's card. "Yep. He's late."

"I doubt he'll make it. You'd better give him another day."

"Can't. Couple's coming in today for their anniversary.

Spent their honeymoon in Four. Reserved it for them myself."

"I'm headed back that way. I'll see if I can rouse him." I still had my wallet out. I kept my eye on the open door and tapped the tin box with the corner of a ten-spot. "Cabin Five," I mouthed.

He looked at the door, snatched the bill out of my hand, and turned to run his finger down a bank calendar tacked to the back wall, leaving the tin box standing open on the desk. There was nothing written on the calendar.

Cabin Five had filled out his registration card in square block capitals:

ROBERT C. BROWN
HOTEL MILWAUKEE
NEW YORK, NY

He'd written the correct number in the license plate blank; it was the one piece of information the motel people could confirm without going to the expense of a long-distance telephone call. I returned the card to its slot, raised my voice to thank the old man for a pleasant stay, and went out, no richer for my ten bucks.

Booth still wasn't answering his door. The shade hung crooked in his front window, leaving a two-inch gap in one corner. I crouched, cupped my hands around my eyes, and leaned on the glass. I straightened quickly and hammered on the door with the side of my fist; hauling back all the way and aiming at the center of a panel. It gave with a crack, the tongue popping out of the groove at upper right. I shoved it in with the flat of my hand and crooked my arm through the opening and undid the latch and then the deadbolt.

No lamps were lit and the curtains had been drawn over the window looking out on the lake. The room seemed as dark as a cave after the sunlight outside. I ran up the shade rather than wait for my eyes to adjust. The rhythmic movement I'd seen through the window was all I'd had to go on, but there is none other like it. Booth's body stirred slightly in the current of air, suspended two feet above the floor from the roof's center beam by his own belt around his neck. I threw my arms about his waist, hoisted him to create slack, and held him with one hand twisted in the waistband of his slacks as I reached up with the other to work loose the buckle at his throat. It took three times as long as it should have because I was straining to support him and the brass tongue was sunk deep in the leather, pulled tight by one hundred sixty pounds of dead weight. Finally I got it free and embraced him again with both arms and lowered him to the floor.

His face told me I needn't have hurried. It was gray-blue and his tongue had grown too big for his mouth. He wasn't wearing his bifocals. His eyes, shot through with ruptured blood vessels, stuck out like eggs. Nothing was happening in the big artery on the side of his neck. His skin felt cool.

The old man from the office was standing in the doorway. He still had on his reading glasses and was raising and lowering them like someone adjusting a TV antenna to improve his reception. I barked at him to call 911. His Red Wings clapped the sidewalk going away.

Booth's belt loops were empty; it was his belt tied to the beam. He hadn't anything in his pockets except his wallet, a scuffed brown leather number containing his driver's license, Social Security card, a creased black-and-white snapshot of a pretty dark-haired woman in her twenties I recognized from her newspaper photo as Allison Booth, and a hundred twelve dollars in cash. I returned it to his hip pocket.

I found a piece of paper containing the telephone number of the Angler's Inn in a pocket of his twill jacket hanging in the closet. There was nothing interesting hidden among the shirts and underwear in the bureau drawers or in his suitcase or the cheap vinyl toilet kit in the bathroom. He used a straight razor and had a nearly full bottle of nitroglycerine tablets prescribed by a Dr. Henry Goldenrod in Belleville. I made a note of the name, address, and telephone number in my pocket pad.

A scrap of coarse paper torn sideways from the bottom of a larger sheet lay slightly curled atop the stack of blank pages on the table beside his old typewriter. On it was written, in Booth's plain hand:

I can't do this anymore.

I left it where it was without touching it. In the distance I heard the first swoop of a siren coming from the direction of town.

I thought of something then and threw open the curtains covering the window that looked out on the lake. It was the double-hung type, with a rotating latch that slid into a socket when the handle was turned. The latch was in place, preventing the window from sliding up or down. The socket wobbled a little when I touched it with a finger. The window's wooden frame was partially rotted and the screws were loose in their holes.

Outside, the grass grew right up to the base of the cabin. It needed cutting. Some of the long wide blades were trampled and broken, but it could have been the heavy rain that did that. The grass wouldn't hold a footprint.

I retreated to the middle of the room and stood with my hands in my pockets, looking around: at Booth's body lying on the Indian rug, appearing smaller than it had when he was using it; at the straightback chair standing at a crooked angle to the door, the way it would have wound up after he stepped off the seat; at an empty bottle on the floor and the half-empty one standing beside a plastic glass containing an inch and a half of amber liquid on the table; at the typewriter, with its wooden case covered in black fabric on the floor leaning against a leg of the table. At first I couldn't tell what was missing.

The siren was slowing down for the turn into the little parking lot when I realized there was only one stack of papers by the typewriter. Yesterday there had been two, a taller one waiting to be filled and a shorter one covered with typewriting and emendations in Booth's hand. The shorter one was gone.

I went over and looked inside the wicker wastebasket next to the table. There wasn't so much as a crumple of paper inside it. The only thing in the room containing Eugene Booth's prose was his suicide note.

16

The sheriff's detective's name was Vaxhölm.

I had to get the spelling from him, because he pronounced it "Foxum" and didn't seem to care whether I got it right. He looked more American Indian than Norwegian, with a nose that was too thick for sunglasses so that the cushions had worn permanent depressions on either side of the bridge, and facial bones that looked as if they might finish gnawing through the skin any time and poke out white and shining against the dusky pigment. His hair was as black and glossy as any Huron's. But it was his eyes that settled the question. They were the harsh glittering blue of a frozen fjörd.

He came in just as the uniforms were finishing up
with me. They were neat in their short brown jackets
and Mountie hats and polite in that detached way that
came with being young and relatively new to the work.
From the start they had shown no more interest in the
corpse than they had to, examined my credentials, asked
who I was working for, and only frowned a little when
I said I'd have to consult with my client before I gave
up the name. I spotted them another five years and an
additional inch or two around their middles before they
started doing the detectives' work for them, frisking the
bodies and cranking up the heat under the witnesses
to break the case on the spot. Ambition in police work
comes in reverse ratio to all other forms of employment; later, when just playing by the rules has gotten
you no farther ahead than being invisible.

Vaxhölm had avoided the five years and the flab. Although he was in plainclothes, there was something of
the uniform in the way he wore his moss-green tweed
jacket with a shooter's patch on the right shoulder and
black knitted tie on a white shirt with a collar that but-
toned down. There was a crease in his olive-drab
trousers and he wore brown leather half-boots that
zipped up inside the ankles. He carried himself like an
athlete, and the thick pad of callus on his palm when
we shook hands spoke of quality time spent each week
with just him and a handball. His speech was clipped,
he bit off his consonants crisply; I thought at first he
was English despite his looks until I realized he was
controlling a bad stutter.

Possibly because of that, he had no small talk. He
went from the introductions straight to the note on the

table, read it without touching it, and examined the window, again without touching. He left the corpse for last. He stood over it for a moment with his hands hanging loose at his sides, noting its position and that of the chair. Finally he took a pair of disposable latex gloves from a pocket and put them on and sat on his heels and went through Booth's clothes and inventoried the contents of his wallet for one of the uniforms, who added them to the information in his steno pad. The detective bagged the wallet in a Ziploc he found in another pocket and attached it to Booth's shirt with a safety pin. He was a walking evidence kit.

He rose and turned his attention to me. "You broke in. Why?"

"I didn't have a key."

"That's the B answer. Why'd you break in and why did you take him down? That's tampering with the scene."

"I saw through the window something big was hanging from the rafter. When something's hanging you assume it's a man or a woman. When a man or a woman is hanging you cut them down. They might still be alive."

"You seem to know a lot about this kind of thing."

"I read a lot."

"I thought maybe you were going to say it's b-because you're a private detective." He bit down hard on the *p.*

"Finding corpses isn't in the job description. I take down more affidavits than carcasses."

That mollified him slightly. "The deceased was the

object of a missing-persons investigation you were con-
ducting?"

I said it was and gave him what I'd given the uniforms. He'd already gotten it from them but there is
no use arguing with cops about the way they do their
job. I didn't say anything about what Booth had told
me or the missing manuscript or the man in Cabin Five.
That was a risk, because the old man might tell them
about the ten bucks I'd paid him for a look at the registration card, but I could always claim I'd forgotten
about it in my distress. Vaxhölm might even believe
me. I didn't know why I ran the risk at all except I
didn't know him or anything about the department he
worked for and I wanted to talk with Louise Starr before I gave them for free what she was paying me five
hundred a day to get.

He must have read my mind, because the next thing
he asked was the name of my client.

"I might, if I thought it had anything to do with this,"
I said. Then I shook my head. "Probably not even then.
Not without permission."

The blue eyes got colder, if that was possible. Then
he surprised me by changing the subject. "Was the door
double-locked?"

I nodded. "I had to work the deadbolt."

"What about the window?"

"It was locked. I left it that way."

"There's no mystery, then. He was locked in from
the inside and we've got a note. Some kind of writer,
was he?"

"Some kind."

"I thought so, from the typewriter. Nobody uses them

anymore except writers that won't give up. On type-writers, I mean. 'I can't do this anymore.' What do you get out of that?"

"I don't have to get anything out of it. My work was finished when I found him."

"Maybe he meant he couldn't write anymore. That's the main reason writers commit suicide, I hear. It's what happened to Hemingway. I guess we should be grateful this one didn't use a shotgun. That must have been a mess."

"It seems like a lot to get out of six words."

"You're saying maybe he didn't write them?"

"Oh, he wrote them. It's his scribble. I'm a little suspicious of suicide notes that don't say anything about suicide. I'd expect a writer to take a little more time with a final draft. There's no date. He could have written it any time and meant anything. You wouldn't think twice about it if it weren't for the body."

"If it weren't for the body I wouldn't know about it. It makes a pretty strong case just by being here. And he was locked in from the inside." He had a sudden flash of extrasensory perception. "What sort of thing did he write?"

I breathed in and out. "Mysteries."

He showed his teeth for the first time and I wished he hadn't. His grin was wolfish, all bottom teeth. "There you have it: a locked-room murder mystery. Only there's no mystery about it, and no murder either."

"You didn't touch the window lock, did you?"

"I don't touch anything until the forensics team's come and gone. They've got enough to do without separating my prints from the hundreds of others they're likely to find in a motel room. D-did you?"

"No." If Forensics could lift my print or anyone else's off a rusted surface they were better than the boys in Detroit. "If you're satisfied he clocked himself, I'll be headed back. I've got a report to file."

He looked at the cop with the pad. "You got an address and phone number?"

"Yes, sir."

"All right, Walker, we'll send you something to sign. Don't take your time sending it back. And don't wander too far from your phone."

"Thanks, Sergeant."

"Officer. I'll take my promotion from the county. This fellow Booth have any next of kin?"

"No."

"What about a friend? Someone to claim the body when the coroner gets through with it?"

I hung back at the door. "Fleta Skirrett. You can reach her at the Edencrest Retirement Home in Marshall."

I went to my car and got in. An unmarked Ford Explorer was parked two slots down with a ton of electronic equipment inside. I looked at Cabin Two, my home for the past nineteen hours. I couldn't believe it could be measured in hours. I got back out.

A gray Pontiac pulled up in front of Four and a short round bald man slid out from under the wheel and went inside carrying a black metal case. He looked like Mr. Pickwick except for his permanent scowl. The old man and the woman in the fishing hat poked their heads out of the office door, one on top of the other like in a cartoon, then drew them back in. There was nobody outside but me.

I used the edge of my photo ID to slip the latch on Two and went in quickly, closing the door behind me. The Seagram's box was where Booth had left it with the necks of the remaining bottles sticking out of the top. I didn't have time to look and see if there was anything else inside. I carried the box to the door, cracked it to look out, then hastened across the sidewalk and shoved it into the Cutlass's front seat on the passenger's side. I didn't waste any time getting behind the wheel and pulling out.

If the old man in the office remembered to tell Vaxhölm about the box, I was going to get a telephone call. I had a hunch I was going to get one anyway.

I put eighty miles and two counties behind me before I felt safe enough to wheel into a rest stop and look inside the box. I didn't expect to find Eugene Booth's missing manuscript, so I wasn't disappointed; whoever had killed him and let himself out the window with the loose lock had to have had something to turn into a makeshift suicide note, and anyway I knew what was in the manuscript. I didn't expect to find anything but half a dozen bottles of a mediocre brand of American whiskey.

What I found was a very old sheet of eight-by-eleven paper, older even than the Alamo stationery and gone nearly as brown as the box itself, so that I didn't notice it at first against the reinforced bottom. It started to tear when I tried to pull it out from under the bottles—it was as thin as tissue—so I took the bottles out one by one and laid them on the floor of the front

seat. The paper peeled away from the corrugated fiberboard with a dry sound, like a mummy being unwrapped.

The report, typed into the prearranged blanks, was
faded so badly I had to hold it up to the sun to read
it. The legend at the top read DETROIT POLICE DE-
PARTMENT. The date, typed into a blank in the upper
left-hand corner, was July 21, 1943. I had to stare hard
to read the spidery signature scrawled at the bottom
by a hand whose bones had long since been picked
clean by sharks on the floor of the South Pacific.

17

I used the pay telephone at the rest stop to call Louise Starr in Hazel Park. I got a chirpy recording telling me I'd reached Debra's machine and if I left a message Debra would get back to me. I hung up before the beep, spent some more change, and got Mary Ann Thaler at Detroit Police Headquarters.

"Where the hell are you?" she greeted. "I'm getting Michigan Department of Transportation on the ID. Are you moonlighting as a trash-picker?"

"I'm calling from a toilet. Did you raise anything on the Allison Booth killing?"

"Plenty. I've been trying to call. You didn't tell me her husband was famous."

"I would have if I thought it was filed under *F*. What's the difference?"

"More column inches equals more paperwork. Same old results: Sometimes you strike oil, sometimes mud. It's a thick file. I cannot give you all of it over the phone. How far away are you?"

"Couple of hours." I looked at my watch. "Say, six o'clock."

"I'll meet you at your office. It's ten blocks closer to home."

I had just enough quarters left to try Louise again. This time when Debra's machine answered I waited for the tone and asked Louise to drop by the office after six.

No Ford Explorer was waiting for me with an angry Officer Vaxhölm inside when I got back to the car. There was no roadblock across the entrance ramp to I-75 and the state trooper stationed at an emergency crossover two miles south didn't give me a second look even though I swept past his cruiser five miles above the limit. Either the old man at the Angler's Inn had forgotten all about the box or the unlawful removal of six bottles of spirits from a vacant motel room at Black Lake was not considered worth the gasoline required to bring them back. I still didn't take a really deep breath and let it all the way out until I hit the first thick knot of rush-hour traffic outside Detroit.

An overheated radiator on a Toyota parked on the apron and five hundred gawkers slowed me to a stop just north of Eight Mile Road. By the time I got to the office it was almost seven and I had two women waiting in my little reception room.

"... sense of humor isn't always appropriate, but I've never known him to violate a confidence, no matter how trivial," Louise Starr was saying when I opened the door. She turned her cool smile on me. "Hello, Amos. Was the drive as bad as all that?"

I was feeling unbuttoned and my shirt was stuck to my back. I'd have felt the same in white tie and a cutaway with her around. She was seated on one end of the upholstered bench with her legs crossed in sheer hose with gray suede pumps on her feet. Today it was a business suit, gray, with a skirt that came to her knees and an unlined jacket not much heavier than her blouse, eggshell silk with a maroon scarf tied bandanna fashion around her neck. Platinum obelisks dangled from her ears, which she'd left exposed by drawing her hair back with barrettes. She was one of the few who had the ears for it, small and well-shaped and flat to her head.

"Cadillac had it worse," I said. "Hello, ladies. Thank you both for waiting."

"Just as long as you don't thank us for our patience," Mary Ann Thaler said. "That would be assuming way too much."

The lieutenant was sitting on the other end of the bench with both sneakered feet flat on the floor and her forearms resting on her thighs. She had on loose faded jeans threadbare at the knees and a University of Detroit sweatshirt with the sleeves pushed up to her elbows. Her hair was gathered inside a black baseball cap with a curled bill and POLICE embroidered in yellow block capitals on the front of the crown. She wore her glasses and no makeup. The only thing missing from the expression on her face was the gun that belonged in front of it.

That made my decision easier. I hadn't been sure which one got first crack, client or cop. *The Miss Manners Guide to P.I. Protocol* didn't cover the situation. But I had to work in Detroit.

I pointed at Thaler. "You. They're reviving *Dirty Harry* tonight at the DIA. You probably want to change."

She stood and looked at the other woman. "Depends on your point of view, Mrs. Starr. In my line, people who are good at keeping confidences are a pain in the butt."

"I never thought of it that way." Louise took a card out of her handbag and held it up. "It was good talking with you, Lieutenant. You can reach me here if you ever change your mind."

Thaler took it. "You've got my number if you need me. Nine-one-one."

I excused myself to Louise and unlocked the door to the private office. Before I could get it open the lieutenant scooped a thick bundle bound with a rubber band off the coffee table and went inside.

"Home sweet stinkhole," she said when we were seated on either side of the desk. "I thought you'd at least have changed the wallpaper by now."

"It's got tenure. Who put the hitch in your holster?" I reached back and switched on the fan on the windowsill. It purred and blew ash off the topsoil in the tray of butts on the desk.

"An hour in your waiting room."

"I've got new magazines."

"I saw. *Architectural Digest;* who do you think you're kidding? I've seen your house."

"Waiting is what cops do best. It wouldn't be that Louise is got up like Katharine Hepburn and you look like one of the Dead End Kids. What happened to the revolution?"

She put on a smile then. A gun could still have gone in front of it. "She's too tall. And someone should tell her you don't wear dangling earrings with a business suit."

"She's wearing earrings?" I was grinning, first time that day. "Change your mind about what?"

"Change my mind." Her face went flat. "Oh, that. She wants me to write about my experiences. You know: *Betsy Billystick, Girl Cop.* I said no. People who write up their life experiences have a habit of not hanging around long enough to have any others."

"That's just superstition."

"Hello?" She tapped the POLICE on her cap, then rapped her knuckles on the desk. "Anyway, I'm no writer. Not like your man Booth. Is he still around, by the way?"

I plucked out a cigarette and smoothed it between my fingers. "He was last time I spoke to him."

"He your client?"

"No."

"Right, that would be Katharine Hepburn. Editor, writer, detective. Triple play."

I lit up and blew smoke at the nicotine smudge on the ceiling.

"Fine," she said, "have it your way. I only put on the back of my closet today and turned down lunch in West Bloomfield with a good-looking inspector from the Fifth to grub around amongst the spiders and forgotten bootleggers in the basement as a favor to you." She shoved the bundle across the desk and sat back.

I unwound the rubber band, releasing a sprinkle of paper shavings and dust into the litter of same already on the blotter pad. "I heard the Fifth's under investigation."

"That's why he had the time for lunch. The feds don't like suspects getting in the way of a paper search. They're just clerks with shoulder holsters."

"Quantico turn down your application again?" I spread open the tattered cardboard file folder. The contents smelled like someone's attic.

"To hell with Quantico. I'm studying for the bar."

"And hoping to marry someone who is not a cop."

"Who's getting married? I was talking about lunch."

"I'll take you to lunch. Not in West Bloomfield, though. How about Greektown?"

"I see more cops in Greektown than at roll call. Anyway I can't be seen breaking bread with no plastic badge. I'm up for city hall detail: nine to five and I don't have to race the rest of the squad to the calendar for my vacation days."

We were both silent while I paged through the old reports, eyewitness statements, inventories of evidence, newspaper clippings, and photos. The grainy black-and-white shots were printed on cheap police stock, without gloss, but the details were sharp enough to liven up anyone's nightmares. Allison Booth didn't look so pretty folded over and stuffed into the concrete square of a basement window well with one shoe off and her skirt hiked up to expose her girdle. Stretched naked on a porcelain table in the morgue she looked less like a department-store mannequin and more like a corpse: one eye swollen shut, the other open and staring, and dark bruised patches all over her chest and abdomen where the knife had gone in.

"The husband's statement," Thaler said when I came to a sheaf of typewritten sheets stuck together with a pitted paperclip, one of the old-fashioned kind that came to a point. "We went after his alibi hard when we found out about that last day, but it wouldn't bend. He was having dinner with his editor and an assistant in New York at the time the coroner figured his wife died in Detroit. The restaurant staff backed them up."

" 'We.' " I laid aside Booth's statement unread and picked up another. "You were how old then?"

"My mother was still in elementary school, thank you. My father was starting junior high and they wouldn't meet for ten years. When I say *we* I'm referring to the sacred and fraternal order of law enforcement professionals. The good guys for short."

"Tell that to the Fifth Precinct. What happened the last day?"

"I told you to read the newspapers. Didn't you take my advice?"

"I never fail. The sacred and fraternal order of law enforcement professionals wasn't any more forthcoming with the press then than it is now. That's why I asked you to grub around amongst the forgotten bootleggers in the basement."

"Spiders too. Don't forget the spiders. One of them tried to steal my hat." She tugged down on the bill as if to make sure it was still there. "You're looking at the eyewitness statement now. A perfume counter clerk at the late lamented downtown Hudson's happened to look out the glass doors just as a car pulled into the curb and the driver got out and opened the door on the passenger's side for Allison Booth and she got in. The clerk didn't know the Booths and she assumed it was the lady's husband picking her up. Apparently they were pretty friendly. There's a description."

I looked at the second sheet. The clerk, whose name was Washington, said the car was dark blue, a late model, and thought it was either a Chevrolet or an Oldsmobile but couldn't say for sure. The driver was six feet tall and well built, in his early thirties, with sandy hair worn in a crewcut. "That's not a description of Booth," I said.

"The detectives figured that out. Saunders and O'Hara their names were, both deceased. I checked them out in the computer. Anyway the fact it wasn't her husband was all the more reason to take a second look at the husband. Especially when Miss Washington picked the driver out of a group of interviewees at headquarters later. That's the next report. No, I'm wrong. That's the autopsy sheet. Keep going."

Death by desanguination was the verdict. I turned over the post-mortem and found a report signed by Detective Michael Patrick O'Hara of Homicide. It was full of typos and strikeovers. He'd have been a lot more comfortable swinging a nightstick than hunched over a department Remington hunting and pecking with two fingers.

Thaler translated. "You can't blame O'Hara and Saunders for thinking they were onto something. The husband and the driver knew each other. It wouldn't have made the papers, though, because they both had alibis that held and there were no other eyewitnesses to back up Washington. The name's there in the last paragraph. Birdsong or something."

"Birdsall," I corrected, reading. "Lowell Birdsall, Senior. Artist."

18

R ight." Thaler was watching me. "He illustrated Booth's books or something. They were pretty tight, or were before the murder."

"Afterwards, too. According to Birdsall's son." I turned to the next sheaf. It was a typewritten transcript of Sergeant Owen Saunders' interview with Birdsall, with no strikeovers and fewer typos; the work of a professional stenographer.

"There's no accounting for people. But Birdsall was cleared, so I guess that was good enough for Booth. The model he was painting that night vouched for him. Fleta Skirrett?"

"Uh-huh." Fleta's statement was there too. She and Birdsall were shut up in the Alamo from a little before six until almost eleven that night. The autopsy report fixed time of death between seven and nine. Her Alzheimer's or something had caused Fleta to leave all that out when we'd talked. "What about the Racket Squad? Booth had a beef with the local mob."

"News to me. There's nothing about it in the file. Didn't they used to have some kind of rule about not going after wives or children?"

"That was the theory."

"Yeah." She made a theoretical sound in her throat. "Saunders and O'Hara closed it out as robbery-murder, assailant unknown. A pair of diamond earrings—a gift from Booth to celebrate a new contract with his publisher—was missing from Allison's jewelry box, and two eyewitnesses in Hudson's said she was wearing them in the store. Her wedding ring was gone too. If any of those items had ever surfaced in a pawnshop or anywhere else, it would have been in the file. Either the thug had a good fence or he dealt them out of town or he panicked and threw them down the sewer grate."

"Didn't there used to be some kind of rule about not wearing diamonds before six?"

"That was the theory." Her tone was arid. "The clothes she had on are in the inventory: blue silk blouse, black skirt, black high-heel pumps, one of those tricky butterfly-shaped hats women used to pin to their hair. It was black too, and so was the little clasp purse she was seen carrying in the store. The purse was never found. She was dressed for a night out."

"Is that the opinion of a cop or a woman?"

"Both. You wouldn't listen if it was just a woman."

"I'd resent that, only I'm too tired. It doesn't sound like you subscribe to the mugging theory."

"I'm Felony Homicide. Murders committed in the course of robbery are my meat. The taxi companies had no record of a fare answering Allison Booth's description leaving Hudson's that night. No one saw her board a bus or a streetcar. The items she bought were easy to carry, but she had them delivered. She wasn't going straight home, and no woman would willingly walk more than a few blocks in high heels. And she wouldn't go shopping carrying a date purse unless she was meeting someone afterwards. Just because no one backed up the perfume clerk doesn't mean she didn't see what she said she saw. Even if she was mistaken about the man she thought she saw giving Allison Booth a lift."

"Maybe it was a friendly thing that turned out not so friendly," I said. "The running-out-of-gas gag was old even in fifty-six, but it still got used. Maybe she smacked him and got out to walk home."

"Maybe. But I'd've made more of an effort to find the man and ask."

"Not if you were Saunders and O'Hara, maybe. And maybe not if you thought she was a tramp and got what she had coming for whoring around while her husband was gone."

"You act surprised. You wouldn't if you were me and spent as much time in police locker rooms as I have. So what if there's one more murderer walking around than there was last week? There's one less two-timing wife."

My cigarette had burned half away in the ashtray. I closed the folder and poked out the glowing coals with the eraser end of a pencil. "How long can I hang on to this file?"

"I doubt anyone will be asking for it any time soon," she said. "Or will they?"

I returned the pencil to the cup. Then I sat back and took another Winston out of the pack; but to play with, not to smoke. "They might. If a sheriff's detective named Vaxhölm up in Black Lake decides Eugene Booth didn't hang himself this morning in his motel cabin."

"I knew when you walked into my office yesterday my weekend was going to be spoiled," she said.

"No reason it should. It's not your jurisdiction. Anyway there's a note and the cabin was locked from inside. A cop like Vaxhölm spends most of his time investigating break-ins at vacation cottages. He'll probably be satisfied with suicide."

" 'Satisfied with suicide.' Sounds like the title of a Gangsta Rap album. Only you don't care if it does rhyme."

"One or two things about it don't. Can you trace an out-of-state license plate?"

"Depends on the state."

"New York."

"New York's dicey. There an officer has to enter his badge number every time he runs a check. Questions can get asked. It seems some members of the sacred and fraternal order of law enforcement professionals have been running a cottage industry on the side. It's

the Information Age. Everybody wants some and is willing to pay to get it."

"Thank God."

We were quiet for a moment. I wondered if Louise
had read all the magazines in the reception room.

"I'd like to break the Allison Booth case," Mary Ann
Thaler said then.

"You won't get any medals. The brass would be just
as happy if it stayed forgotten. That's the nature of old
cases. You might even lose your shot at city hall."

"Yeah, well. You can only fetch sandwiches for the
chief so many times before it gets old."

"Like maybe once."

She took off her glasses and pulled up the bottom
of her sweatshirt to wipe the lenses. She had a nice
tanned midriff, but it couldn't compete with her eyes,
blue as robin's eggs and nearly as large. "Even if it is
suicide, it could have something to do with what happened in fifty-six. It could shake something loose. If
she was a tramp—okay, but it didn't entitle her to a
death sentence. And if by some chance her killer is
still around, I'd have the satisfaction of clamping the
cuffs around his withered old wrists. That's why I took
the oath and the twelve-week course. Doughnuts make
me bloat. Is the plate connected?"

"I won't know that until I know who it belongs to.
Maybe not even then." I told her about the man in the
Yankees cap in Cabin Five.

"Robert C. Brown," she echoed. "The middle initial
is a nice touch. It's safe to assume he had a gun if he
kept his hand covered. Keep me current and I'll run
the plate. I got on pretty good with a sergeant with

NYPD Narcotics when he was here last year on an extradition. He might be able to slip it in with a bunch."

"I'll call you right behind my client." I took out my notepad and gave her the number.

She put on her glasses, wrote the number in her pad, and put it back in her hip pocket. "What was Booth's beef with the mob?"

"He knew something and got drunk. He might have opened his mouth. He wasn't sure. His wife might have been killed as a warning."

"What did he know?"

"He swung from his belt before he could tell me." I didn't want to confuse her with details. One confused detective in town was enough.

"It doesn't wash," she said, and I thought my poker face had slipped. "They don't kill wives as a warning. That's what dogs are for."

"They can't all be Don Vito Corleone. Anyway it worked, if gagging Booth was what was intended. He shut his mouth and the weight of it broke him and his career."

"Then he opened it again and the weight of him broke his neck."

"Ironic," I said, "but not accurate. He strangled."

"They always do. A crime writer of all people ought to be able to come up with a better way to clock himself."

I picked up the cigarette I'd been playing with earlier. "If you spend all your time with inspectors and sergeants, you're never going to marry that dull character with the gas grill."

"Look who's talking. Your gig is missing persons. Your job ended at Black Lake."

I centered the butt on the blotter and circled a finger around it; part of a trick I couldn't get the hang of in Southeast Asia and hadn't had any luck with since. "You know a limerick that begins, 'There once was a lady from Niger'?"

"I've heard about the man from Nantucket, but nobody ever finishes it. What are you doing?"

"Trying to magnetize the tobacco. The limerick goes something something 'ride on a tiger.'"

"It would have to. Is it a static electricity thing?" She was watching the cigarette.

"Search me. I'm trying to tell you about this limerick."

She flicked her nails at the back of my hand and I withdrew it. She stared at the cigarette for a moment, then traced an index finger around it slowly. On the second pass she picked up the pace, tightening the circle. By the fifth lap the movement was a blur. On the seventh and eighth she slowed down. The tenth time around, the cigarette twitched. Twice more and then it revolved in a full circle, following her finger as if it were attached with an invisible filament.

She got up. "Keep the file. If anyone asks for it they won't be expecting it right away. I'll call you if I need something I haven't already committed to memory. Don't forget my number if you raise anything on your end. Right, the limerick. I don't see much point to it if the lady doesn't wind up inside the tiger."

She left while I was rising to open the door for her.

*   *   *

I got there in time to hold it for Louise, who drifted in carrying a folded copy of the *Free Press* under one arm. She glanced back toward the hall door. "Interesting woman. I offered her a chance to write her memoirs. Women doing traditional men's jobs is a good market."

"She isn't a writer."

"These days that doesn't matter. There are plenty of talented writers out there who are willing to ghost." She looked around. "Same charming office. Gene Booth would approve."

"Sorry I kept you waiting."

"That's all right. I took the liberty of reading your paper. Debra subscribes to *USA Today*. That news I can get from the TV networks." She put the newspaper on the desk and let me pull the chair out for her. "I see you don't keep it bolted to the floor anymore."

"Some of my clients don't use mouthwash. But a lot of them feel more comfortable if they can push up close and whisper." I took my seat. It was uncomfortably warm from my own body heat and I turned the fan up another notch. "Have you been taking in the sights?"

"You mean the casinos? Are they open?"

"Not yet. The MGM Grand is renovating the old IRS building."

"Appropriate. I do want to check out Greenfield Village and Henry Ford Museum."

"Don't try to do both in one day. The Wright Brothers' bicycle shop and the chair Lincoln was shot in is too much history all at once."

"Small talk." She smiled. "The news must be bad."

"Uh-huh." I picked up the magnetized cigarette and plunked it into the wastepaper basket. Then I folded my hands on the blotter. That made me feel like an undertaker so I rested them on the arms of the swivel. "Booth is dead. I found him this morning hanging in Cabin Four at the Angler's Inn."

One hand went halfway to her mouth. Then it drifted down and found the other one in her lap. "Oh, dear God. Suicide? No, what a ridiculous question to ask. Of course it was suicide. The poor man."

"Why 'of course'?"

"He was old and miserable and sick. He told me the first time we spoke he had a bad heart. It seemed likely. Do you mean it wasn't?"

I'd been a detective too long. For the smallest piece of a second a light showed in her eyes. It didn't have to mean anything. It could have been the sheen of tears.

I ran a test. "You could get a book out of it I suppose. But you'd need a murderer. Otherwise it's a long joke without a punchline. Anyway, who would you get to write it, one of your ghosts?"

The delicately chiseled face went stony. "That's a despicable thing to say." Her tone was barely audible.

"I'm the one who took him down."

"I'm sorry." She looked it.

"Me too." I stirred myself finally and opened the file drawer at the bottom of the desk. "Scotch is all I have. I'm sorry about that too. You're welcome to join me." I stood the bottle on the desk and the two shot glasses I kept for genteel company. It was the good brand I'd bought out of the spring's largesse. Spring seemed a long time ago.

"Thank you, I will."

I poured hers first and then mine. I didn't propose a toast out of respect for the deceased. *Bullshit*, he'd said, the one time I asked. I wanted to put mine down in one easy deposit, but I made myself sip it. The sip Louise took was healthier than expected. It brought a flush to her smoothly tanned cheeks.

"Tell me all of it," she said.

I told her all of it, including the part I hadn't told Lieutenant Thaler. When I finished she was thinking like a publisher. I decided I hadn't misinterpreted what I'd seen before, but what the hell. The Scotch was already working. It paid to buy the best.

"Do you think this Robert Brown did it?" she asked. "He's a mobster?"

"If he is his name isn't Brown. It probably isn't anyway. This year's Robert Brown is last year's John Smith. I'd need a lot more help than you could afford to look them all up, even if I confined myself to New York State, and then he wouldn't be one of them. I'm having his plate run but that will be a dead end too. If it isn't he's probably innocent. If all my hunches played out I'd be down at the Grand now, waiting for the doors to open."

"It had to be murder. If it wasn't, the manuscript would have still been in his cabin."

"The manuscript didn't mean anything. He was writing fiction. It wouldn't hang anyone without proof. If he was killed and the killer took it, it would just be to satisfy someone's curiosity about what Booth knew. It wasn't worth killing for."

"Duane Booth's original police report would be, though. That's why he put it in your cabin. He must have known his life was in danger."

"Only an idiot doesn't," I said. "He told me his brother destroyed the report and signed his name to Roland Clifford's. He hadn't made his mind up about me yet. Either he did before he left my cabin or he was too drunk to remember it was in the case of whiskey. Either way he left me with a grenade and walked away holding the pin."

"Where is it now?"

I patted my breast pocket. Her eyes widened a little, but they still weren't as big as Mary Ann Thaler's.

"Do you think it's wise to carry it around? It should be in a safe deposit box."

"Hiding it in a safe place didn't help Booth. Anyway I don't think anyone knows it exists. Otherwise whoever strung him up would have tossed the cabin looking for it."

"Why is it still important? Clifford's dead. His reputation is of no use to anyone."

"It is to the city of Detroit," I said. "They've built this latest renaissance on his shoulders. A white hero in a black cause might go a long way toward reversing white flight. I don't think they'd kill an old man to protect his memory, but I've seen worse done by people high up."

"Alive he was an asset to the underworld. Dead he's a boon to society. How ironic."

"There's a book in that."

She gave me the violet stare. "I'm sorry a man got killed, but I'm fighting for my life. If Booth's manuscript still exists I want it."

"Are you making a pitch?"

"You don't have to take the job if it repels you. There are other private detectives who will, some of them just as good as you and maybe better. But they'd lose at least a day catching up to where you are now. Meanwhile whoever has the book may burn it."

"It's probably burned already. It's evidence of murder."

"The chance is worth taking. I'll double your fee and add a bonus if you manage to deliver the script. Ten thousand dollars."

"You can't afford ten thousand. Even if I find the book, you don't own it."

"I'd have advanced him a lot more to publish it. I can scratch up the difference to deal with his literary estate. If he didn't have one I'll enter a claim in Lansing. In any case that's my headache. Yours is to continue the investigation. If you agree." She leaned forward and touched my hand. "Do it for me if not the money. We have a history."

I patted hers and sat back. "I'll do it for the money."

Nothing changed in her face. Everything else had. She opened her purse and drew out a checkbook bound in gray suede leather.

"I'll pay you what I owe so far, along with three days' advance based on the new terms," she said, uncapping a silver pen. "That should cover your expenses until you know something definite."

"Just make it out for the fifteen hundred I've earned.

I'll bill you at the other end, the old fee, and I'll hold you to the bonus, just to keep it interesting. The cops get suspicious when a private star butts in on an open case for nothing but his health. I want to see this out."

She regarded me. Then she shook her head and began writing. "I can't make up my mind whether you're the shrewdest man I ever met or the most ridiculous. Perhaps that's how you survive."

"It sure isn't my diet." I drank the rest of my Scotch.

She handed me the check and stood. Her gaze fell to the copy of the *Free Press* folded on the corner of the desk. "I forgot to mention I'm not your only out-of-town visitor this week. I see Glad Eddie Cypress is coming to sign his book."

"I thought you turned him down."

"My boss didn't. The book's number three on the *Times* list. Eddie's doing a twenty-city tour." She unfolded the paper and touched a corner article with a clear glossy nail.

It was a publisher's handout about the Mafia hitman-turned–government witness and his appearance that coming Sunday at Borders Books in Birmingham, with a picture of Cypress smiling with pen in hand. The smile caught my eye, possibly because it was the last thing some fifteen people had seen when he had been holding something else. When I covered the top half of his face with my hand I recognized it myself. He looked older without the Yankees cap and dark glasses.

19

I didn't tell Louise about Glad Eddie. It would have led to more questions I couldn't answer, and I had enough of those already to qualify for associate membership in the Detroit local of the philosophers' union. When she was gone, leaving behind that faint trace of foxglove, I switched off the fan and locked up.

I drove home through the chalky half-tone of early dusk, stopping only for a sandwich and a cup of coffee at a place on Warren that was got up like an old-time diner in hopes of snaring the casino trade; only the casinos had run into a legal snag and the whites of desperation showed in the eyes of the proprietor behind the counter as he filled the orders of half a dozen customers scattered like coins in a beggar's hat. The sandwich was good and I hadn't eaten since breakfast, but I didn't finish it. I kept thinking that my last meal had been steak-and-eggs with Eugene Booth.

TV had nothing better to offer than three sitcoms about young divorced mothers of small precocious children and an hour-long drama about lawyers. I'd brought in the package that had come for me at the Angler's Inn and I broke it open and admired Lowell Birdsall's cover, a study in reds and yellows of a bent-nosed brute grappling with a blonde in a fringed taxi-dancer's dress on a ballroom floor ringed with human apes in deep shadow. But I wasn't in the mood for Booth's prose and laid down *Some of My Best Friends Are Killers* halfway through the first short chapter.

I lit a cigarette and put it out. I poured myself a drink and abandoned it after one sip. I couldn't seem to stick with anything. I thought about going to bed. Although my eyes were burning and my shoulder blades stung from the long drive south I saw nothing in front of me but a night of rolling out the lumps in my mattress. So I did what I always did when I didn't feel like thinking. I called Barry Stackpole.

"Hello, Amos." He sounded bright and youthful. People who spend all their time stewing over blowtorch murders generally do.

I hesitated. "So you caved in and got Caller ID. I guess that makes me the last Mohican."

"I didn't neither. The people who place the threatening calls I have to worry about are smart enough to dial star sixty-seven first. Only two people have this

number and the other one's on Death Row in Texas."
Ice tinkled on his end. He swallowed. "You sound like
you're in the next cell. Divorce business getting too
lively?"

"Go to hell. I drove four hours today on top of a
police interrogation."

"Well, the drive is new. Which police, Chicago?"

"Cheboygan County."

"You're kidding. They got law up there now? I thought
everybody settled their differences with dueling pistols."

"No, that's Detroit. I ran into someone you might
know."

"If it was in Cheboygan County he must have been
floating facedown in a lake."

"Why a lake?" Barry had been working on develop-
ing a sixth sense for as long as I'd known him.

"Nobody goes north in Michigan for the culture. Take
away the lakes and you might as well be in Nebraska.
Was I right about the floater?"

"No, this one's still alive and doing a good job of it.
Cypress is the name."

Ice tinkled and clanked, but this time he didn't drink.
"That cocksucker." It was barely audible.

"So you know him."

"I haven't had the pleasure. I haven't had the plague
either, but I know enough not to make pets of strange
rats."

"Your sense of humor's wearing thin," I said. "You
make your living reporting on the comings and goings
of rats like Glad Eddie."

"If you can call cable TV a living. I get along with
goons just fine. You ought to see the Christmas cards

I get from Sing Sing and San Quentin. They skim a little, burn down buildings for the insurance, and occasionally beat some poor schmo to death with a baseball
bat for missing one too many loan payments. They get
caught or they don't, do the time or they don't, rat
each other out for immunity or a plea to a lesser charge.
But so far only one of them's slid out from under fifteen contract murders and wheeled and dealed it into
his own star on the Hollywood Walk of Fame. If I got
a Christmas card from him I'd shove it up his ass with
a bayonet. What's a fuck like him doing up in the
pines?"

"That was yesterday. Sunday he's in Detroit. Well,
Birmingham. He's schlepping a book."

"I heard. I hope it goes big and he celebrates with
vodka and Valium."

"Twelve hours after I saw him at Black Lake the man
staying in the motel cabin next to his strangled to death
with his own belt. Are you interested?"

The silence on his end was just long enough to register. "Your place or mine?"

"Are you drinking?"

"I jumped off the wagon to make a deadline. I can
cab it over if you're beat."

"Do that."

"Haig and Haig?"

"Chivas."

"Barbarian. Be there in twenty."

A Checker delivered him at the front door. He paused
for a quick handshake, then strode in fast, the way he
always did when in his current condition, to keep the

effects of the alcohol from catching up. They showed only in the metallic brightness of his eyes and a minor limp. When he was granite sober, an orthopedic surgeon couldn't tell which leg was artificial. The white cotton gloves he wore to disguise his two missing fingers gave him the air of a country club gentleman, an image he could carry off when it suited him, although he was just as comfortable in the company of Hell's Angels and guys named Vinnie the Aardvark.

Considering the hours he keeps and the circles he travels in, Barry should look ten years older than he is. He's my age and could pass for a college senior. Tonight I wondered if the hairdressers at the cable station where he kept weekly on-air tabs on the underworld elite might be responsible for the absence of gray in his sandy temples, but he had the complexion of a kid at church camp.

He glanced around at the living room, made no comment—the place hadn't changed since his last visit, and anyway he'd spent three years sleeping in roach motels and underground garages after a bomb in his car failed to carry away more than a quarter of his anatomy—and flung himself into the only completely comfortable chair I owned. He had on an orange sweater, windowpane-plaid slacks, and well-worn moccasins with pink socks. "Pour," he said.

I'd brought in an extra glass from the kitchen, filled it, and handed it to him. "Where's Veronica and Jughead?"

"What, the outfit? I met my prospective father-in-law today. He thinks this is how they dress at Harvard."

"Who's the lucky mafiosa?" I topped off the drink I'd been nursing for a half hour and sat on the sofa.

"Cynic." He drank and screwed up his face. Then he lifted his brows. "It *is* Chivas. I thought maybe you'd saved the bottle. Stuff still tastes like iodine. The bride-to-be's name is Tatyana, and she's the prettiest little linebacker you've ever seen in a size fifteen."

"Russian mob?"

"Ukrainian. Her old man's silent partner in a couple of Indian casinos up north. He's got his eye on Detroit. That's the deadline I'm working on. Gaming Commission decides on his partner's license application first of next month."

"June wedding?"

He nodded with his eyes closed. The steel plate in his skull gave him migraines. "If the commission postpones I may have to ask you to be my best man."

"Ever consider an easier line of work?"

"Back at you. At least the food's good at an eastern European wedding. And they don't serve Scotch." He put his down, but not before helping himself to another sip. "Well, well. Glad Eddie Cypress. As I live and breathe. Which is not an expression he'd be used to hearing. I read his book."

"Already? It's just out."

"His publisher sent me an advance copy. I guess you didn't catch my review. I blew it to pieces with the sawed-off shotgun the boys in ATF took out of Joey Grenada's place on Lake Michigan last summer. I can't wait to see if they quoted that on the dust jacket."

"Eddie got under your skin."

"It's the country I ought to be mad at. We gave

Capone his day, but then we put him in jail. You and
I must have been in Cambodia the week someone de-
cided it was supposed to go the other way around.
But you can't fight the country, so I'll just go ahead
and hate Cypress. You know why they call him Glad
Eddie? It's not because of that shit-eating grin of his."

"I thought it was."

"They call him that because every time he completed
a contract he sent a tasteful bouquet of gladiolus to
the funeral. It was in the way of submitting a statement to his customers for services rendered. You can't
accuse him of being a piker; some of those hits took
place out of season. But I imagine he deducted his
florist's bill from his taxes as a business expense. I can't
help wondering what went through the widows' minds
when those bouquets showed up."

"His testimony sent a don to prison."

"For putting out a single contract. The feds thought
swinging a conviction was worth forgiving more murders than Jack the Ripper committed. But let's not kid
ourselves. Washington and Quantico don't care about
killings. Murder isn't in their jurisdiction. Paul Lippo
was costing them too much in uncollected taxes and
all the accountants on their payroll couldn't uncover a
paper trail to save them. So they dug up Eddie and
got him to corroborate a couple of wiretaps and let
him walk without so much as a Hail Mary. And the
gladiolus on fifteen graves are doing splendidly."

"What else can you tell me about him?"

"First tell me about Black Lake."

I rolled my glass between my palms. "I don't want
to turn on my TV tomorrow and see it."

"You won't. You don't have a cable box. You won't anyway. Not until you give me the high sign. How long have we known each other?"

"Don't go there, Barry. You won't like the ride." I drank.

He looked at me blandly, his fake leg slung over one arm of his chair. "Okay. I'm off the air until this Ukrainian thing breaks anyway. My future father-in-law might tune in and find out I'm not a Harvard man. How's that?"

"Better." I told him the Black Lake part; more than I'd told Lieutenant Thaler but less than I'd told Louise Starr, and he didn't have to know the name of the client. I left out Lowell Birdsall and Fleta Skirrett. Their connection with Allison Booth's death fell outside Barry's area of expertise.

"I read Eugene Booth when I was a kid," he said. "Dynamite style, but he had the establishment sitting on his face like a fat dominatrix. I never bought Roland Clifford as a saint. My old man sold cut-rate suits out of a second-floor joint on Clairmount in forty-three. He didn't see any heroes that weekend. Not in uniform. I wrote a piece on the riot when I was with the *Free Press*, but my editor spiked it. Too one-sided, he said. He was right. The only people who would talk to me were the blacks who survived it. The whites all had bad consciences and even the police officers who were retired were afraid of losing their pensions. Freedom of Information only bought me the runaround. The files were always in some other precinct. Bad karma. But you can't publish that without a source."

"So much for Barry Stackpole's autobiography."

"Twenty-three ninety-five will buy you Eddie's, complete with his signature. I can't add much, just everything that counts. He got ten of his notches the old-fashioned way, two soft-nose slugs in the back of the head close up, which says a lot more for his bedside manner than his marksmanship. He's a charming fucker. He garroted three others, which is the *really* old-fashioned way, if you're up on your Sicilian history. He favors nylon fishing line, fifty-pound test."

"He said his old man was a fisherman."

"His old man was a shark, which is as close as he ever got to a fish. Genovese mob gunned him when they moved in on the loan action in Manhattan midtown. Eddie wouldn't tell you that if he was incognito."

"That was just an impression. He had on a cap and sunglasses in his cabin and he was disguising his voice."

"All the more reason his former bosses wouldn't tag him for a quiet hit in a jerkwater town in northern Michigan. He's not your boy."

"Then why was he carrying?"

"You didn't see a gun." He broke into a grin when I looked at him. "Okay, okay. It just doesn't make sense they'd use a high-profile character like him and then have him go through all the trouble to make it look like suicide. And copping Booth's manuscript. I mean, come on."

"That might have been curiosity. And maybe he was just spotting the job. He checked out the night before."

"He would have anyway. Even if he was only casing the pigeon for another shooter, he's still Glad Eddie, the talk-show kid. That's a job for an invisible man, a nebbish. You're sure it was him? Don't take that wrong;

two years ago I blew half a season's budget collecting footage on a Nazi war criminal who turned out to be a retired baker from Brooklyn named Israel Feinstein."

"I'm never sure of anything until someone rubs my nose in it. But he's in town this weekend and I don't like coincidences. They screw up the odds for the rest of us."

"If anyone paid attention to the odds we wouldn't have casinos coming in all over like blackheads. But putting aside all the things I've been saying, we have to ask ourselves why Eddie would muck around with this at all. That's his old job. He's too busy being a celebrity, and making more money on the legit than he ever did tipping over stoolies and working whatever crumbs the made guys threw at him to keep him solvent between hits."

"I don't know why he's still around to make money. Whatever happened to omerta?"

"Went out when RICO came in," he said. "Ever since Uncle Sam threw out the Bill of Rights in mob cases they're more afraid of him than they are of the God-father. They're rolling over on each other to beat raps they used to do in their jammies. But I am a little surprised someone didn't hang his cat or something, just to keep their hand in. He got away too clean to suit me."

"Maybe he didn't."

He moved a shoulder and drank. Then he realized I was still looking at him. He swirled his ice. "Meaning this is the price he's paying for his early out. One last job."

"It'd be like them to make it unpleasant," I said. "He

told me himself he hated the country. He said the frogs were driving him nuts."

"Yeah, but it's still crazy. He might as well be walking around with George Washington's face from the dollar."

"Maybe that's the idea."

That troubled him enough to set his glass on the table beside the chair. "Setup?"

"It's a theory." I finished my drink.

"Damn it, Amos. I'm in this Ukrainian thing up to my steel plate."

"So what? You can't use it yet."

"That's not the point. How am I supposed to keep my mind on the Gaming Commission when you hand me Eddie Cypress on a plate with an apple in his mouth?"

"I haven't yet. Coincidences happen. It might have been Robert C. Brown in Cabin Five. He might have had a TV remote in his hand."

"Right. And this time next month I'll be Mr. Tatyana Ostrokovich. Your theories have a rotten habit of holding some water. Goddamn it."

I got to my feet and poured myself another. My appetite was returning. "So Glad Eddie shot ten and strangled three. What about the other two? Do I have to watch for a knife?" I thought of Allison Booth in the morgue, punched full of holes; but that would have been before his time.

"You should be so lucky. He went Golden Gloves in seventy-two but didn't turn pro. He beat the poor dumb bastards to death with just his fists. Smiling all the time, would be my guess."

20

Barry was asleep in the armchair when I came out of the kitchen carrying a plateful of fried-egg sandwiches to absorb the alcohol. I dug an extra blanket out of a closet, threw it over him, then ate two of the sandwiches and turned in. When I got up with the sun in my face and the Tet offensive replaying in my head, he was gone and so was the rest of the Scotch. I made a note to enter the bottle on the expense sheet and drank coffee until the mortars stopped pounding.

It was Saturday. The neighborhood was alive with the ripping of power mowers. The grown son of the retired GM foreman across the street was using the chainfall that lived in the branches of the oak in the front yard to hoist the engine out of the Chevy Suburban he'd been working on since Kissinger was a pup. As I stood with cup in hand watching him through the kitchen window, a herd of bicyclists in helmets and kneepads whooshed past. Weekends in Detroit always have something to do with wheels.

The combined edition of the *News* and *Free Press* was unenlightening. There were two paragraphs on Eugene Booth's death buried inside, culled from an old library file on the Michigan writer with a tacked-on lead stating that he was an apparent suicide. Glad Eddie Cypress' Sunday signing at the Birmingham Borders got three lines in the local section and the Tigers were hosting the Orioles at home that afternoon. Detroit was starting its last season in the old ballpark. I decided to go.

Before I did I swung around to the Alamo Motel. In the parking lot I watched the scarlet sharkfin sail of a ketch bucking the current in the river, then climbed the gridded iron steps to 610.

The young man who answered the door stood six-two in sandals and cutoff jeans and a black open-weave tank top that ended just above his navel. He had gold rings in his nose, eyebrows, and upper lip, and his hair was shaved close to his scalp. He might have been wearing eyeliner; looking at the hardware on his face made my eyes water so I didn't study it too closely. He was holding a plastic tub of some kind by its molded handle down at his side.

"Yes?" His voice was a deep thud.

I glanced at the number on the door to make sure I hadn't miscounted. "Lowell Birdsall."

"He's out of town."

"Business?"

"Hobby. He's at a pulp collectors' convention in Cleveland. I'm in six-oh-nine. He asked me to come in and empty the tank in his dehumidifier." He lifted the tub and let it fall the length of his arm. Water sloshed around inside. "He'll be back Monday. Can I take a message?"

"No message." I turned away.

He slid his free hand from the knob to the top of the door and struck an S-curve with one hip. "You don't look like a collector. Are you one of his customers?" He put a lilt in the question. It sounded like a tight end playing Juliet in a college production.

"No. I don't have any systems that need analyzing."

"Too bad. I thought you might be hiring. I'm thinking of changing professions. My knees can't stand it."

"Are you a baseball catcher?"

He giggled and pushed the door shut. I squared my shoulders and went back down to the car.

The peeling casserole of Tiger Stadium—Bennett Park, Navin Field, Briggs Stadium, the Rusty Girder, call it what you will according to your generation or where your loyalties lie—stands at the corner of Michigan and Trumbull avenues, although for more than a century all you have had to do is tell the cabbie to take you to the Corner, and in due course of time he will deposit you in front of the cavernous entrance. You pass through the usual smells of mildewed concrete, stale grease,

sharp mustard, spilled beer, and glove oil, up a ramp
that hasn't been mopped since Nixon, and then there
you are in bright sunlight, dazzled by the impossible
green of the infield; the same one where Ty Cobb
bribed the grounds crew to hose down the area in front
of the batter's box to make sure all his bunts died on
arrival. On a blistering Saturday in August 1920, Cobb
nailed a vicious line drive hit by Babe Ruth in right
field, not too many blocks from the alley where legend said Cobb, mean cracker that he was, beat to death
a would-be mugger early in his career. On June 4, 1984,
Dave Bergman stood like an iron jockey at home plate
with two out in the bottom of the tenth and fouled off
seven Toronto pitches before drilling one into the upper
deck to win the game. Game Seven, 1968 World Series, sixth inning: Beerbelly Mickey Lolich picked Lou
Brock and Curt Flood off first to clinch the champi-
onship after coming back from three games to one
against St. Louis, first time ever.

Kaline and Greenberg, Leonard and Cash, Northrup
and Trammell, Whitaker and Parrish, Horton and McLain
and Gibson and Schoolboy Rowe and Gates Brown and
Bird Fidrych and all the rest; flashing signals, spitting
tobacco, and doffing their caps to the bleachers. There
were too many ghosts running the bases and warming
up in the bullpen for the live players to move around
and so a new stadium had to be built downtown. They
had decided to name it after a bank.

The game was unworthy of the venue. An umpire
made a bad call, the scattered crowd uncorked some
favorite obscenities and halfheartedly threw their beer
cups and crumpled popcorn bags down on the field.

An easy Baltimore pop fly plopped onto the ground between right and center while the fielders watched. Detroit carried a two-run lead into the fifth inning and came out the bottom down by seven. In the eighth they loaded the bases with one out, then struck out and flied to the shortstop. The Orioles scored an inside-the-park home run at the top of the ninth, just for fun, and put Detroit down one-two-three to win.

Free agency and a string of indifferent owners had managed to do what the Gashouse Gang, Murderers' Row, and two major race riots couldn't: break the spirit of a proud team. But they'd come back. Coming back was what they did best, after spoiling New York's shot at the pennant.

By the bottom of the eighth you could have counted the fans who had remained to see it out and still had time to go for a hot dog. Most of them were there for the park. Me too; I didn't know any of the younger players and they were too busy trying to make routine catches look like Willie Mays to hold my attention for long. The only thing I got out of the experience was a tan and a program and a chance not to think about Eugene and Allison Booth or Louise Starr or Fleta Skirrett or the Birdsalls, Senior and Junior, or Glad Eddie Cypress for three pitches at a stretch.

Until the end.

Trickling out with the rest of the diehards I spotted something lying in the grass outside the Michigan Avenue exit and went over and picked it up. It was a piece of brick about the size of an egg. I looked up, but I couldn't tell what part of the wall it had fallen from. In a year or two or ten, when they stopped try-

ing to save the building and finally tore it down, the
bricks would sell for up to twenty-five bucks apiece. I
juggled the chunk on the palm of my hand. Then I
arranged my index and middle fingers on it in the Au-
relio Lopez three-fingered grip, pounded it into the
palm of my left hand, and went into the wind-up, one
foot raised and my eyes focused on a spot of white
paint on a streetlamp ten yards away.

"Hey!"

A Detroit cop as big as a bus stepped in front of
the lamp, thumbs hooked in his belt and his big jaw
drawn up into the shadow of his visor. He looked like
an umpire. I lowered my foot, tossed the piece of ma-
sonry back into the grass, and waved at the officer on
my way to find where I'd parked. He waved back.

21

Winter got in one last slap Saturday night. The thermometer dipped below forty just before dawn, brewing a heavy fog and stacking a honey of a pileup on the downtown John Lodge when a truck loaded with furniture jackknifed and dumped over near the Howard Street exit, scattering lamps and loveseats and an Ethan Allen four-poster bed as far as Lafayette. Detour traffic was still heavy on the surface streets just before noon, and it was Sunday. How the people who live in the suburbs and work in the city get in on time when that happens during the week is not as big a mystery as why.

Glad Eddie Cypress had a jam of his own on the front porch of Borders, where a crowd was waiting to get inside and form a line. There were posters in the window with a blowup of the book jacket and the same picture of the author that had run in the *Free Press*, along with the date and time of the signing. There was also a bulky black party in a midnight-blue serge sportcoat and Ray-Bans standing next to the door facing in the opposite direction.

I was still thinking about him when I beat out a square green barge of an Olds 98 for a parking space freshly vacated by a station wagon full of kids. Although it went against the grain to confront a character like Cypress carrying nothing but a book, I unsnapped the holster from my belt and tucked it and the .38 into my glove compartment. The 98 blasted its horn and took off with a chirp to find another spot.

A pair of women in fresh permanents carrying shoulder bags as big as rucksacks were admiring Eddie's picture when I joined the crowd.

"He's so good-looking," one of them said. "I can't believe he did the things they say he did."

The other one snapped her tongue off her teeth. "I heard he had plastic surgery."

"To disguise himself? They say the Mafia is offering a million dollars for his head." The first one whispered the word *Mafia*.

"No, just a nose job. It used to bend to the left. Honey, if the mob was offering a million, I'd take a crack at him myself."

The crowd slid forward under the eye of Blue Serge. He had a two-way Motorola radio on his belt. His sportcoat covered whatever else he had on it. As I came abreast of him he took a step my way. "Watch your step, sir. No pushing, ladies and gentlemen. You'll all get your turn." He put a steadying hand against my chest, then swept it down to brush my hip pocket on the right side. It was as neat a frisk as I'd seen, and as thorough as could be managed without discouraging the people in back. He'd noted I was carrying a book in my left hand and that it was too small to conceal a gun.

Our gazes met through the tinted lenses of his Ray-Bans. He lowered his voice to a murmur. "No trouble, okay, cowboy? We don't want to upset customers."

"I'm a customer myself," I said.

"You don't look like one, cowboy. You just look like work."

"U.S. marshal?"

He shook his head, but a little surprised smile tugged at the corners of his mouth. "Secret Service, retired. Running my own shop now. Does it stick out?"

"You ought to let your hair grow out a little. You looked too smart for FBI."

"I've got fibbies for friends. Beat them all the time at Scrabble. Their letters never spell anything."

The crowd moved again. It was time to say goodbye. "At least they don't work for Glad Eddie."

"Everybody needs protection, cowboy. You too. Don't browse."

A store employee in shirtsleeves and a necktie whittled the crowd down to a single-file line inside the door. We shuffled forward briskly after that. A long table covered in green crepe stood across the center aisle bearing stacks of copies of Cypress' book, another poster free-standing on one end, and on the other a printed sign asking customers to refrain from engaging the author in conversation. As I drew near I picked out a white version of Blue Serge standing behind the table among a group that included a woman in a red blazer with a badge pinned to the lapel identifying her as the store manager and a man in a gray suit that had not been cut in this hemisphere, with his steely hair worn in a stiff brush and glasses whose metal rims matched his hair. He had taken his degree at the same university that had turned out both bodyguards years later.

Seated at the table was a mass of thick hair that had been frosted to mask the gray. The face that belonged to it came up with a smile as Eddie Cypress flipped shut the cover of his book and handed it to the customer standing in front. He was fifty, but looked younger thanks to medical science—I'd heard he'd had his face lifted and his teeth straightened and bonded about the time of the nose job—and his leather sportcoat was scuffed to the accepted degree at the elbows. He wore his blue button-down shirt open at the throat without a necktie and no jewelry, not even the standard mob-issue Rolex. That would be an old habit; you didn't wear anything that might snag on the door after you dumped the murder weapon.

The customer in front of me was the woman who thought he was too good-looking to have killed fifteen men in cold blood. She asked him to sign her book "To Eleanor: An offer I can't refuse." He wrote

the inscription without hesitation, signed it with a
swooping final *s*, and surrendered the book grinning.

The grin didn't slip a notch when I stepped up to
take her place. His eyes didn't flicker. They were golden
brown and warm. You hear a lot about killers' eyes,
but it only holds true among the amateurs. He had a
long jaw, shaven close, and high Mediterranean cheekbones. I was sure they were the ones I'd seen in the
doorway of Cabin Five, but there was no recognition
in the eyes.

The store manager took a book off the top of the
stack and opened it to the title page for him to sign.
I said, "I brought my own," and laid the book I'd carried in on the table. It was *Some of My Best Friends
Are Killers.*

Cypress hesitated only a split-second, his eyes on
the book and the expression in them invisible. He
picked it up and held it out. "You made a mistake,
sport. It's not mine."

"No mistake," I said. "Trade. If you're finished reading Booth's latest I'd like to take a look at it."

I was still watching his eyes. Something flashed in
them this time—consternation or bewilderment, I wasn't
sure, except he hadn't shown either when he'd looked
at me the first time. There was a brief frozen tableau,
Cypress holding the paperback, the store manager still
holding Cypress' book open at the title page, while a
grumbling murmur made its way through the line behind me over the delay. Then his perfect smile found
its earlier warmth. He laid Booth's book on my side
of the table.

"I'd like to continue this, sport, only the sign says no conversation. Maybe you got in the wrong line."

The man in the gray suit said, "Herb." He was looking at me and the name dropped into the air without inflection, as if it didn't belong in his mouth and he had decided to get rid of it. The younger man at his side started around the table. He was in no hurry but he made good time and I turned toward the end where he was coming from, going up on the balls of my feet. There was a general collision behind me as the people at the head of the line backed up to make room.

Cypress said, "It's okay, Sarge. This is my publicist, Sargent Hurley. Sargent's his first name, not his rank. I didn't get your name, sport."

I waited until I was sure Herb had stopped moving. He was on my side of the table now, facing me with both hands clear of his sides. I opened my coat slowly so he could see I didn't have anything on my belt and drew out my wallet and stuck out a card for Cypress to take. He took it and read it. Then he put it down, took the book from the store manager's hands, and wrote something on the title page with his fat felt-tipped pen, finishing with his signature. He held it out. "This one's on me."

I didn't take it. "Thanks. I buy my own books."

The store manager cleared her throat. She was a blonde in her fifties with a mole on her cheek like Miss Kitty's. "The store will take care of it. We're grateful to have you here, Mr. Cypress. We wouldn't take your money." She was watching me. Glad Eddie could have taken poker lessons from her.

I thanked her and took the book. Some pressure went out of the air then.

"Where were we having lunch, Sarge?" Cypress asked.

"The Blue Heron. It's on—"

"Walker can find it. He's a detective. I'm stuck here for a couple of hours, Walker; can't disappoint the literate public. Lunch is on New York. Unless you prefer to buy your own." He opened his smile another quarter-inch. "Two o'clock?"

"Better make it three," Hurley said. "It's a long line."

"You heard him, sport. Don't forget your two-bit book. They've got me on a short leash. I don't have a lot of time to read."

All of this was conducted in a low tone that didn't reach any of the people waiting for their signed books. I picked up the paperback and let him keep the curtain line. The leash part was too easy. I trailed glares all the way out. If this kind of thing was repeated, Detroit wouldn't be able to draw the really first-class felons.

Blue Serge No. 1 was shoving the antenna back into his Motorola when I came out. He wasn't wearing his dark glasses. "Had to try it on, didn't you? Didn't I have you tagged for a cowboy?"

I looked at him. He had a chiseled square nut-brown face with thick skin on the cheeks. He wouldn't be a bleeder. He had hard sad eyes, as unlike Eddie's as a good guard dog's were to a wolf's. "What's an ex–Secret Service man doing tasting peas for a goon like Cypress?"

"That's Herb's job, inside. He works for Eddie's boy Hurley. I'm just local talent. A gig's a gig, you know

what I'm saying? I never made the White House detail or I sure wouldn't be doing this."

"Would you take a bullet for him?"

"Haven't met anybody I'd do that for yet. That's why
I didn't make White House." He slipped two fingers
into his shirt pocket and gave me a card. "You're going
to need me someday, if they don't kill you first."

It was good stock but plain, just his name and telephone number and an address on Grand River. "Russell Fearing. Were you born with that?"

"Hell, no." He put on his Ray-Bans. "My real name's
Ogolo Zimbabwe. I just changed it to get back to
my roots in Cambridge. Don't come back, cowboy. I
wouldn't want to have to throw you through any windows."

Back in the car I opened Cypress' book and tucked
Fearing's card inside. While I was there I read the inscription. It was in Italian: "*Senso vostra angoscia.*" He'd
signed it "Glad Eddie." I laid it on the passenger's seat
for translation later and got out of there.

I had time to kill, but not enough to go back home
or to the office, so I caught the last two-thirds of a
techno-thriller playing at a multiplex in Bloomfield Hills.
It was as full of holes as a flute and the special effects just brought back my hangover. I left an hour
into the closing credits, bought a two-pack of Alka-
Seltzer at the concession stand, and chewed them on
my way out. I had just enough time to make it to
lunch with Jack the Ripper Dot Com.

The Blue Heron is West Bloomfield's answer to
Oscar's at the Waldorf and the only five-star restaurant
in the state of Michigan. The low yellow brick build-

ing is planted all around with trees strung with lights, but they only twinkle at night, so if you miss the tasteful sign at the end of the driveway you have nothing to look forward to but the Pizza Hut in Orchard Lake. The fog had burned off and the sun was coming hot through the windshield. There were plenty of parking spaces at that hour of the afternoon, so I pulled into a spot in the shade. I thought about the gun in the glove compartment but didn't take it out. I didn't think I'd need it to get a look at the wine list.

I put one foot on the asphalt and a train hit me. Anyway something hard and heavy and moving fast struck the door, pinning me between it and the roof of the car and forcing the wind out of my lungs. I got my hands up to push back and then something like the blunt edge of an axe bounced off the big muscle on the side of my neck.

It was over then, but my body didn't know it. I twisted sideways, forcing the door open a little, and my left arm came loose and I swept the heel of my hand up toward a blur of pale face. It's a killing blow if you catch the nose just right and drive splinters of bone up into the brain, only you almost never catch the nose right. I missed it entirely, dislodged a pair of glasses from the bridge, tried for a handful of hair but couldn't hold on because it was cut in a short brush, and before I could reverse the momentum a black hole opened in my vision; the blow to the neck having its effect. My hearing was the last thing to go. I heard a sharp crack, as of something hard striking bone, and a dull thump right behind it, but didn't feel anything. I was on my way down.

Any time you're out more than a few minutes from a blow, you've suffered permanent damage of some kind. That was why, when someone shook me by the shoulder asking me if I was all right and I got up on one elbow and turned my head and spat out a mouthful of bile, the first thing I looked at was my watch. I'd checked it just before I stepped out of the car; unless I'd been lying on that oil-smelling pavement twenty-four hours I'd only been out of competition two minutes. My neck was sore and my face ached. I touched a doughy swelling on my left cheek and decided right away not to touch it again with anything but a Ziploc bag full of ice. I was going to have a shiner to make a Norman Rockwell model proud.

"Man, you was out. I was scared I'd have to call the morgue wagon. That ain't good for bidness."

The door to the Cutlass hung open. I got a hand on the rocker panel and pulled myself into a sitting position with my back against the door post. The man who was talking was black and skinny, in black formal trousers, a white bibfront tunic, and a white chef's hat as tall and stiff as a smokestack. His apron was spattered with grease.

"Compliments to the kitchen." I cleared my throat, spat again, and repeated myself, this time in English. "How much did you see?"

"I come out for a smoke and seen a gray Lincoln pealing out onto the highway with two guys inside. Then I seen a open car door in the lot and a shoe laying in the aisle. The shoe had a foot in it and you was attached. First thing I think is, Holy shit, I hope it wasn't the abalone. You get mugged or what? Only

West Bloomfield muggers drive Lincolns. Want me to call the cops?"

I didn't answer him. When I tilted my head back, the black hole opened up again and I drew up my knees and leaned my forehead against them until it went away. My head ached, but it wasn't the hangover. The back of my head must have struck the roof of the car when I took the hit to the cheek. Well, it wouldn't be my first concussion. I don't know how many you get but the supply must have been thinning out.

"Mister? You're scaring the shit out of me."

I looked up at him. His forehead was pleated but the rest of his face was as smooth as good brandy. "I couldn't scare you with a car bomb. Can you drive a stick?"

"Better'n I can make a soufflé, and I got a wall full of certificates for that. Where you want to go?"

"Hazel Park."

"I never heard of no hospitals there. Sure you don't want to go to Detroit General?"

"I don't need to see a doctor. I've already been mugged." I reached for my wallet, but the movement drained too much blood from my brain. "I'll pay you fifty, but you'll have to get it out yourself."

"They left you fifty? That's the trouble with living here. Nobody's hungry enough."

"You can catch a cab back in time for the supper rush if we don't hit too many red lights."

"I ain't hit a red light since the first time they took away my license." He stooped to help me to my feet. He smelled of baked bread and sherry.

When I put my hand down on the pavement for leverage something cut into my palm. I'd been aware before I'd sat up that I was lying on something uncomfortable, but since discomfort was the order of the hour I hadn't given it any thought. I picked up the twisted remains of a pair of gray steel-rimmed glasses. One lens was shattered and I guessed Sargent Hurley hadn't thought they were worth moving me to reclaim. I flipped them onto the floorboards of the Cutlass.

Leaning on the chef as he got me around to the passenger's side I found out I had some cracked ribs. I didn't bother counting them. I'd cracked plenty and I hadn't run out yet.

The lights were green all the way, a trick I'd given up trying to acquire; you have to be born with it, like perfect pitch. He changed gears smoothly and never used the brake until he ran out of road. Once he jumped the curb to beat the car ahead into a right turn. I bet he didn't cook out of the book either.

I was feeling lightheaded again when we swept into the driveway in Hazel Park. He blew the horn and Louise Starr came out tying the sash of a quilted blue satin robe and stopped when she saw the strange face behind the wheel. She'd recognized the car. Then she saw me and clattered around to that side on tiny mules. I hadn't enough energy to roll down the window. I popped the door and had to hang on to the handle to keep from spilling out.

"Give Chef Boy-ar-dee fifty bucks," I said. "Charge it to expenses."

She stepped forward to help me, but he was already there. "Keep your money, ma'am," he said, stooping.

"Next time you have a real fine meal out, send a couple of bucks back to the boys in the kitchen."

22

'd be very interested in seeing an X-ray of your skull," Louise said. "I'll bet it looks like Omaha Beach."

We were breathing the countrified air in the Hazel Park living room, she in a maple platform rocker with an afghan slung over the back, me sunk in one of the slipcovered armchairs with my feet up on an ottoman made out of an antique doll trunk. We were drinking coffee. She'd offered alcohol, but I'd declined. I didn't explain that it wouldn't do to ingest an anticoagulant on the off-chance of an intracranial hemorrhage.

"I've seen a couple," I said. "It looks more like a

spider sac. The bone's pretty thick. I didn't need a guy with eighteen years of schooling to tell me that."

"I don't suppose I'm the first person to suggest you consider changing professions."

"Detecting isn't a profession. It's a job, like pouring steel or operating a crane. You do what you're trained for. I'm a good detective. It just so happens I get doors slammed in my face and occasionally someone drops a piano on my head. Complaining about it would be like a goalie carping that people keep bouncing pucks off his chin. Anyway a skull like mine would be wasted in Accounts Receivable."

"I don't see how you get insurance."

"I don't have insurance. I don't drive a Porsche or live in Grosse Pointe either. I've made my peace with these things." I closed my eyes against the throbbing going on behind them; or rather my eye. The left was pretty much shut all the time. "Your roommate wouldn't have any ice, by any chance. It's okay if the cubes are shaped like ducks."

She set down her cup and saucer and went into the kitchen. After a minute she came out wrapping a clean dishtowel around one of those blue gel-packs. I got rid of the towel and applied the pack directly to my eye. I could feel the heat of the swelling right through the gel.

"I don't suppose it will do any good to insist that you see a doctor."

"Probably not, but don't let it stop you. It isn't often somebody cares."

She sat down again and crossed her legs. The robe fell open, exposing a stretch of tanned thigh. She covered it without undue haste. "Okay, we've discussed your condition and analyzed your career choice. Is this the place where we talk about what happened?"

She was entitled and I told it. I couldn't tell it without Eddie Cypress and so I went back to the picture she'd showed me of Cypress in the *Free Press* and continued from there. She and Barry Stackpole shared the same view of Glad Eddie—I'd never heard her call anyone a son of a bitch before, and she interrupted me to do it—and I thought it was a shame they hadn't gotten together years ago when Barry had a book and Louise wanted to publish it. It had been a memoir of Vietnam; the bottom had fallen out of that market quicker than slide rules.

When I finished, she picked up her cup, sipped, made a face, and put it back. The coffee had grown cold while she was listening.

"You should have told me," she said.

"I wasn't a hundred percent sure it was Cypress I saw at Black Lake. I had to see him face to face. When he called me 'sport,' I knew he remembered me too, and didn't care whether he confirmed anything when he said it. He's a pretty confident character."

"Why not? He'd decided to have you killed. I guess he's too good to take care of it himself these days."

"If he wanted me killed I'd be on ice right now instead of the other way around. What happened at the Blue Heron was in the way of a message."

"Maybe the mob's getting civilized. Forty years ago their idea of sending a message was killing Eugene Booth's wife."

"I'm not married. Anyway if murder was called for

it would have been cleaner just to do me. I'm not a famous writer. The cops would close the file in a week, with or without an arrest."

"So what was the message?"

"Lay off. Butt out. Take a hike. Whatever's current. I haven't seen a rock video in a while. In a way it's a compliment to me he didn't have Hurley or his boy Herb say hello from him. He figured I'd get it." That made me remember something, but she was talking then.

"Are you sure it *was* from him? You said yourself pianos fall on you from time to time."

"I found a pair of smashed glasses where I fell. I don't need the prescription to know they were the ones Hurley was wearing at Borders. Everything happened too fast for me to count, but our chef friend said he saw two men laying rubber in a gray Lincoln. He'd have Herb with him on a job like that. It wasn't your usual publicist work. Do you read Italian?"

She blinked. "My ex-husband and I spent a winter in Rome. I understand it better than I speak it. What a question. Are you sure you're all right?"

"There's a copy of Cypress' book in my car. I might have been able to remember the inscription he wrote if I hadn't been hit on the head, but I doubt it. Can you take a look at it and translate?"

She got up and went out. While I was waiting for her to come back I finished my coffee. It was nearly as cold as the ice pack but I needed the caffeine. It's important to stay awake for a few hours after sustaining a concussion. She returned with the book open in her hands and a tight-lipped smile. "It's too bad you're not multilingual," she said. "You might have spared yourself a beating. Do you mind a loose interpretation?"

"Punt."

"The man has a sense of humor. He wrote 'I feel your pain.' "

Grinning hurt; but I'm a tough guy. "If he didn't have any imagination he wouldn't have written a book."

"It was probably ghosted." She stopped smiling. "Amos, you should call the police."

"They're the competition. In any case it doesn't prove anything, except that he's not worried enough to cover his tracks. Which makes me think I'm not as right as I thought I was."

"He's pretty sure of his protection."

"Either that or he doesn't think he needs any. Maybe he doesn't know Booth's dead."

She was still standing, holding the book open. She closed it gently. "But if it *was* suicide, what was Cypress doing staying in the next cabin?"

"I'll ask him."

"You're going to confront him again after what happened the last time?"

"He owes me lunch."

"Not on my time," she said. "One man has died already. If Booth was murdered, I want to know why and if it had anything to do with the book he was writing. I need to know if in some way I'm responsible. If he killed himself, well, that's that, and if it has anything to do with me—I don't know, maybe I gave him hope just when he'd resigned himself to life as a has-been and when he found out he was right all along it put him over the edge—I'll live with that. What I can't live with is two men dead before their time over a book with a shelf life of three months maximum. I'll take you off the case before I let that happen."

"So am I fired?"

She pressed her lips tight. Standing there in her robe with her hair loose, holding a book, she looked like an Annunciation painting. "What if you are? Will you forget Glad Eddie and go back to whatever it is you do that doesn't involve getting roughed around in restaurant parking lots?"

"Don't let that enter into your figuring. As parking lots go I've kissed the asphalt in places a lot less classy than the Blue Heron. I don't usually have to make a reservation. I wouldn't have gotten roughed around at all if I'd remembered I was meeting a hoodlum instead of a literary celebrity. I won't make that mistake twice."

"You didn't answer my question. If I fire you, will it take?"

"I don't know. Fire me and let's see."

A heavy truck detouring around construction on I-75 shuddered past on the street, its load shifting over a break in the pavement. The noise made her flinch. She tossed the book into the rocker and sank down onto the slipcovered sofa. One half of her robe slid sideways, showing the whole of one bare leg. She'd been walking around Central Park Sundays.

"I don't know what to say," she said. "I don't know what's right: abandon Eugene Booth and risk another life or cut our losses and risk letting a murderer go free. It isn't like deciding which book to publish."

"I'll make it easy, since it's my life. If Booth killed himself, someone walked around his body hanging in his cabin and walked out with his manuscript. It makes more sense that whoever did that also strung him up to begin with. It takes strength to hoist a full-grown man, dead or dead drunk, and hold him up long enough to slip a noose over his head. Eddie's a healthy-looking fifty. If he needed help he has Hurley and Herb, which sounds like a magic act in Vegas. Then there's the very good point that I don't like getting my head and my ribs kicked in next to a Dumpster when I ought to be inside choosing between the rack of lamb and the pan-roasted veal. When I'm through bouncing Siegfried and Roy off a few walls and the cops show up to nail me for battery, it might help my case if I can claim a client, but whether I'm on the clock or not I'm going to pay them a visit. Did I mention I don't like getting my head and my ribs kicked in?"

"A couple of times." She smiled. "Do you make enough from this hobby of yours to pay taxes?"

"The government seems to think so. Some days I'm not so sure. It pays better than bungee-jumping, and the risk's not as high. Cords break."

"So do skulls."

I had nothing to throw at that. I turned the ice pack over and pressed it against my eye. It was just as warm on that side. "Is there another one of these in the freezer? I sucked the life out of this one."

"It was the only one. I can put some ice in a plastic bag."

"Don't bother. I'm beginning to feel like broccoli."

"Would you like to lie down?"

"I thought I was."

"I meant over here."

I flipped the ice pack onto the table beside the chair. It was supporting a lamp with a hunting scene in the base. She had lowered herself to one elbow and crossed her legs, hanging a mule off one slim foot. She had a high arch.

I said, "I take it I'm still employed."

She wasn't insulted. She never was when it came to that. "Tell me something?" she said. "When that nice young man picked you up off the pavement, why did you tell him to take you here?"

"It was closest. Hospitals make you watch soap operas all day and charge five bucks a pop for aspirin."

"Your house is just as close."

"You've been boning up on the local geography."

"I rented a car yesterday. The man at Hertz gave me a map. Detroit certainly has a lot of suburbs."

"White flight. All I had to do at home was sleep, and that's not a good idea when you've taken a hit to the head. Conversation with you has never put me to sleep yet."

"Don't you have friends?"

"I also had a report to make. Combining things saves my clients money."

"I don't believe you. When a dog gets shot he limps out of his way to the place where he can find love and sympathy."

"Poetic, but not zoologically correct," I said. "He crawls under a porch."

"What are you, a dog or a man?"

I said nothing. She took a base.

"We have a history, you know," she said.

"So do France and Germany. That doesn't make us Romeo and Juliet."

"Romeo and Juliet were teenagers. We're grownups."

She had me beat in literature.

"New York's a village," she said. "Publishers' Row is even smaller. It's like incest. I've been busy for two years trying to find a hole to get my head above water. I haven't seen a show since *Sunset Boulevard* closed, or been to a good restaurant where I didn't put the check on my corporate card since I can't remember when. It's been a long dry spell, Amos. I'm not a camel."

I glanced toward the front door. She saw it.

"Debra called this morning. She's stuck in Terre Haute. If anybody walks in on us, you have my permission to shoot them down."

"I left my gun in the car."

She tugged loose her sash with an impatient jerk. The robe fell open the rest of the way. There were no swimsuit rules in the tanning beds in Manhattan.

I got up out of the chair without a grunt or a gasp and managed not to sway while the blood charged out of my head and made the long circulatory journey back. She made room for me on the cushions and I went over and sat on one hip on the edge. A rib pinched. I caught my lip. "You might have to do most of the work."

"I'm the boss. I'm used to it." She put her arms around me and drew me down beside her.

23

I ghosted away from there an hour past dark. We'd
moved to the guest room, the only room in the house
that didn't look as if Heidi might wander in at any moment, and I left Louise sleeping. I found a pad and
pen in the kitchen, but all I could think of to write
was *"Senso vostra angoscia."* That didn't seem appropriate. I didn't leave a note.

The night air was cool and damp and smelled of
fresh-cut grass. The driver's seat felt clammy when I
eased under the wheel. I wouldn't be taking any deep
breaths for a couple of weeks, but my head was clear
and the business with the ice pack had opened up my

left eye enough for driving. Back home I mixed a drink
from the everyday bottle, got the rest of the fried-egg
sandwiches I'd made that morning out of the refrigerator, and sat in the breakfast nook to wash them down
with Scotch and tap water. Fourteen hours old and cold,
they tasted like cork coasters. It was a far cry from the
lunch I hadn't had at the Blue Heron, but it was better than what fifteen others had had after they met up
with Eddie Cypress.

I'd brought his book home. There was a full-length
photograph of Glad Eddie on the front of the jacket,
in his working uniform of blue Oxford shirt, loose-
fitting sportcoat, pleated slacks, and Gucci loafers, which
were the only things Italian about him apart from some
phrases he'd picked up on the job, unless some Roman
centurion had docked at his great-plus-grandmother's
Greek island for an olive to put in his martini and fell
in love between tides. The family name, according to
the copy on an inside flap, was Kyparissia, but an evergreen tree was as close as the civil servant who had
checked his grandfather through Ellis Island could come.

The book's title was *Prey Tell.*

I laid it facedown on the table. I didn't feel like reading. Reading seemed to be all I'd been doing on this
one when I wasn't driving or getting my face punched.
The left side of it from the eye down ached and felt
tight. I knew what it was like to be the Phantom of
the Opera, except my tenor sounded like a teakettle
with a sore throat.

A white rectangle on the table caught my eye. Russell Fearing's business card had fallen out of the book
when I opened it. The calm black bodyguard with the

Secret Service resumé had told me I'd need him someday if they didn't kill me first.

I knew the office would be closed, but I went into
the living room and called the number anyway. A female contralto with a crumpet in it confirmed in a
recording that I'd reached the headquarters of Russell
Fearing Security Services and told me the hours of op-
eration were 9:00 A.M. to 6:30 P.M. Monday through Friday. She offered me the opportunity to record a
message. I didn't take it.

It was still early, but I had put in a full day for a
sabbath, with the most exhausting part at the end.
Louise Starr was a cool cypher only when it came to
the publishing business. My face ached, my ribs hurt.
My blood had ceased to circulate in my extremities,
bagging like lead shot in my feet and hands. I shuffled when I walked and had to rest my arms before
unfastening the next button. I dumped myself into bed,
not bothering with the sheet or blanket, and woke up
ten hours later in the same position, on my stomach
with my head twisted to the right. I drove to the office making all right turns because I couldn't turn my
head left.

No one was waiting to throw money at me in the
reception room and the mail hadn't come yet, but the
cops were at work. My answering service told me Mary
Ann Thaler had called. I couldn't get her on the ex-
tension so I called the switchboard, worked my way
down the menu and up through a sergeant at the desk
and a detective third grade to a detective sergeant named
Richman who said Lieutenant Thaler was away from
her desk. I left my name and rang off. The whole thing

had taken just twice as long as it had before they'd updated the system.

The telephone rang as soon as I took my hand off the receiver. It was Thaler.

"You sound like Monday morning," she said. "Big weekend?"

"Bigger than both of us. How was yours?"

"It was a weekend. They come around every sixth day, no surprise. Life's short enough without blowing it away in five-day increments waiting for Saturday."

"Did your laundry, right? Run out of quarters?"

"I send out my laundry. I don't cook either if I can help it. I'm not the girl of your dreams, Walker. I'm also not the policeman of your dreams. I heard back from my friend in the Big Apple. Those plates you saw at Black Lake don't belong to a GMC pickup. They're registered to a five-year-old Ford Escort, and they were reported stolen in Manhattan a week ago."

"I'd have been disappointed in him if they weren't. The pickup was probably hot too."

"Undoubtedly." There was a short silence. "Got pretty chummy with him on two minutes' acquaintance, did you?"

I'd speared a Winston between my lips. I struck the match at a bad angle and burned my fingers. I got rid of it and blew on them. My brain was still soft on one side. The man in Cabin Five was still Robert C. Brown to her, a guy in sunglasses and a Yankees cap. If this kept up I was going to have to hire someone to edit an A. Walker Investigations newsletter to help me keep my half-truths straight.

"I'm talking about a basic human type," I said. "They learned to hunt by pack rules."

Someone trundled a metal file drawer shut on her end. It was a warm morning; the door to her office would be open to circulate air. "Where were you yesterday, Walker? I tried your home phone all day. One of my nines looked like a seven and I wanted to make sure I got the plate number right. I had to read it out both ways. It hadn't been assigned with a seven in that spot so we were all right, but it was a headache I didn't need."

"I went to a movie." I told her which one. I stopped before I told her what theater. People who are establishing alibis are full of such helpful information.

"All night too? I tried you at nine-thirty and eleven, let it ring ten times."

"I was asleep, working on a stiff neck."

"The movie must have taken a lot out of you. Was there a cartoon?"

"If you were lonely you should have called your inspector friend. I don't wear this office home."

"Since when?" She didn't wait for an answer. "So you got laid. Congratulations. The blonde lady editor with the stick up her skirt, no doubt. You could have said something up front without naming names. Why do you figure you have to lock everything up? You live your life like a suspicious person."

"I've been reading too many paperback mysteries." I cracked another match. This time I got the tobacco going without personal injury.

"I'll tell you how I spent *my* Sunday," she said. "When

I wasn't trying to get you on the line, I was thinking about Allison Booth."

"What did you think up?"

"Nothing worth bringing to court. I never owned a pair of black lace panties until I was twenty-five. Would you care to know why?"

"If you care, I care." She wasn't the kind who locked things up.

"It was something my mother told me. 'Never wear black lace panties, because if you get in an accident the doctors will think you're a tramp and they won't work as hard to save your life.' What's that say to you?"

"Right off the bat it says your mother never dated a doctor."

"My mother is an angel and it's not your privilege to soil her good name. She taped my first police-range qualifying target on her refrigerator. What it says is nice girls finish first and bad girls are just finished. Or were, when my mother was a girl and Allison Booth got stabbed full of holes and two cops named Saunders and O'Hara went through the motions of looking for her killer and hung them up as soon as their first suspect went sour. All because the night someone stuffed her into a window well she met a man outside Hudson's who was not her husband. I'm not reopening this case to get a promotion. I'm doing it for all the women who want to wear black lace panties even if nobody ever gets to see them."

"Are you wearing them right now?"

"Go directly to hell. What's on the list today?"

"Lowell Birdsall was out of town yesterday. I want to ask him if he knew the cops liked his father for the

Booth murder in the beginning. He might not have known, but I want to be looking at him when he tells me. If he says he knew I want to ask why it didn't come up the first time we spoke."

"I'll go with you. I'll be Tweedledee."

"Why should you be Tweedledee? You're badge-carrying fuzz."

"I'm also a girl. He'll expect me to be the one who offers him a warm cup of tea and my pillowy bosom. You're the ape who wants to tie him around a banister."

"You don't have a pillowy bosom. And I thought you girls didn't like to be called girls."

"Nobody asked my opinion when the subject came up. If they had I'd have convinced them it's one weapon we should never trade away."

"You're making sweeping assumptions about Birdsall's experience of the opposite sex. Don't forget, he grew up on a steady diet of hardboiled dames and vixens in black sable. Also he's a big muscular baldy. That's just the type that runs toward women who buy dog collars by the gross even though they live in apartments where pets aren't allowed. If you confuse him he'll clam up."

"Okay, I'll be Tweedledum. Just don't tell the inspector. He thinks I'm demure."

"You cops have no ambition. The trunk's full of tricks but you're too lazy to dig down."

"So dig. I'm a quick study."

"I'm swimming solo on this one," I said. "It will be less awkward if you don't ask me why."

"Why?"

I stubbed out the butt. "Because you're an officer of the court, and you won't have to answer so many embarrassing questions if you don't see me hang him out a fourth-floor window by his shoelaces."

"Do you think four floors are enough?"

"It's all I've got to work with at the Alamo. You need to pay me out some line, Lieutenant. I'll never hear the end of it if you wind up walking the halls of the Hotel Nobody Gives a Shit talking to yourself on a Motorola."

"Such language in front of a lady. You did have a tough night."

"I'm sorry."

When she laughed, genuinely laughed, she did sound like a girl. "Cheer up, Walker. Jitterbug's back and so will you be, someday. Just don't hand me that bull about my career. You want to cowboy the job."

"That's the second time in two days somebody's called me a cowboy. I can't think why. I don't know a fetlock from a Yale."

"It was an observation, not a criticism. I gave up trying to corrige the incorrigible when I passed the L.T.'s exam."

"Tell that to Allison Booth." I looked at the fan to make sure the blades were still turning. They didn't seem to be stirring any air. "You know, you can't answer all the lost voices. If you start trying, in the end you won't be able to answer even one."

"That sounds like a pep talk you give yourself."

"Another lost voice."

A swivel chair squeaked on its rocker. "Just tell me what you found out when you find it out, okay? Forty-year-old police business is still police business. And

you need to do downtown a favor. It's been a while.
You don't call, you don't write. Next time you need
the latchstring left out, Mama might not be home." She
hung up.

24

The talk with Lieutenant Thaler made me change the order of things. I try not to lie to women. I dug out Lowell Birdsall's business card and dialed his number at the Alamo. His machine played five seconds of sirens and machine guns—a scratchy old transcription from *Gangbusters*—then an announcement that sounded like Jeanette MacDonald doing an impression of Humphrey Bogart, asking me to leave a message. I didn't leave one.

My watch read a couple of minutes past nine. He might have been sleeping in after the trip back from Cleveland. It was all of a two-hour drive, but for a man who worked out of his apartment it would seem like the Bataan Death March. Anyway it freed me up to go back to my original plan.

Grand River Avenue extends most of the way across Michigan. If you don't like expressways and don't mind traffic lights and construction delays and can avoid the occasional stygian detour, you can drive from downtown Detroit almost into Lake Michigan without ever using a turn signal; but you'd need a week to spare to get the thing done. Fortunately I needed less than fifteen minutes, because Russell Fearing and I worked in the same ZIP code.

I'd probably driven past the building a couple of hundred times and hadn't noticed it. A dozen blocks west of the little pocket canyon of skyscrapers in the heart of the business district, it stood a story high and a block long, built of white-painted cinderblock, and contained a half-dozen businesses separated by interior partitions. A beauty school operated out of one end with its name in white on a blue plastic awning over a display window with wigs on Styrofoam heads inside, while a store that sold plumbing fixtures advertised a sale on flush valves on a sandwich board on the other end, the sign holding open the door to offer the throngs easy access. Accordioned between were a hearing-aid shop, a Christian Science reading room next to a medical supply outlet, and RUSSELL FEARING SECURITY SERVICES lettered in tasteful gold on a glass door that sparkled from polishing. Only when you parked in the cramped lot and stood in front of the door could you read *R. I. Fearing, U.S. Secret Service, Ret'd*, etched in one corner.

A pleasant little buzzer sounded when I pushed open the door. The reception room was a perfect square, carpeted in silver-blue pile, with soundproof navy panels on the walls and four white scoop chairs cornered around a glass table containing the usual magazines. In the corner opposite sat a woman of about sixty, sitting straight-backed before a small computer screen. She wore her gray hair short in back and swept into a Woody Woodpecker crest in front and glasses with heavy black frames. She hadn't an ounce of fat on her. She had on a red blazer with black patches on the lapels and a white silk riding-stock around her throat, and when she looked up alertly and asked if she could help me, I wasn't surprised to hear a Mayfair accent.

"Fearing," I said. In the right mood there is something about Merrie Olde England that brings out the Detroit in me.

"He's in a meeting at the moment. Is he expecting you, Mister—?"

"Drummond. You can call me Bulldog." I twisted the knob on the door at the rear marked PRIVATE and went on through. She squeaked and got up to stop me, but there's never any sincerity in that. They teach elementary physics even in British public schools.

Fearing's office wasn't any bigger than the waiting room, and less comfortable. There were no seats for visitors, only a plain chunk of desk holding up desk stuff and the man himself sitting behind it in his shirt-sleeves holding a slim black telephone receiver. There was a color photo framed on one wall of a younger, less bulky Fearing shaking hands with Gerald Ford and a glass case mounted on the wall adjacent with a Remington pump shotgun and a teargas gun with a wire barrel in racks and a number of revolvers and automatic pistols on pegs. It had a large round brass lock and the glass was gridded with alarm wires. Aside from those things there was no decoration, not even a window. The carpet and walls were the same as in the other room, as if whoever decorated the place had not bothered to draw a line between public first impression and personal privacy. Fearing had made all the decisions himself and hadn't taken five minutes doing it.

He looked up at me with those hard sad eyes in that nut-brown face, as surprised as a turtle at the dawn, and said, "I'll call you back, Mr. Ford." He placed the receiver on its shallow standard and looked at the woman vibrating in the doorway behind me.

"He just walked right in, Mr. Fearing. Should I call the police?"

"No. That would be poor advertising. Leave us, please. I know this fellow. He answers to Tom Mix."

"Tom Mix?"

The tight smile tugged at the corners of his mouth and gave up. "Well, Errol Flynn."

"Robin Hood?"

"I was thinking of *Virginia City*. The one where he was a cowboy?"

"You Americans and your westerns. You'd think the frontier never closed. Even we Brits let go of the Empire finally." The door banged shut.

Fearing said, "You should put some steak on that eye."

"That's an old myth. Anyway, T-bones are six bucks

a pound. I thought you bodyguard types never bothered with the face. Too hard on the hands when an undercut to the stomach's just as good."

"That's true. Are you telling me you were hit by a bodyguard? Just how many celebrities did you harass over the weekend?"

"One seemed to do the trick. How often do you eat at the Blue Heron?"

"Twice in the last four years. I was working both times. Am I being accused of something?" He sat with his palms up on the desk, a gesture of wary submission known only to certain related fields of endeavor. It added a split-second to one's fast draw—unless he had a spring rig up a sleeve. The French cuffs of his white shirt looked pretty snug for that. I let a little of the tension out of my shoulders; about enough to add a split-second to my fast draw. I'd come armed.

"Your client Eddie Cypress asked me to lunch yesterday. Two men I never got a good look at pinned me with my own car door and played a fast game of hacky-sack with my head. They left these behind." I slid my left hand into my side pocket and laid the twisted and smashed pair of glasses on his desk.

He looked at them without touching. "Did you check the prescription?"

"I don't have to prove anything in court. When I find Sargent Hurley I'll try them on him, just like Cinderella. Then I'll turn him into a pumpkin."

"You said they pinned you with the car door?"

"They cracked a couple of ribs doing it, but I'm not beefing about that. I need my head to hold up my hat."

"You're not wearing a hat."

"I'm keeping my options open."

"Get them taped up?"

I shook my head.

"Right. Why pay the AMA by the yard? Either way they knit. Well, that explains why they hit you in the face. The door was in the way. You must have made Glad Eddie pretty sore at the bookstore. I'm sorry I was stuck outside. It would've been worth getting fired off the job to see you wipe the smile off his face."

"I didn't. It's nailed on. What's the matter, didn't his check clear?"

He sat back then and smoothed down his necktie. It was clipped to his shirt with a gold clasp bearing the Secret Service seal. He folded his hands across his flat middle.

"I'm a gentleman so far," he said. "You bust in, frighten my assistant, accuse me of a Class-A violation of the civil code, and I don't raise my voice. One thing the service teaches you is patience, along with every home remedy ever invented to cure piles. But the cures don't all work, and right now nobody's paying me to be patient. I took a call from New York saying a celebrated author was coming to town and his security needed an extra man at the door. I didn't hire on for any other kind of work, and I wasn't asked, then or yesterday. I'd heard of Cypress, but I hadn't thought anything about him either way: What business is it of mine how many mob lowlifes he stamped out or how much legit money he gets paid for writing about it? We've got presidential advisors advising the president to accept campaign money from the enemies of our country and cashing their government paychecks in the same bars in Washington where I used to cash mine. Okay, I don't like him when I meet him. If I only worked for people I liked, I'd be buying my ammo with food stamps. I put up with what I have to put up with to pay my overhead. That doesn't include putting up with characters like you. It doesn't cost me a penny to show characters like you the door at forty miles an hour."

I looked at his boxer's face, the thick skin on his cheeks and the hard sad eyes made for looking up from under with his head sunk into his shoulders like a turtle's, and I relaxed. It would have been a sin to put a hole through an arrangement like his, and my draw might not have been fast enough anyway. The fisted black combination butt of what would be a short-barreled revolver stuck out of a holster behind his right hipbone.

" 'R. I. Fearing,' " I said. "What's the *I* stand for?"

This time he let the smile run out a little before taking in the hitch. "Icarus. My old man could barely read and write his own name, but he was a nut on the classics. So now you've got three names for me and I've got none for you."

"Amos Walker. My old man named me after half a radio show."

"You're way too white for either half. Is that private cop I smell?"

"I'm going to have to buy a better brand of soap."

"Wouldn't help. It's the way you hold your head and how you let your right hand hang open and the questions you ask that don't count, like a polygraph expert getting a level. You're not a cop or I'd have seen a shield before this. Given the choice between his metal and pictures of his grandkids, a cop will go for the metal every time."

"Sweet."

"Reflex. After fifteen years in Washington I can't see a kid licking an ice cream cone without looking for a wire running from the cone to his shortpants pocket. It's ruined me for Norman Rockwell."

"*The Man with the X-Ray Eyes.*"

"You got that right. Can't admire an apple without seeing the worm."

"How come you got your picture taken with Jerry Ford if you never worked the White House?"

"Whip Inflation Now rally. Chief of Staff was afraid not many people would show up for the photo op. The order went out for warm bodies. I don't vote Republican but the wife thought the kids might like a memento of their old man in case I got run over by a surveillance van. It attracts business. I think you've got a level by now."

I accepted the invitation. "Were you at the restaurant?"

"No. My job was to work the door at the bookshop. It ended when Cypress finished signing. Where he went from there nobody told me and I didn't ask. Hurley handed me my check on the spot. I went home to drink beer and sleep and wait for the bank to open. You can check with my wife on that, not that you'd believe her or I'd give you my number at home. If you get it from any other source I won't go to court. I'll come see you."

"Okay."

"Okay means what?"

"It means you probably wouldn't lie in your own ballpark. Also it means I don't want to go another round with this eye. It would just give you something to work on. Finally it means I think you're too smart to throw in with Hurley on a job not connected with your specialty. He probably wouldn't even ask. He's got Herb."

"Herb. The service turned away a hundred Herbs a week, and fifty Hurleys. Did he tell you he's Eddie's publicist?"

"Eddie told me."

"I know a bit about the work from hanging around the press corps. He couldn't write a release if you held a knife to his throat and dictated. When a strongarm starts to slow down, you either kick him upstairs or put him out to pasture. Hurley knows how to put studs in a dress shirt, so he didn't go to the Old Pugs' Home. He loves his work. I doubt he's married. He sits home at night and cleans his gun."

"Did he and Herb fly out with Cypress?"

"They didn't fly out. They're still in town."

That left me silent for a minute. I hadn't expected that big a break. "Where and why?"

"He's doing an interview at the NPR station in Ypsilanti this afternoon. They're running a network feed to New York on account of he's flying out to the Coast tonight and working his way back east at about five cities per week. He's sharing a suite with the Brothers Karamazov at the Pontchartrain." He gave me a number on the twelfth floor.

"Why are you so good to me?"

"I've been at this twenty-two years, counting government service and private. I held up my right hand

and swore and I didn't cross any fingers when I did it. People who do ought to be called down. I can listen to a coon joke and not turn a hair, but jokes about gorillas in blue suits make me want to spit. Guys like Hurley and Herb are the reason those jokes get told. Are you figuring on carrying that piece into the suite?"

I bought my jackets and coats one size too big so the tail would hang over the gun without snagging; to someone like Fearing, that was the same as if I had on crossed bandoleros. "I was thinking about it. The last time I left it off I was mishandled."

"If you wear it in I'm going to call the suite as soon as you leave here and tell them you're coming. That thing I swore to included not being an accessory to murder. I don't know you that well."

I unsnapped the holster and placed it and the Chief's Special on the desk.

"Good arm," he said, again without touching. "I'm glad to see you're not one of the cannon boys. A bullet ought to stay inside the man you fired it at if it's going to do any good. We used half-loads in the service. The PR was to avoid blowing a hole through a bad guy and hitting an innocent. There's things I miss about Washington, but PR isn't one of them. Put it back on. Just try not to use it."

I returned it to my belt. "Guess you know me better than you thought."

"If you'd beefed about leaving the gun I'd have known just as much. I don't suppose it's any of my business to ask what this is all about."

"It wouldn't do you any good to know it. So far all

it's done for me is gotten me slapped around and made me the toast of two police departments."

"City?"

"One city, one county."

He sucked air through his teeth. "Those rural boys hunt to eat."

"I can stay out of that county. It's the Detroit cops I'm worried about."

"Need a side man?"

"I don't hire muscle."

He got mad for the first time. "I wasn't drumming up business. I was thinking of taking an early lunch."

"I didn't mean it that way. I get my own dirt on my own hands."

He backed off. "Not many of you left."

"For obvious reasons."

He raised a hand. It wasn't quite a gesture of benediction but it increased the distance between the hand and his gun, so I took it in that spirit. On the way out through the reception room I smiled at the woman seated at the computer. She stared back hard. No benediction there.

25

No ghosts wander the halls of the Hotel Pontchartrain. It was named for the hotel where shortly after the turn of the twentieth century Ransom E. Olds, the Dodge brothers, and even teetotaling Henry Ford gathered in the bar to discuss their dreams of an industry based entirely upon the manufacture and sale of automobiles, but the original building in Cadillac Square was torn down in 1920. The one at Jefferson and Washington was built in 1965, in the middle of a decade known more for free love than architecture. Its 450 rooms climb a glass wall perched on a horizontal base like one domino stood atop another. I crossed through a lobby that Russell Fearing might have decorated when he was preoccupied and shared the elevator as far as the fifth floor with an old woman in a long white canvas coat like a duster with her hand on the collar of a Rottweiler with a clouded left eye who didn't like me by half. From there on up to twelve I had the car to myself. They say the hotels will be full when the casinos come. This one hadn't run out of vacancies since the Republican National Convention in 1980.

I stepped out into a shotgun corridor carpeted in quiet industrial pile with surveillance cameras mounted at the ends. On the way to the Cypress suite I passed a room service cart parked halfway down containing a disorderly pile of smeared crockery, wadded linen, and thick aluminum tray covers shaped like dog dishes. Without pausing I scooped one up by the finger-hole in the center and continued walking, holding it down at my side. The action wouldn't have attracted even passing interest from whoever was watching the monitors, if anyone was and if the cameras had been activated at that very second; in standard practice they clicked on and off in a random pattern using a half-dozen screens.

I knocked at the door to the suite. "Beverage."

Feet thumped the floor on the other side. I leaned in, breathed on the convex bubble of glass in the peephole, and stood close, turning away the side of my face with the bruised eye.

There was a pause while whoever was inside tried to see me through the fogged glass.

"What's that you said?"

I said, "I'm here to restock the mini-bar."

Another little silence. I hoped he'd given up on the peephole. It would be clearing by now.

The deadbolt opened with a grinding snap. I stepped back to brace myself. If he had the chain on I was out of luck. The door opened, no chain, and I thrust the tray cover into Herb's broad blank face like a custard pie in a Keaton film. It made a dull clang. I kicked him in the left kneecap. He gasped and lost his balance and I dropped the cover and grabbed him by his nubby knitted black necktie and pulled him forward onto his face. As soon as he hit he tried to roll over onto his right side. That made him a lefty, so I put my foot between his shoulder blades and pushed him flat and leaned down and groped at his belt on the left side, got nothing, and tunneled up under his blue serge suitcoat and grasped a handle and sprang a .44 magnum from an underarm clip. It was the portable model with the four-inch barrel, no plating. I had him figured for the chromed one as big as a T-square, but it must have been too uncomfortable even for him.

I wasn't through with him—a cracked kneecap and a pie in the face was only interest on the principal I owed him—but the door on the other side of the sitting room was opening. I just had time to stretch out the arm holding Herb's magnum like an old-time shootist in a Remington print and catch Sargent Hurley with one hand on the doorknob and the other hitching up his pants. He had his coat off and he was growing a belly; hitching up his pants would be a thing he did every time he stood up from a chair.

He had on a spare pair of glasses just like the ones he'd lost in the parking lot, but he didn't seem to be seeing through them too well. He stopped short for the gun but there was no recognition on his big spreading face, an older version of Herb's. I was pretty sure then they were related.

"Fearing was right," I said. "I guess I am a cowboy, at that."

"You," he said, remembering. "What—"

"You, what." I crossed the room in two strides and laid the four-inch barrel above his left ear. His glasses went one way, he went the other. His shoulder struck the doorjamb hard enough to shake the entire twelfth floor and he slid down it onto his left hip, not smoothly but in jerky little stages, lowering himself gently like a man climbing into a scalding tub. He was dazed, but he wasn't out.

Covering him, I picked up his glasses and slid them into my pocket with the other pair. "You ought to consider contacts," I said. "I don't suppose a spook like you would ever let anyone get near him with a laser."

"I'm astigmatic. How the hell—" He groped blindly for the jamb.

I leaned down and tapped him with the gun, the right temple this time. When you've been slugged on the coconut as many times as I have you develop a feel for the pressure points. He went out like the Rat Pack. "I liked 'You, what' better," I said, to no one who was listening.

By the time I was through with him I had Herb back on my plate. This was getting to be like cleaning the Augean stables. On his feet again, he came at me sideways in that praying mantis position that meant someone had dropped a couple of grand at Colonel Yi's

Academy of Self-Defense and Szechwan Kitchen. The length of a man's own body is as far as he can kick without a running start, and I let him get almost that far before I raised the magnum to the level of his clavicle and rolled back the hammer.

"Next time ask Uncle Sarge just to go ahead and buy you an ICBM," I said.

That made him stop to think; or maybe it was the bore of the .44. "He's not my uncle. He's my cousin, once removed."

"Looks like twice. Sit down."

"On what?" He was several paces from the nearest chair.

"On the floor. Make like I'm going to tell you a story."

He hesitated. He might not have been disobedient, just reluctant to get back down when getting back up had been so much trouble; he'd have a stiff knee for days. In any case he took too long and I stepped in and gave him what I'd given Cousin Sargent. He had a harder head. He managed to form an expression of indignation before his eyes turned to glass. He folded into a tidy pile at my feet.

"Finished?"

The voice belonged to a new piece on the board. I moved to one side to broaden my field of view. Eddie Cypress stood in the doorway that led to the rest of the suite. He had on a thin blue cashmere pullover against bare skin and gray corduroy slacks. The nickel plating on the light automatic in his right hand shone like a mirror. He seemed as comfortable with it as he was with the presence of Sargent Hurley's crumpled form blocking his way. It didn't annoy him even so much as a misplaced suitcase.

I said, "A thirty-two, Eddie?"

For the first time his made-over face showed pain. "It's all I could rustle up. None of my old contacts will have anything to do with me. I can't even make out what language is stamped on this piece of shit. But it goes bang when I pull the thingie, and like the man said, no one wants to get shot with anything. You the exception?"

"Are you?" I had the magnum trained on him.

His trademark smile was as shiny as the .32. "Well, we can do this all day, except I called the desk when I heard Herb hit the floor the first time. I'm registered in this suite. Who do you think the dick will shoot?"

"Hotel dicks don't shoot. And you didn't call. You haven't been legit long enough to pick up the habit."

"Why don't let's wait and see?"

I moved the shoulder not connected to the gun. "I cleared my calendar."

"Shit." He laid the pistol on a lamp table and turned away from the door. "Try not to trip over Sarge. We wouldn't want you blowing a hole through the next two rooms. You might hit a low-flow toilet and drain a lake somewhere in Pakistan."

I held the magnum at hip level and stepped over the publicist. This room contained a white-enameled sleigh bed, neatly made, a sitting area, and a massive breakfront containing rows of books behind leaded glass with a refrigerator and mini-bar built in. Tasteful watercolors of Lake St. Clair and the Detroit River hung in frames on the wall adjacent the window, whose drapes were open to provide a view of their inspiration. Cypress broke a can of Coke out of the refrigerator and poured it into a glass containing ice cubes and nothing else. "Booze? Soda? I guess you call it pop here. I gave up the hard stuff after Crazy Joe went down clear back in seventy-two, and I had a hollow leg even then. Haven't touched a drop since."

"I'm fine."

"Only thing I miss is the noise the ice used to make when I poured the liquor. It sounded like the polar cap breaking up. But not as loud as the guns that night in Umberto's. I can still see Joey sitting there with his face in his side of steamed clams."

"You shot Joey Gallo?"

"No. Hell, no. I still had my cherry then. I was in the party. It was Joey's wedding anniversary, he wanted everybody to have a good time. I was running the juke route in Jersey for the Profaci family. It was like delivering papers, only without a bike and with a cheap Saturday-night buster in my pocket—cheaper than that fucking thirty-two—because I expected some Puerto Rican son of a bitch to cut my throat any minute for a bag of quarters."

"Youth." I was beginning to feel like a plaster saint standing there holding the .44.

He drank a slug of Coke and walked over to the window. "Some view. Lots of bones at the bottom of that river. Wish I was around in Prohibition. My old man told me stories. I hate these glass buildings. I keep asking them to book older hotels. Publishers don't listen. These places make me feel like a germ on a slide."

"That's a reach."

"Now you're just a disappointment. You had my attention there when you stepped on Herb and Sarge, but then you had to go and spoil it. I didn't see your tambourine when you came in."

"That's because I traded it for a P.I. license years ago." I took the deep-bodied revolver off cock and laid it next to the .32. "That the same piece you had covered up north?"

"Sport, I don't know what you're talking about."

"You'd be a lot more convincing if you didn't keep calling me 'sport.' You should have gotten rid of it when you took off the sunglasses and cap."

"You nailed me. I'm guilty as hell of buzzing up to Styxville, U.S.A., for a little p and q in the middle of a twenty-city book tour. That a felony in this state or do I just fork over a fine?"

"You checked out just in time. Your next-door neighbor swung from his belt the next morning. That would have just brought back memories of the bad old days."

He turned away from the window. His age showed through the cosmetic work when he wasn't smiling, as if he'd asked the surgeons to tailor it to his grin. Aside from that he didn't look upset or surprised. It wouldn't have meant anything if he had; Booth's death had made the papers, and even if it hadn't he'd had a lifetime of practice at controlling those muscles that give away most of the rest of us, with eighteen months of legal coaching and three weeks of federal grand jury testimony on top of it. "I don't know a damn thing about that, Walker. That's the truth, swear on my father's grave. You know how he finished."

"I heard he got greedy. Then he got dead. I'd swear

on the grave of a mook like that I went to bed with Mother Teresa."

He held up a manicured finger. No polish; that was very Frank Costello. "That's one. One's all you get. I loved my old man. I bawled like a baby all the time they were cremating him."

"Then you went back to your juke route. Working for the same mob that killed him."

"I bet you rent *The Godfather* every chance you get." The smile this time was tired, not the one he wore for company. "What'd you expect me to do, declare war on the entire Cosa fucking Nostra? Eugene Booth might have written it that way, but books end. The world doesn't and you have to live in it. I swallowed what happened to the old man, choked it down like the sourest goddamn potato since Job got boils and went to work running numbers for Genovese. The juke route came later. I gave all my pay to my mother and it spent just as good as if none of it ever passed through the same hands that made her a widow. That's the year I turned thirty-five. Except I was fourteen. So when I swear on Tommy Cypress' grave I'm making an oath on the only pure thing I know."

I fished a Winston out of the pack in my shirt pocket, looked at it, and put it back. "That in the book?"

"Go fuck yourself, Walker." He gulped from his glass.

"So you knew it was Booth in Cabin Four. He didn't know who you were. You hadn't met. It takes a good eye to spot a celebrated author forty years after the celebration ended."

"I read his obituary. That's how I knew he was dead.

I didn't kill him. My score stands at fifteen and that's where it's going to stay."

"I'd like to believe that. I'd like to believe you just happened to go up there to breathe the clean air the same time as Booth, who has a history with your late employers. You'd register under a phony name for privacy and disguise your famous face with a cap and glasses for the same reason. You've got enemies, so when someone knocks on your door you answer it with artillery support. Stealing someone else's license plates is taking incognito a bit far, but let's stretch and say that's why you did it. It's still not a serious enough beef to send the Cousins Hurley after me when I called you on it. Add a little murder and it all lines out."

"The last part was Sarge's idea. I'm out of practice in that area or I wouldn't have gone along with it. You can take that as an apology if you want. I got scared." He smiled at the thought, the Glad Eddie grin. "Hell, I guess I did. Funny, I never was scared all the time I was working the other side. This legitimate enterprise isn't for sissies. Sit down, Sarge. You look beat. Ha."

Hurley was swaying inside the doorway, squinting to make out who was which without his glasses. The violet swelling was more prominent on his left temple than his right. I'd been too enthusiastic the first time.

"Son of a bitch blindsided me," he said thickly. "Otherwise—"

"Otherwise you'd be a rack of ribs. I know a little bit more about characters like Walker than you do. You're not used to being the target. Grab yourself a drink. How's Herb?"

"Still out. This bastard cracked his skull."

"Not nearly," I said. "I know the sound." I excavated his latest pair of glasses and held them out. He squinted, then snatched them out of my hand and put them on.

He was braver when he could see. "We should have kicked the extra point in the parking lot."

"I should have bought Microsoft at twelve. We all have our regrets. I'll just lay these here." I put the ruined pair on the same table with the guns. He'd walked right past them without seeing. "Let them sit till I'm gone. I might get the wrong idea."

"And do what?"

"Ask Herb when he comes around."

"Sit the hell down," Cypress snapped. "Next time I'll hire a real publicist. They know when the tour's over."

Hurley slammed a defiant handful of ice cubes from the brass bucket into a glass, emptied a dwarf bottle of Jack Daniel's over it, and took the glass to a deep divan covered with thick gray fabric.

Cypress gestured with his glass toward a pair of club chairs in the opposite corner. He shook his head when I glanced at Hurley.

"Sarge used to work for the Democratic Party," he said. "He's heard worse."

"I haven't been in a booth since Reagan."

"I never was. I was all set to vote for Muskie when eighteen months in Elmira got in the way."

"It might have made the difference."

He grinned.

I decided I was thirsty after all. I found a can of Vernor's and threw in half a pony bottle of Absolut, which in Detroit is called a Joseph Campau. The glass fizzed all the way across the room.

Glad Eddie sat, crossed his legs, then put his Coke on a disk of pebbled glass with a floor lamp stuck through it and never touched it again, talking while the ice melted and turned the liquid from chocolate brown to the color of gun oil. He uncrossed his legs and rested his forearms on his thighs and slid his palms back and forth against each other with a rasping sound.

"I'm out now," he said. "Out as you can get and still stay vertical. I'm relieved as all hell, but not for the reasons you might think. I'm sick of doing professional work for idiots."

"So you went into publishing." I drank. The vodka and ginger ale had a sweet clean bite.

He was looking at me, but he wasn't listening. He was so caught up in what he'd started he even forgot to smile.

26

You ou heard there's a million-dollar tag out on me?" Cypress asked.

I said, "It's on the flap of your book. I figured if it wasn't just hype you'd be part of some highway by now."

"It's real enough, but they put a hold on it until I'm yesterday's news. Cops, reporters, and people who show up on *Entertainment Tonight* a lot are off limits; nobody's death is worth the heat that comes after. It's an incentive to stay on the *Times* list, I tell you."

"Publish or perish."

"My contract is for three books; but if whatever I

write next doesn't fly like *Prey Tell*, there won't be a third. In a year or two you'll find it on the remainder tables at ninety-nine cents a crack, by which time I'll be on another kind of table, getting my organs harvested for science. The kicker is, what's the next one going to be about? I told my life the first time. That's what I meant about being scareder on this side of the blanket than I ever was on the other."

"So hire another ghost."

He frowned, going against the grain of his face work. It made him look like a wounded author. "Hey, I *wrote* every word that went into that book. The editors fixed the spelling and put in some commas and moved a couple of paragraphs around, but it's one hundred percent Eddie Cypress, no soy substitutes. I sign my own work."

"That's what I heard."

"Yeah, okay, I walked into that one." The grin flared and faded. "I only sent glads to the first three funerals, in the beginning when I figured I needed to advertise. Third time was in February, when they were out of season. I wound up paying through the nose in a little shit florist shop in Flushing for the sorriest display you ever saw. That cured me. But you know that. You read the book."

I shook my head. "I thought I'd wait and not see the movie."

"The *point*," he went on, "is I'm not all that much of a priority or someone would've found a way to get rid of me before this. I put a fat shark in the tank and a couple of pilot fish, but the school swims on. I'm an

open sore, not a mortal wound. I get to keep drain-
ing if I do New York an occasional favor."

"Eugene Booth, for one."

"Booth was just a test. You read *Paradise Valley*?"

"Depends on which version you're talking about."

"That answers my question. Roland Clifford, what a
nosebleed. The Detroit bosses built him up like a bad
fighter, bought off all his betters and made him champ—
hero to you. They owned him down to his skivvies, a
cop on his way up, and that never hurts when you're
trying to build something permanent on the killing you
made in the wartime black market. Booth's brother part-
nered Clifford during the riot. When *Paradise Valley*
came out the first time, Detroit blew a big old sigh of
relief because the book backed up the official version.
Not only that, it made Clifford out to be Paul Bunyan,
which is something you can't buy; it's like tenure, it
just keeps building and building."

"Until the guy that started it has a change of heart."

"Not even then. Not then, anyway. This was the fifties,
remember. You could say MacArthur was an arrogant
fuck and Ike whored around with a WAC and James
Dean took it up the ass and nobody'd listen. Vietnam
and Watergate changed all that. Now when someone
goes up like a balloon we all admire him with our fingers in our ears waiting for the pop. New York's a
small town. When it gets out Booth's back and signing a new deal for *Paradise Valley*, New York decides
to do Detroit a favor and find out what he's got in
mind."

"That's stupid. Clifford's dead. What harm could the
truth do the Detroit mob now?"

"Not any. The legit crowd's a different story. You've got a nice little renaissance going and Roland Clifford's part of it. They want to name a street after him, throw up a statue or two and probably a scholarship. See, when he died, the organization was through with him. That's when he became the property of the straights. When I said New York put me on Booth as a favor to Detroit, I didn't mean the mob. I meant Detroit."

"Who signed off on that?"

"Nobody confided in me. At a guess? New York's idea. New York meaning the organization. A little fence-mending with the organization in Detroit, by way of a peace offering with the city. Buying cops is Cold War thinking. You've got to buy cities if you want to compete."

"All this without checking to see if it's what Detroit wanted," I said. "Amazing."

"I told you I was sick of working for idiots."

"You're telling me you killed Booth."

"I told you I didn't. I was just there to spot the job. I did the homework, found out where Booth liked to work, and traced him to Black Lake and the Angler's Inn. If I gave it thumbs up and they decided to go ahead, they would've rung in somebody local to cap it off. Somebody invisible, which I'm not. The only reason they risked using me at all is they wanted to keep me nervous. Also I was going to Detroit anyway to promote the book, which gave me a cover."

"Which you blew by using stolen plates."

"Somebody's idea of a joke. They gave me the keys to the truck and the address of the garage where it was parked. Don't forget I'm a running sore. You can bet the trail would've stopped with me if I got pulled over. I'd have a brand new beef and it didn't matter if the job got blown, it wasn't important. Just a favor. I didn't know about the plates until you told me."

I drank. The Campau was losing its fizz. "Any idea who drew the Booth job?"

"Not Detroit. Not the organization, I mean. I nixed the job. You check out those locks when you were at the inn?"

"I pushed one in. Took about two seconds."

"What'd you do with the second second? He went out one night for a walk and I let myself in and read what he'd written. It was red hot, but it was fiction. There wasn't anything to back it up. I put the pages back the way I found them and went out and called New York and told them Booth wasn't worth the investment."

"Toss the cabin?"

"I'm rusty. I ain't broke down. I went through his suitcase and the closet and under the bed. I checked out the typewriter case and turned the machine upside-down. I didn't want to make a mess and I didn't have the time to do it neat and thorough. Did I miss something?"

"How would I know? I'm just being neat and thorough. If you put back Booth's manuscript, who took it? It wasn't there when I cut him down."

"Find it and you've found the one who strung him up. Just a guess."

"Maybe New York didn't like your report."

"Maybe. Fuck that. Why bother sending me in the first place?"

"Setup."

He shook his head and rasped his palms. "That's the first thing I thought of. Only they didn't need to go to the trouble. Back when the feds gave me immunity, a couple of things didn't come up on account of they didn't know about them. If they came out now I'd be on my way to the Marion pen in a New York minute, ha. So the boys back home don't need Number Sixteen."

"Uh-uh." I grinned over my glass. "If that were true, New York would have rolled over on you months ago."

"It wouldn't be as much fun as what they're doing to me right now." He wasn't grinning.

"Poor Glad Eddie."

"Go to hell."

"Not today. Who pushed the button on Allison Booth in fifty-six?"

"Nobody. That was an amateur job."

"It's a lot easier to make a professional job look amateur than the other way around."

"Not as easy as you think. Ever try to arrange some things on a table so it looks as if they just landed there? Anyway it wasn't an organization act."

"You seem pretty familiar with the details."

"Right. I was seven. I rode over from Brooklyn on my hobby horse and stuck her with my rubber Zorro knife. I do my homework, Walker. When I do a job—did a job—I tracked it clear back to the womb. Booth's wife was a stepper. She stepped one time too many and got stepped on herself."

"Booth didn't see it that way. He figured her death

was a warning to keep his mouth shut about Roland Clifford."

"He wrote fiction. Out here in the world you don't kick in a wife or a close relative when you can get the same effect by throwing a dead canary on someone's doorstep. You take too much from a man, he stops caring. You might as well set up the press conference yourself. And that's another thing. Booth didn't believe she was hit either. Otherwise he'd have burned Roland Clifford in effigy in the middle of Cadillac Square. Whatever else he told you, he spent forty years talking himself into. He didn't believe it when it counted."

I said nothing. He rasped his hands. "Anyway, like I said, after *Paradise Valley* nothing Booth could say would've slowed down the momentum. Not unless he had proof."

I was looking at him. Mob guys are great liars and lousy at coming clean. His gaze darted about and if he rubbed his hands together any faster he'd start a fire. That's when I knew he was telling the truth.

27

Herb wobbled in from the other room looking like a man who had not survived Everest. He was a colorful bruiser, all eggplant and yellow and royal blue, not the best quality to bring to his line of work; but then I couldn't see him taking a civil service exam either. He hesitated by the table containing the guns. I could see all his gears and pulleys working from where I sat.

So could Cypress. "You're off duty. Pour yourself a slug and park it."

"I don't drink." But he wobbled over and sat down

on the upholstered bench at the foot of the bed with his head propped in his hands.

I said, "Whoever did Booth tore out a piece of his writing to look like a suicide note and walked off with the manuscript. Who'd do that, if Detroit or New York weren't doubling up on you?"

"Without evidence or Booth alive to back it up with an affidavit—which would be hearsay—it was just fiction. It had to be worth something to someone for some other reason." Cypress remembered his Coke, picked it up, looked at the weak yellowish syrup, and put it back without drinking.

I drained my glass, held the contents in my mouth for a moment, then let them go on down. I stood up, fast enough to startle Sargent Hurley and make Herb lift his shop-damaged head.

"Something?" Cypress' brows followed me up.

"Nothing you could use. I think you're out of it. If you'd gone ahead and met me for lunch, you could have spared your publicity staff a rough morning."

"They were getting fat." He rose. "I might call you from Denver or someplace. I'm curious to see how this comes out."

Neither of us made a move to shake hands. I said, "Just a suggestion. Write the next one about what it's like to promote a book instead of kill people."

"That's not bad. Got a title?"

I thought. "How about *Crime and Punishment*?"

"That's not bad, either," he said. "Hasn't it been used?"

"Not in a long time."

He grinned. "I'm starting not to hate you, Walker. We've got a lot in common."

"About four quarts of blood and thirty feet of intestines. After that, nothing."

The grin went. "Maybe I won't call you."

"*Senso vostra angoscia.*"

Here I was, back at the Alamo, standing in front of 610. A couple more visits and I could start using it as my voting address.

There was no answer after five minutes. I stepped over and rapped on 609. The young man with the gold rings and shaved head opened his door in nothing but a skimpy pair of red Y-fronts. There was a blue shadow on his narrow chest where he'd shaved there too. His eyelids were puffy. He was having trouble focusing. It was a few minutes past eleven-thirty.

"Sorry to drag you out of the sack," I said. "We met Saturday, sort of. I was looking for Lowell Birdsall. I still am."

"I remember." There was a gurgle in the deep thud of his voice. He cleared his throat and swallowed. "He got in late last night."

"You were up?"

"Along with about half the building. The owner's thinking of renaming it the Anne Rice Arms."

"I couldn't raise him."

"Who, the owner?"

"Birdsall. Maybe he's sleeping in too."

"I don't think he ever gets more than four hours together. He never goes out during the business day. He must be in the can."

"I knocked loud. I need to talk to him. Do you still have a key?"

"I can't let you in if he isn't there. If he is and he isn't answering he must have his reasons."

I got out my ID folder and showed him the county star. "I just want to look around. You can go in with me."

"Let me put something on."

He started to push the door shut. My shoulder got in the way and he turned inside without so much as a shrug.

There was a yellow telephone on the wall next to the door to the bathroom. He walked past it without a glance and went on through and closed the door behind him. What I could see of the place from the front door was tidy except for the rumpled bed. There were books and plants on shelves, a rack of stereo components, a CD tower shaped like the Capitol Records building, and a concert poster in a transparent Lucite frame of The Artist Before He Became Formerly Known As Whatsizname, decked out in Viennese court dress with a lace ruffle at his throat. The palette seemed to be purple and yellow. It looked better than it sounds. His and Birdsall's apartments represented the artistic corner of an address that generally looked like a hastily packed suitcase.

He came out wearing the same black net top, cut-off jeans, and sandals he'd had on the other day, jingling a ring of keys in rhythm with his walk. He locked up, went to Birdsall's door, tapped a panel, waited, whistling pieces of some tune through his front teeth, then slipped one of the keys into the lock.

Something struck the floor with a bang and a clatter when he pushed the door open. I thought at first he'd hit something, but the door swung all the way around on its hinges and he froze with one foot on the threshold, blocking most of the view. Looking around him I saw the plywood underside of a kitchen chair lying on its back with two tubular steel legs in the air. I shoved him hard from behind and when he stumbled I circled wide around him and went for the white thing wriggling and jerking twelve inches above the floor.

Birdsall's reflexes were just fine. I bit a piece off my tongue when a white-clad knee jerked up and caught me on the chin, but I got my arms around his waist and lifted with everything I had. I was getting to be good at that. He was as hard as a tree trunk under the top layer of flab and heavier than a sofa, and he was twisting in my grip like a live marlin. I had barely breath enough to call for a hand. The neighbor got hold of him and I let go and righted the chair and climbed up on it, clawing out my pocket knife. I sawed at the cord tied around the white metal runner of one of the track lights Birdsall had installed to show off his collection. The cord was insulated with brown fabric with a yellow stripe, the kind they used to put on irons and toasters, and the knot had sunk deep into his thick neck.

The copper wire inside parted with a twang and the neighbor caught his weight with a grunt and lowered him to the floor. He had the noose yanked open by the time I stepped down.

My cracked ribs burned holes in my sides. I bent over with my hands on my knees and dry-retched for the better part of a minute. Then I knelt beside Birdsall.

His face, hairless except for the goatee and moustache, was changing color. The purple-black hue of congestion was fading, but his pale gray-pink tongue stuck out and his eyes were rolled back into his head so that only the glistening whites showed. I slapped his cheeks, using both sides of my hand, and called his name. He wasn't breathing. I signaled for more room and when the neighbor stood up and away I stretched Birdsall out on the floor and pinched his nostrils and blew into his mouth. I did that seven times, counting the seconds in between, before his chest began to fill and empty on its own. His face had gone dead white in the meantime, as white as his T-shirt, but now the pink was coming back.

Beep-boop-boop. The neighbor on the telephone, pipping out the three notes to salvation. I pried back each of Birdsall's eyelids. His irises were back where they belonged. The pupils matched. He was breathing evenly. I dragged down one of the nubby green cushions from the loveseat and put it under his head. Then I got up and took a walk around the apartment.

With the chair back up on its legs there were no signs of disturbance. His weight had pulled the light track into a V. Much more kicking like he'd been doing and he'd have torn the screws out of the ceiling joists. Cheap places to live are almost never easy places to die. The noise I'd heard had been the chair falling over when he kicked it out from under himself. There was no one hiding in the bathroom, a dank little closet with specks of black growing on the plastic shower curtain. It was a do-it-yourself job.

"No, no," the neighbor was saying into the receiver.

"*West* Jefferson. The Alamo Motel. Jesus. It's only been here longer than the Penobscot Building. No, not the Penobscot. The Alamo. Apartment six-ten. Yeah. You be sure and have a nice day."

Fleta Skirrett bared her teeth at me from a canvas. Her blue eyes gleamed like the bottoms of polished china bowls, as big in the painting as half-dollars. Her dress was tiger orange, ripped loose from one white shoulder to expose her cleavage, and she had one orange-nailed fist wrapped around the handle of an automatic pistol, a shiny .32 like the one Glad Eddie Cypress had pointed at me. Her black pupils were as big around as my thumbs and had tiny flaws in their centers.

I stepped closer. They weren't flaws at all, but twin reflections of a brutish-looking male coming her way with a knife; not in the melodramatic overhand grip so popular among pulp artists who had never taken part in a knife fight or even witnessed one, but in the scooping underhand of the professional blade man. That was impressive. That was research. The reflections themselves wouldn't have shown at all once the picture was reduced for reproduction on the cover of a cheap paperback. Lowell Senior was an artist. The industry hadn't known what it had, in him or Booth. The definition of art in America.

"Creepy shit, huh?" The neighbor's voice shook a little. "No wonder he got depressed. Think he'll be all right?"

"He'll live. If he were all right he wouldn't have stepped off the chair."

"Well, duh."

I was only half listening, to him and myself. Bird-sall's dehumidifier was whirring in its corner. I went over and turned the dial all the way to the left. Silence came down with a thump. The reservoir had been emp-tied recently. He'd thought to preserve his collection beyond his own death. That was dedication. He was his father's son.

The Domino's pizza box was gone from the vintage laminated table. A green marbleized clamshell box took up half the space it had occupied. It was the kind archivists use to store and display valuable papers. I knew what was inside, but I went over anyway and tipped back the lid.

I looked at a stack of coarse discolored sheets with dog-eared corners. They bore the Alamo letterhead, with the old two-letter telephone prefix and no ZIP, because the code had yet to be invented when the sheets were printed. Motels were still a novel concept then; even vis-itors to the Alamo didn't mind letting the folks back home know where they'd landed. The sheets were cov-ered with dense typing, with here and there whole para-graphs scratched out and thickly scribbled notes substituted between the lines. I'd seen it before and knew what it was, but I got out the note Eugene Booth had written Louise Starr when he returned her check and compared them. Handwriting can be forged, but not the wandering *a* and *o* of Eugene Booth's old Smith-Corona.

Someone groaned, a long grating sound like rusted metal parts scraping against each other, and I turned away from the box. Lowell Junior was coming around.

28

It was early afternoon when I got back to the office. I wasn't hungry, but I'd stopped at the desperate diner for a BLT to boost my protein and help out the owner. When he rang up the sale on his old-fashioned cash register, the little number tab looked like a tombstone. I circled my block twice, then found a space two streets over. I walked through one of those spring rains that doesn't do much more than stamp circles in the dust on the sidewalk. It didn't even get my head wet.

I smelled an official visit all the way from the landing. It reeked of leather and gun oil and the lime-based aftershave they give away with a year's subscription to

Police Times. I sagged against the hallway wall and smoked thirty seconds' worth of cigarette. Then I flipped it into the fire bucket and went on.

Sheriff's Detective Vaxhölm was standing in front of the framed *Casablanca* poster when I let myself into the waiting room. He had on the same shooting jacket with the leather patch and what might have been the same black knitted tie and button-down white shirt. He didn't turn as I entered. The Huron nose and cheekbones stood out against the door to the inner office like an advertisement for chewing tobacco.

"Never could see what the shouting was about," he said. "If he were any kind of man he'd have ignored the woman and kept the nightclub."

I said, "The woman was Ingrid Bergman. Anyway the movie would've been over in half an hour."

"It looks old."

"It's an original."

"You ought to lock your door. Someone might steal it."

"I need the business more than I do the poster. Run into much construction on the way down?"

"I drove around it, on the shoulder. There are some advantages to being a cop. Not damn many." He turned his frozen blue eyes on me. "What did you do with the box?"

"It didn't come in a box."

"I'm not talking about the poster anymore. Old Man Erwig says you told him there was a box belonging to Booth in Cabin Two. There wasn't any box when I checked."

"His name's Erwig?"

"Let's g-go inside."

I unlocked the door and held it for him. He looked around, but that was just habit. He turned in the middle of the floor to face me. "My aunt would prescribe a leech for that eye."

"Medicine woman?"

"No, just nuts. Should I know how you got it?"

I shook my head. He pulled the customer chair to the side of the desk so it wouldn't be between us and used it. I picked up my mail from the floor under the slot, shuffled through it on the way over, and laid it alongside the blotter when I sat down. It didn't contain any checks or ransom notes.

"It's at my house," I said. "There isn't anything in it but a few bottles of liquor, Booth's brand. We can swing by there and you can take it back with you. Whiskey isn't my cup of tea. It isn't even a good label."

"What else was in the box?"

I shook my head. He could take that any way he wanted and I was too tired to care which he chose.

He changed directions. "We got the report back from Lansing this morning on the blood and tissue samples we took from Booth. You didn't answer your telephone so I buzzed down to deliver it in person. You want raw numbers, or can I do it in English?"

"I flunked math."

"He had enough alcohol in his system to rub down a rhinoceros. County M.E. says with a load like that he couldn't have gotten out of bed, much less buckled his belt around his neck and climbed up on a chair and jumped off. So what looked like a tidy little suicide

isn't. And what were *you* doing when Booth was making like a piñata?"

"Sleeping it off, like I said. I had enough alcohol in
my system to rub down an Impala. A sixty-seven Impala with chrome-reverse wheels."

"What was in the box, Walker?"

"We can talk about that after I tell you who killed
Booth."

He sat back and crossed his legs. His olive-drab
trousers were starched and pressed into a lethal crease
and his brown half-boots gleamed like furniture. "Theory?"

"Confession."

"Yours?"

"Lowell Birdsall's. You don't know him."

"I'd like to. When were you planning to tell me this?"

"I just found out myself. I guessed it this morning,
but we both know what you'd have said to that. I went
over to his place to ask him about it and wound up
saving his neck. Literally. He tried to hang himself the
same way he did Booth. He's a big boy, lots of bulk
and muscle. He didn't need help."

"He told you this? Where is he now, jail?"

"Detroit General. It's a hospital. Talking killed time
while we were waiting for EMS. The local cops don't
know he's anything more than an attempted suicide. I
was saving the rest for you."

"What's to stop him from walking away?"

"I can see you don't handle many suicides. It's illegal in this state. It's the only crime they can't nail you
with if you pull it off. If you fail, you're committed for
seventy-two hours of mandatory psychiatric evaluation.

There's a pair of eyes on you the whole time. So your department has three days to obtain a warrant and ship him back to Black Lake."

"Cheboygan," he corrected. "That's where the county lockup is. Give me the rest."

I gave him everything about the case except Glad Eddie Cypress and the existence of Officer Duane Booth's written report on Roland Clifford's conduct during the 1943 riot; in fact I left out the mob angle altogether. It didn't figure in and I had a promise to keep that involved the old police report. Vaxhölm, writing in his notebook, asked me for the details on the Allison Booth killing and I referred him to Lieutenant Mary Ann Thaler.

"That one's fuzzy as hell," he said. "Who killed Booth's wife?"

"According to Birdsall Junior, it was Birdsall Senior. For a gifted artist his powers of observation were spotty. Every time he looked at a woman outside his work all he saw was the bottom half. He hit on Allison while Booth was in New York and she was feeling lonely. Maybe she thought it was innocent, dinner and drinks with a friend of her husband's; the cops who investigated the case didn't spend any time on that angle once they'd made up their minds about her, so we may never know. Say she put up a fight when she found out it wasn't so innocent. Birdsall Senior panicked, or became enraged when he found out he wasn't God's gift to this particular woman. That many stab wounds doesn't suggest premeditation."

"Why'd he have a knife if he didn't plan it?"

"It was the fifties. You weren't a man or a boy if

you went out of the house without a folding knife in your pocket. The deepest wound was less than three and a half inches. That's consistent with a Boy Scout blade. He punched her full of holes, probably in his car, then drove her to the first deserted street and dumped her into a window well."

"The investigating officers must have impounded his car."

"They didn't find anything. Remember, they didn't have the equipment we have now, and Birdsall did a good job cleaning up after himself. He was an artist, a detail man. You ought to see his paintings. He knew how to use a knife, too. He did his homework."

"You said he had an alibi."

"One of his models said they were working that night. She was probably one of his conquests; Junior said he bedded all his models. The cops could have cracked her if they'd leaned hard enough, but they had only the salesgirl's identification of Birdsall as the man she saw picking up Allison and it was one woman's word against another's. Also they were just going through the motions. A dead tramp is a dead tramp."

He frowned at his notebook. "The son knew?"

"He suspected. He's sure his mother knew, or suspected, and that's why she drove her car into a bridge abutment. Suicide's getting to be a family tradition."

"That doesn't explain why the son killed Booth."

"Sure it does. He's practically a shut-in, living and working out of the same room his father used for a studio, surrounding himself with Lowell Senior's paintings and thousands of lurid paperback murder mysteries. All those stories have one thing in common, aside from flashy dames and tough talk: the hero always wins and the murderers are punished. It's been a comfort to him all these years, living with his father's crimes— murder *and* betrayal—and the fact that he was never punished. He couldn't kill his father. His father's dead. When I came around asking questions, stirring up all those old emotions, the books weren't enough."

I got *Bullets Are My Business* out of the belly drawer of the desk and skidded it across the top. "P.I. yarn," I said. "That character with the broken nose is Booth. Birdsall Senior used him as the inspiration for all the tough monkeys on the covers he illustrated. Birdsall Junior grew up looking at those paintings and later reading the books, and got confused. He told his neighbor he was attending a pulp convention in Cleveland last weekend. I called the *Plain Dealer* today before I went to see him. There weren't any pulp conventions going on within a hundred miles of the city last weekend. Instead Lowell drove up to Black Lake where he knew Booth would be working, strung him up by his belt, and tore a piece of handwriting out of Booth's manuscript to stand for a suicide note. He was no stranger to suicide, and when he let himself in and found him passed out on the bed, the rest was just muscle. He knew everything he needed to about slipping locks and arranging a crime scene from the hundreds of books he'd read. The loose window latch even gave him a chance to lock up after. Of course the manuscript went with him—he was a collector. By the time he confessed to me he had himself talked into believing that was the reason he killed Booth. It wasn't. The motive wasn't strong enough for murder. It wasn't even strong enough to make him kill himself. That takes guilt. Guilt and rage.

"Booth let him down," I said. "He wasn't there to protect his wife from Birdsall's father, and he didn't do anything about it after she was murdered. He looked like a hero, but he didn't behave like one. What's a boy to do when he can't believe in his own father and the substitute he picked out of a book betrays him too? He writes his own ending."

The telephone stepped on my closing line. I snatched up the receiver and snarled into it.

"I didn't expect flowers," Louise Starr said after a pause. "I can get along without a call. I wasn't pre-pared to have my head bitten off. Is this a comment on last night? I get better reviews from Kirkus."

I apologized. I apologized for not calling her too. I shut my mouth before I could think of something else to apologize for.

"Are you all right? You sound terrible."

"I'm more tired than terrible. I've been lifting weights. I found Booth's manuscript." I met the blue-ice depths of Vaxhölm's glare.

"Does that mean you know who killed him?"

"Yeah. Can I call you back? I'm in the middle of an official visit."

"The police?"

"Yeah. You'll have to wait for the manuscript. They'll want it until they close the file."

Vaxhölm sat back and directed his attention to *Custer's Last Stand* on the wall beside the desk.

"I hope they clear it in time to make next year's

spring list. Is it complete? How long is it? Could you tell if it needs much fixing?"

"I didn't have time to read it. I can't think why. I called nine-one-one before I started, just to make sure I wouldn't be interrupted for a couple of hours. I really have to call you back." I cradled the receiver.

"That the client?"

"She's a publisher."

"A lot of people tell me I should write about my adventures. You'd be surprised what goes on in a rural county up north. Did you see *Deliverance*?"

"I live it. She probably wouldn't be interested. Lady cops are in this season."

"I'll use a female pseudonym. I wish you city folk would settle your differences at home. Most of the murders we deal with happen in winter, when the snow's piled ten feet high and wifie cracks open her husband's head with a meat tenderizer because he complained about the casserole. The locals respect the tourist season."

"I'd believe that if I hadn't counted a dozen satellite dishes between town and the lake. Nobody uses meat tenderizers anymore, not even in Mayberry. You're going to have to write a new speech."

He flicked at one olive-drab knee. There was nothing on it. "I don't like it that Booth and Birdsall Senior went on being friends after Senior killed Allison. He must have known he was a suspect."

"Who can ever figure out how a writer thinks? Maybe he wanted to use him in a book. Maybe *Some of My Best Friends Are Killers* was more than just a title."

He watched me for a while. It was hard to tell which

was worse, the part that was some kind of Indian or
the part that was related to the Vikings. Or whether it
was just that he was all cop.

"Where is the manuscript?"

"In Birdsall Junior's apartment. I know how you are
about removing evidence from the scene of a crime so
I left it where I found it."

"You didn't know that then."

"I had a better than even chance of being right." I
drew a pencil out of the cup and bounced its eraser
on the blotter. "You can expect my client to put in a
claim for the manuscript when you're done with it.
Booth didn't leave any next of kin and I doubt he
made any arrangements about his literary estate."

"I look forward to reading it. Detective fiction relaxes
me. Those writers sure know how to tie up all the
loose ends."

"Speaking of those, do you still want that case of
whiskey?"

"I'd just drink it up. I got a little problem in that
area. You know I'm three-quarters Ottawa."

"I would've guessed Iroquois."

"They're overrated. Pontiac was Ottawa. We almost
took Detroit away from you."

"On days like this I'd let you have it."

29

"haler, Felony Homicide."

I grinned at the telephone standard. "I bet you get a lot of hang-ups. People think you're offering a service."

"I am. I hope you've got news for me."

"I've got Allison Booth's murderer. Actually I've got two. I saved the best one for you."

"Who got the worst?"

"A sheriff's detective from Black Lake named Vaxhölm. But I can always avoid Cheboygan County."

"That leaves you, what, three counties in Michigan?

A trip across the state for you must be like a game of checkers."

"It's not quite that bad. The Allison Booth case is just filler for him. I gave him Eugene Booth's killer a few minutes ago."

"Lowell Birdsall, right?"

I was still playing with a pencil. I stopped. "Lieutenant's intuition?"

"Kindly go screw yourself. That's a John Wayne remark got up in Alan Alda clothing. Last time we spoke you were on your way to dangle Birdsall out a window by his heels. Details, please."

"The story takes telling. Are you free this afternoon for a three-hour round trip?"

"Black Lake?"

"I said *round* trip." I told her where. "You'll be back in time for dinner with the inspector from the Fifth."

"That's over. The FBI arrested him this morning and I'm nobody's idea of Hillary Clinton. I'll drive. That bomb of yours wouldn't pass an emissions test in New Mexico. The antipollution equipment's all dummy."

"When did you join Greenpeace?"

"I just don't like getting pulled over by those horses' necks on the state police."

"I'll spring for gas," I said. "Regular or premium?"

"Economy. It's a company car. Pick you up in front of your building in ten minutes."

A gold Chrysler LeBaron, last year's model, took the corner on the yellow and chirped to a stop at the curb. I climbed in on the passenger's side and buckled up.

Cops are among the worst drivers in the world and it's always the passenger who gets hurt.

"This is a no-smoking car," she said.

"You're kidding." But I put the cigarette back in the pack.

"Holdover from the last chief. The evil men do lives after and like that. We can stop when you need a fix."

"Not necessary. I only smoke them because I never met a happy ninety-year-old."

"That wouldn't be a concern for you even if you jogged and ate yogurt." She wheeled out into traffic. She was wearing a white plastic hairband, a white blouse, and a mauve Ultrasuede skirt with three buttons unfastened at the hem to let her right leg breathe. A matching blazer hung from a hanger over the left rear window. Her flats were mauve too and she worked both pedals with one foot. She had on sunglasses with blue-tinted oval frames. I asked her if they were prescription.

She shook her head. "Contacts. I'm thinking of RKT."

"I hear you need reading glasses after."

"Better than glasses all the time. They called me Goggles in first grade."

"Not twice, I bet."

"Small talk." We entered the John Lodge Freeway. A tanker air-braked when we took its lane and blatted its horn. "Tell me what you didn't tell Black Lake."

"When my heart slows down."

"Trucks. My daddy drove one back when you had to be good."

"Mine too. Teamster?"

She shook her head. "He was long-haul. They had a different union. How's your heart?"

"Ask me when we've stopped. I hung on to the Mafia angle. It cost me some grief when Vaxhölm asked why Booth stayed friendly with a suspect in his wife's murder, but that's not a direction I wanted to go."

"Vaxhölm's the county cop?"

"Yeah. Half Chingachgook, half Eric the Red. You ought to recruit him. He's wasted up there."

"He'd be wasted down here. The best ones always are. You think that was a good idea? Booth convinced Allison was a mob job."

"He wanted to be, so he was. The only other explanation was she'd been sleeping in more beds than Goldilocks. It wasn't a hit. Those old boys couldn't use the word *cat* in a sentence, but they knew killing his wife would only make him open his mouth that much wider."

"Tell me about Birdsall Junior."

I gave her what I'd given Vaxhölm. It went quicker the second time.

"If Birdsall killed Allison, why are we making this trip?"

"To prove me a liar."

That opened a whole new area of discussion, which I ended by turning on her radio. She'd programmed classical, country and western, hard rock, soft rock, and all-talk. The subject of the program was a civil war in Europe. This time we were on the side of the rebels. I turned it off without comment.

"Classical's to get me through traffic jams without chewing off my lipstick," she said. "Hard rock's to blow off steam on the drive home. Soft rock gets me ready for a date, and I like to yell at the idiots on the talk station."

"What about country?"

"I like country."

"No jazz?"

"I don't like jazz. I don't like monster truck rallies either. Don't tell the other cops." She slowed down as we passed a traffic stop. The trooper seemed to have the situation in hand and she sped up again. "Why all the mystery? I don't even know if I'm supposed to be Tweedledee or Tweedledum."

"It may not be that kind of interrogation. This will be a more pleasant drive if you don't ask too many questions."

"The drive back will be a lot less pleasant if this turns out to be a wild goose chase." But she didn't ask any more questions. After a little while she switched the radio back on and punched up Mahler.

The weepy rain kept up until we passed Jackson. Beyond that point it was a full spring day, with fat crocuses blooming in the grass on the median and a Crayola sun beaming all alone on a construction-paper sky.

We hit Marshall just as the early-bird special was starting at the German restaurant. The parking lot was filled with Jurassic Park–size sedans and we braked for a covey of white-haired pedestrians in Ban-Lon shirts and brocaded mother-of-the-bride jackets crossing the street against the light.

"You wonder how they got to be that age," muttered the lieutenant.

"Wait till we get to Edencrest."

The retirement home sat in a patch of obese sunlight with the same employee vehicles and a scatter of
visitors' cars parked in front. No ambulance today. Mrs.
Milbocker stood up from her desk in the office and
shook Thaler's hand. "When Mr. Walker said he was
bringing a police detective with him, I expected someone more along the lines of Dennis Franz." The smile
on the leathery face was brighter than the one she'd
given me the first time; but she hadn't been trying as
hard then.

The lieutenant looked at me. "When did you call?"

"Just before I called you."

The smile flickered. "Did I say something I shouldn't
have?"

Now Thaler smiled. "No, it's all right when it's official. A girl doesn't like to be taken for granted."

"How is she?" I asked Mrs. Milbocker.

"There's been no change since we spoke. Physically
she's fine. She's in remarkably good health considering she's sixty pounds overweight. Mentally, not so
good. She went into a bad spell after your visit last
week. She had her good days and her bad days before, but she may have seen the last of her good days.
Then again she could snap right out of it and remain
lucid for weeks. We know so little about Alzheimer's
as opposed to Princess Di's wardrobe." She frowned
for the first time since we'd met; but she couldn't sus-
tain it. "Let's go see if she's up to receiving visitors.
Friday night she threw a pitcher of water at a nurse's
aide. Luckily it was plastic. She has quite an arm."

The old man in the heavy sweater was asleep in his
wheelchair when we passed him in the hall. He might

not have moved since last week. Mrs. Milbocker checked his vitals on the fly. Thaler noted it.

"Mr. Goldstein was the first American on Corregidor," I said.

She said nothing. Her face was green around the edges. In the Wayne County Morgue I'd seen her probe the skin of a corpse that had been bobbing in Lake St. Clair for three days, to test its consistency. I asked her how she was holding up.

"I was just thinking I haven't visited my grandfather in months. He pitched a no-hitter for the Toledo Mudhens in forty-eight. Now they've got him singing the Alphabet Song in Stockbridge."

We stopped before the purple door. Mrs. Milbocker knocked, said, "Mrs. Skirrett?" When there was no answer the second time she opened the door and went in.

The small bedroom looked as cheerful as it had before. The curtains were pulled aside from the window, letting sunlight fall onto Lowell Birdsall Senior's original oil painting for the cover of *Paradise Valley* and the massive bulk that was Fleta Skirrett, squeezed into a wheelchair beside the bed. The pink-and-white crocheted coverlet had been removed from the bed and draped across her lap, above which showed a yellow cotton blouse with birds printed on it. Her plump pink face was a cardboardy color beneath the cotton-candy pink of her hair, with her blue eyes roaming around a pair of sunken hollows as if someone had pushed them in with his fingers. The fat of her great bare arms lay in folds on top of the coverlet. Her wrists were tied to the arms of the chair with strips of white cloth.

"We make it a point to dress them every day and sit them up," Mrs. Milbocker said. "The ties shock some visitors, but without them they can slide right out the bottom and break a bone. How are you, dear?"

It was the first time I'd heard her address the woman in the high affected voice of a parent talking to a small child.

"Rita?" The cartoony voice had a crack in it, like a worn-out Betty Boop soundtrack.

"No, dear, it's Mrs. Milbocker." She looked at us. "Sometimes she thinks I'm her sister."

I grinned. "Rita and Fleta? Are they twins?"

"Not so you'd notice. She only comes to visit at Christmas. She's as bony as a hatrack and acts as if a smile would violate her warranty. There's a theory that says you shouldn't agitate them by setting them straight. Even if I agreed with it I'm not about to let her go on thinking I'm Rita."

"I hope you brought something to eat, sis. They never feed me."

"You had lunch an hour ago. You're supposed to be losing weight."

"If I drop three more pounds I can get into those step-ins for the Hudson's catalogue."

Mrs. Milbocker said, "Now she's back to being a model."

"Tell me the truth, Rita. Do I look like Virginia Mayo? If I get the book-cover job I can say good-bye to lingerie ads."

Thaler said, "This is useless."

"Fleta, you got the job," I said. "Birdsall says you're perfect."

It wasn't going to work. The sunken eyes, of a shade so far removed from the glacial blue of Detective Vaxhölm's as to belong to a separate spectrum, continued to roam in their fleshy prison like inmates pacing their cells. Then they seemed to come forward a quarter-inch and she sucked in first one lip, then the other, wetting them.

"Oh, I'm so glad. A book is so much more permanent than a catalogue. And Mr. Birdsall is such a fine artist, and handsome. He looks like Van Gogh ought to have. Except for the ear, of course."

The worn-out quality was gone from the voice. She sounded even younger than she had when she was smoking a forbidden butt and talking about sleeping with Dali. Thaler and I exchanged glances.

Mrs. Milbocker wasn't smiling. "You won't upset her, will you?"

"Fleta," Thaler said, "do you remember me? Sergeant Saunders. This is Officer O'Hara. We're with the Detroit Police."

"I remember." Fleta's smile was brilliant. "You said I look like Marilyn."

"That's right, only prettier. You don't look made over."

I turned to Mrs. Milbocker and lowered my tone. "You can stay and make sure she doesn't get too worked up. Try not to say anything meanwhile."

Thaler said, "I've had emergency training."

Fleta said, "What?"

Mrs. Milbocker pressed her lips together for a moment. "I'll come back and look in on you in a few minutes. Poke your head out into the hall and yell if she becomes hyper. And don't untie her."

"Nothing, Fleta," Thaler said when we were alone. "We're still investigating what happened to Allison Booth. You remember Gene Booth's wife?"

"Of course. That poor woman. How horrible. You haven't caught the man?"

"We've got a suspect. You know who he is."

I shook a cigarette out of the pack and lit up. "She knows, all right." I spat smoke. "You know plenty, don't you, sister? Everything except where your boyfriend Birdsall was the night she got poked full of holes, and you can guess that."

"No. I know exactly where he was. He was in his studio, working late. I was posing for him. He had a deadline."

"He had a deadline, all right," I said.

Thaler said, "Shut up, O'Hara. It's all right if you got your nights mixed up, Fleta. That happens. We won't hold it against you if you remember it differently from the way you told us the first time."

The fat cheeks jiggled when she shook her head. "I didn't lie. He isn't my boyfriend. We were together, working."

"It isn't just the salesgirl anymore," Thaler said. "We've got a corroborating witness who saw Birdsall driving with Allison that night. This one got the license number. It was his car."

"It's a mistake." She tried to raise her hands and encountered resistance. She looked down at her wrists and her face twisted. She looked like the blonde waving the broken bottle in the *Paradise Valley* picture. "Why am I tied up? I don't do bondage. Who am I, Betty Page?"

I ground the filter between my teeth. "You'll be tied up a lot tighter if you don't start telling some truth. Let's tank her," I told Thaler.

"O'Hara's right, Fleta. Right now we can help you, put in a good word. Nobody can blame you for trying to help out a friend. If we give this to the lieutenant it's out of our hands. He's got the press on his neck. You could do five years as an accessory."

"Untie me!" Her voice rose. "Untie me or I won't say another word!"

I looked at Thaler. She bent over the chair and tugged loose the cloth strips. Fleta rubbed her wrists. Her lower lip stuck out. "Look at those marks. I won't be able to work for days. I cut my mouth licking an envelope last month and Lowell sent me home for a week, without even an advance to hold me over. He said it was distracting."

"Lowell, is it?" I laughed nastily. Thaler scowled at me and made a lowering motion with one hand.

"They aren't bad," she said.

"Modeling is hard work." Fleta rubbed with one broad thumb at a nearly invisible pressure-mark at the base of her left hand. "Everyone thinks you're getting paid all this money to do nothing. If I eat any more than a cracker for lunch I blow up like a balloon. I have to buy all my own makeup, and let me tell you, you can go through a whole lipstick in one session. I'm lucky when I don't have to buy my own clothes to model in, and when I do they're almost never any good for anything but modeling. I can't go out on the street dressed like Diana, Goddess of the Hunt. And the cramp-

ing's awful. Some mornings I feel like I went fifteen
rounds with Primo Carnera."

"Cut it," I said. "You'll have me bawling in a minute.
Tell me something, Fleta; when you strip for Lowell,
does he paint you before or after?"

The coverlet slid off her lap. One massive arm swept
up in a pink flash and the side of my head exploded.
It was the side with the bad eye. I was blinded for
half a second. I groped and caught one of her wrists,
but she slapped me again just as hard with the free
hand and twisted out of my grasp. Her voice was shrill
and she knew every name that couldn't be printed in
the book. Thaler moved in to get a hammerlock on
her, but nothing that big had ever moved that fast and
Fleta ducked under her arm, scrabbling among the litter of items on the nightstand beside the bed. She got
hold of something and hurled herself at Thaler, pinning her to the wall with her huge bosom and belly
and swinging her right arm up and down, up and
down, stabbing and slashing.

"Tramp!" she screamed. "Nymphomaniac! How many
men you need? Bitch! How stupid did you think I was?
You think I wouldn't follow him? Whore!"

Up and down, up and down and up while Thaler
got one foot to the side and twisted a shoulder into
the wall for leverage and pushed out, shoving against
that flesh avalanche with all the strength in her wiry
body while the object clenched in the pudgy dimpled
fist raked up and down, striking her on the head and
neck and behind her back and into her breasts. I lunged
and got one arm across the mad old woman's throat
from behind and hauled back with every crack in my

ribcage spreading and catching fire. I hauled back and back and hit the bed with my calves and fell over, holding on and dragging her great weight down on top of me while she clawed at my arm with the nails of her free hand and flailed out with the weapon in the other, shrieking names at the top of her lungs. I couldn't breathe, but I tightened my grip, flexing my biceps until I could feel the veins standing out on them like ropes. She stopped shrieking and started gurgling, fighting now for breath as I increased the pressure. Very slowly her strength began to fail. She stopped clawing and the other hand drifted down.

"Enough!" It was Lieutenant Thaler. "She's through. Let up."

I let up. The old woman lay atop me like a sack of bowling balls, wheezing but no longer struggling. I stretched my neck to see past the mound of her shoulder. There were other people in the room now, white heads mostly, with Mrs. Milbocker's bushy red perm bobbing among them as she forced her way through. Thaler was standing in front of them. The tail of her blouse was pulled out on one side and she'd lost her hairband, but there was no blood. She groped at Fleta Skirrett's slack fingers and held up a blunt hairbrush made of molded white plastic with a tangle of pink hairs caught in the bristles.

30

The roar of the .45 shook the room. Char-
lotte staggered back a step. Her eyes were a
symphony of incredulity, an unbelieving witness to truth. Slowly, she looked down at
the ugly swelling in her naked belly where
the bullet went in. . . .

"How c-could you?" she gasped.

I only had a moment before talking to a
corpse, but I got it in.

"It was easy," I said.

—Mickey Spillane
I, *The Jury* (1948)

It was another pretty day and most of the people who
had gathered in the red-brick structure modeled after
the capitol building in Philadelphia were buying tickets

for Greenfield Village across the street; but Louise Starr had said Henry Ford Museum and so I opted for the indoor attraction. I found her just inside the museum entrance, putting on lipstick with the aid of her reflection in the shimmering finish of a black-and-nickel 1949 Mercury in the automobile exhibit. She had on a beige jacket with the sleeves rolled halfway up her forearms and a matching skirt of some material that looked like burlap but was probably unbleached silk. A tricky arrangement involving amber-and-mica combs caught some of her hair above her ears and allowed the rest to fall down her back in a pale spill. She smiled when she saw me and dropped her lipstick into the woven-leather bag she'd been carrying the day we met in the Caucus Club.

"I like the way they display the cars in their natural habitat," she said. "Façades of old-fashioned drive-ins and like that. Clever."

"The new curator's idea. They used to have them in plain rows like a time-release parking lot. What have you seen so far?"

"I don't know where to start. Let's see, I've seen the chair Lincoln was sitting in at Ford's Theater—I thought you were kidding about that—and some kind of aluminum tube said to contain Thomas Edison's last breath. Is that genuine?"

"That one was Henry Ford's idea. He sent his son Edsel to get it. He was as nuts as he was brilliant."

"I even saw *The Spirit of St. Louis*. I thought it was in the Smithsonian."

"Jimmy Stewart flew this one in the movie. Washington had even deeper pockets than Henry. Wait till you see the Village. Edison's laboratory is within walking distance of the Wright brothers' shop."

"I wish I had the time. My luggage is outside. I leave here straight for home in an hour. But I've been meaning to see this place every visit, and I don't know when I'll be back. I hope you don't mind. Debra's back from Indiana. We can't talk at the house without having to answer a lot of pesky questions."

"I don't mind. It's been years since my last visit. If I have to wait till you misplace another Detroit writer I may never make it."

"The other night was wonderful. I hope you don't think Booth's book was all I cared about."

"Save it until you've read it." I held out the briefcase I'd carried in. It was brand new from Kmart, vinyl over cardboard with the leathergrain printed on.

She hesitated. "What is it? Not the manuscript."

"Black Lake still has that. These are Booth's dictation tapes. The manuscript's probably a long way from complete. When you get it your ghost might need the tapes to finish it."

She took the case. "I may just make an editor out of you yet."

"Too risky. I might hop on the wrong subway train and finish up in Brooklyn."

"Thank you, Amos. I'm sorry it went so hard for you. I still think you should swear out a complaint against Cypress. Possession of a handgun alone would land him in prison."

"He'd just bargain his way into another immunity. Guys like Glad Eddie only show enough of their cards to win the current hand. Anyway he didn't have anything to do with what happened to Booth."

"Poor Gene. Poor Fleta, too. I shouldn't feel sorry for her, but I do." I'd given Louise a complete report over the telephone.

"Me, too," I said. "I liked her even when we were wrestling."

"Thank God it was just a hairbrush. Is Lieutenant Thaler all right?"

"Just bruised. She can still write her memoirs."

"You know that's not the reason I asked. I like her. Anything there?" She turned her violet gaze on me.

"I make it a point never to date anyone who knows more submission holds than I do." A rib pinched me at the thought.

She saw the face I made. "I hope you saw a doctor."

"Sports physician in Dearborn. I cleared him of a narcotics charge a couple of years ago. He taped me up for the cost of the roll. It'll be on the expense sheet."

"You're a little old to be taking as many beatings as you do."

"If that's a contract offer, I'll quit and learn to type with all my fingers."

"Sorry. Nobody wants to read about good guys anymore. It's all hitmen and serial killers and people who lied for the president. Maybe I'm the one who should think about making a change."

We went on to a red Edsel. Four decades of shag rugs, polyester neckties, Beanie Babies, and feminine hygiene commercials hadn't done a thing to make the horsecollar grille look any more beautiful.

"What's going to happen to Fleta?" she asked.

"Probably nothing. Thaler isn't keen to hand it over to the county prosecutor, even if he'd thank her for cracking open a forty-year-old egg under his nose. Fleta's losing a piece of herself every day at Edencrest. Prison wouldn't be any worse."

"So Allison Booth's murder was an old-fashioned crime of passion."

"It was a little more cold-blooded than that. After Birdsall left Fleta in his studio, she waited for him to come back with Allison. She picked up one of his palette knives and hid behind the folding screen where the models changed. She didn't know who she was going to use the knife on, Birdsall or Allison or both, but she'd made up her mind to use it. She was candid about all this after she calmed down. That tussle in her room got the blood flowing to her brain. It was a lucid confession."

"The police were right, then. Allison was running around behind her husband's back."

"For all we know it was the only time. I imagine it's tough being married to a writer. They live in their heads most of the day. Birdsall was the whore in the picture. He seduced Fleta the way he did all his models and didn't mind bragging to her that he was out to seduce his best friend's wife too."

"But he helped her get rid of the body."

"It was the only thing he could do, after he got the knife away from her and quieted her down. He was afraid of Booth. Booth was a boxer, remember. The studio was already stained all over with paint. He splashed some cadmium red on top of the blood, wrapped Allison in a dropcloth, and waited till past midnight to smuggle her down to the car and out to that window well. Later, when Fleta told the cops she and Birdsall were working that night, she wasn't providing an alibi for him. It was for herself."

"But won't it all come out now because of Lowell Junior?"

"He's the main reason it won't. He believes his father killed Allison. I never met the man, but what I've heard doesn't make me feel a bit uncomfortable to let the cops go on thinking the same thing."

"What a terrible secret to carry around all these years. No wonder Fleta lost her mind."

"That was Alzheimer's. If it weren't for that she'd still be carrying it. Anyway it was more terrible for Eugene Booth. It was too hard for a tough-guy writer like him to accept the fact his wife was cheating on him, so he told himself the mob killed her because he talked too much about Roland Clifford and the riot. In the end he'd convinced himself of it. Only that was harder on him, because it meant he was indirectly responsible for her death. That's the ironic part. If he'd just believed the truth in the first place, he'd have gotten over it years and years ago."

"Maybe not. If there was anything to brood over, he'd have brooded over it, and if there wasn't, he'd have found something to brood over in its place. For a certain kind of person, that's as close to happy as they ever get."

"Could be," I said. "Fortunately I don't have to be deep."

"Right. Everything beads up on you like water on plastic."

I looked at her. She was hugging herself, stroking one arm. Part of it was Booth, but we happened to be standing in front of the black Lincoln convertible in which JFK had been killed, parked in line in a phantom motorcade made up of automobiles that had carried FDR, Harry S. Truman, Dwight D. Eisenhower, and LBJ; all dead men with middle initials and long-kept secrets of their own. Broken heroes all, like Roland Clifford and Eugene Booth.

"Lowell Junior was a victim of his own lies too," she said. "Will he survive?"

"His hanging, yeah. I don't know about the lies. You can put that in the preface. It'll help flesh out the book."

"You think all I care about is the book."

"Give me back the briefcase and I'll apologize."

She shook her head. "That would be like killing Gene Booth all over again. He wanted to set the record straight. That's why he sent back the check."

"Don't pay any attention to anything I say. My ribs hurt and I've got a black eye on top of a black eye that was the black eye to end them all in the first place. You've got a publishing house to launch. It's okay if you do it on top of a few corpses. They won't mind. Booth would sure as hell mind your saying it was all for him, though. I didn't spend much time with him, but what I spent bought me plenty."

"There's no moral law against doing something for someone and yourself at the same time. It will be a dignified promotion. I'm thinking of approaching Maya Angelou to write an introduction."

"She'll sell fifty thousand copies," I said. "Breaking the Clifford story just before publication will move another half million."

"*Just* before. If it breaks too soon, it will be old news months before we can get the book into production. I have to ask you for Duane Booth's original police report."

"That wasn't part of the deal."

"I thought you and I were beyond deals, Amos."

"No good," I said. "Some women can get away with the look. Not you."

"What look?"

"A torn slip and a broken bottle. You're too refined to trade a night in Hazel Park for services."

"That's a crude way to put it. I wasn't talking about that."

"Okay. Let's just say I was off the clock. The police report's promised to someone else. In my work you have to put up information in return for information received. I stonewalled two police departments to hang on to it."

"Am I allowed to ask who?"

"I think that's *whom*." When her face didn't change I said, "You know him. Barry Stackpole."

"Oh, Barry. Why didn't you say so in the first place? I'll talk to him." She looked at her wristwatch, a tiny one with an amber face on an alligator strap. "I need time to return my rental. We'll have to say good-bye here."

She kissed me on the cheek. Her lips were cool and the foxglove scent was there. "Thank you for everything. Don't you dare come through New York without calling me."

After she left I browsed among the exhibits, but they weren't doing anything for me. I got my car out of the lot and drove to the post office, where I bummed a priority envelope and slipped into it the police report Eugene Booth's brother Duane had written on the 1943 riot before he changed his mind and filed another. I tore a sheet out of my notebook and started a note to Barry about Louise Starr, then crumpled it up; Barry's a big boy. I sealed the flap, addressed the envelope to him, paid the postage, and gave it to the clerk.

I had the afternoon ahead of me. I'd cleared the entire day for the museum. I smoked a cigarette until the meter ran out, then started the motor and drove to the Corner to watch Detroit lose one more time in the old ballpark.